WHY CAN'T I EVER LEARN?

Joe Campbell was yet another dark prince. She should walk away, leave him alone, but when her tears and rage at herself subsided, what did she do? Like an idiot, she punched her answering machine play button again.

"Look, I'm sorry for the way I behaved. I wish... I wish we'd met under different circumstances.... Because I like you."

She made a fist and brushed the tears from her eyes. *You can't let yourself want him. You can't love him or save him. You can't save anybody. Haven't you learned anything?*

Frantically, she dug the phone book advertisement that had his picture on it out of her trash can, smoothed it out and lost another piece of her soul the second she glanced into his fierce, predatory black eyes.

Because I like you.

Joe Campbell was a lost soul. Just thinking about him made defeat slump her shoulders.

"I like you, too," she whispered. "But don't you dare tell anybody."

ANN MAJOR

THE HOT LADIES MURDER CLUB

MIRA®

ISBN 1-55166-741-X

THE HOT LADIES MURDER CLUB

Copyright © 2003 by Ann Major.

To my readers:

Love doesn't transform.
It forms.

What if we smashed the mirrors
And saw our true face?

ELSA GIDLOW

Prologue

The wages of sin must always be paid. That's what his headmaster used to say right before he tied him up and locked him in that awful cupboard. It came as a pleasant surprise that the familiar phrase, as well as thinking about *her* punishment, could give him such a thrill.

Yesterday the handsome, debonair Sir Dominic Phillips had lunched at his club in London. Today he was sweating like a pig in a nondescript rental car in a shadowy parking garage in south Texas contemplating his wife's murder.

Please… Please, sir, let it be her.

He used to say please, pretty please to the headmaster. It had been part of their ritual.

This wasn't the first time Georgina had tempted him to murder. The trouble with murder was the risk that it would catch her unawares. That wouldn't do.

He wanted Georgina to feel the blow coming, to dread it with a morbid, soul-destroying anticipation. That was part of the game. He wanted to overwhelm her in death as he had in marriage. He wanted her last dying thought to be that her precious, darling Georgia, whom she'd unwisely favored over him, was now his to do with as he pleased. And Georgina knew his tastes when it came to little girls.

His heart beat in a frenzy. Maybe it was the late-summer, south Texas heat that had him so feverish and crazy. Even in the dark garage the sun seemed to scream out of a too-bright, almost-hostile blue haze. Two minutes ago he'd turned off the air conditioner. Two minutes, and already his Savile Row suit that was a blend of silk and wool was dripping wet, and his fine silk shirt was sticking to his armpits. It wouldn't be long before he stank, too.

Even though he'd rolled the windows of his car down, he was suffocating. He wiped his damp brow with his soaked handkerchief.

Had he found her?

According to Morrison's report, she was to be deposed at three o'clock by an unscrupulous, hotshot local attorney, Joe Campbell. Apparently, Campbell had been run out of Houston for his shady legal dealings with a CEO by the name of Rod Brown. Together they'd looted Brown's company and run off with the funds. Brown was living it up in a mansion in the British Virgins while Campbell was exiled to this backwater hellhole doing personal injury law. The creep was representing former clients of Georgina's, who were suing her for not disclosing mold growth in a property she'd sold them.

Georgina, or rather Lady Phillips, a Realtor—here? How appalling!

As always Morrison had been painstakingly thorough. So thorough, Dominic nearly laughed out loud as he thumbed through the detective's report.

And she'd thought she could hide. If the plain-looking woman in Morrison's grainy photos really was his dazzling, wild Georgina, he now knew everything about her new life, her address, little Georgia's school—everything.

When he heard her ancient Mercedes rumble up the ramp of the parking garage, he felt as devilishly excited as a child playing hide-and-seek. As he was about to crouch behind the wheel, a woman laughed close by. She was short with red hair. Walking toward her car, she fumbled in her purse for her keys.

Bugger. This could ruin everything.

A man in the truck that she climbed into started the engine and drove toward the exit. Dom held his breath until he heard Georgina's Mercedes, closer now.

With her fear of dark, enclosed places, he hadn't expected her to dare the garage even in broad daylight. Nevertheless, just in case, he'd parked in a reserved spot two floors beneath Campbell's plush offices, so there'd be no danger of her parking anywhere near him.

You should've killed me when you had the chance, darling.

That last hideous night in their ultramodern flat on the Thames, she'd enraged him by begging for a divorce. He'd grabbed her, and when his hands had closed around her throat she'd hit him with a paperweight. Just the memory was enough to contort his aristocratic face into a mask of rage.

He'd plummeted to the floor and landed with a resounding thud. He remembered staring up at her in a
weird, semiconscious state as she knelt over him in
fear and alarm.

"You'll be all right," she'd whispered in that
throaty voice of hers.

"Help me," he'd mouthed, the way he'd once
begged the headmaster for mercy.

"I'll get help, but I can't stay. This whole thing,
us, is getting worse and worse. Please try to understand."

Understand? He'd tried to talk, to say he was sorry,
but because of the coke he'd been on, his words had
slurred. He'd struggled to move, but it was as if his
limbs had been made of lead and he was paralyzed
from tongue to toe, helpless to do a thing to stop her
as she'd gotten to her feet and packed and taken Georgia. Finally, he'd regained sensation in his limbs and
had been able to crawl to the couch and then to stand.

Slut. That night she'd taught him she was like all
the others, who'd made him love them and then used
and abandoned him. Unlike the others, she was his
wife, and she still consumed him. Constantly he imagined her with other men.

A diesel engine purred up the ramp. He knew he
shouldn't risk her seeing him, but when her Mercedes
inched past him, belching plumes of black diesel, he
couldn't resist a glance just to make sure.

One look had his heart trilling with excitement and
he got hard.

Yes!

Huge sunglasses hid most of her pale, slim face.

Sure enough, just like in Morrison's pictures, she'd dyed her hair and swept it untidily into a cheap plastic clip. Neither the color nor the style flattered her. Still, how clever of her to mute her dazzling beauty, to dye her honey-gold hair and discard her beautiful clothes and glamorous sense of style, to hide here, of all the dull places—Corpus Christi, Texas—which was so far away from who and what she really was. So far away from him and their glittering life together.

You shouldn't have told me about your grand-mother in San Antonio. Nor about that year when you were nineteen and lived with her when you got your Realtor's license.

He scowled. *He* was the clever one. He was the one who planned while she just drifted, hoping for the best. Her disguise wasn't *that* good. As soon as his detective had shown him the pictures, he'd put two and two together and had boarded a plane.

She was his wife. *His.* She belonged to him forever. She had no right to run away, no right to take little Georgia. No right to leave him all alone. No right to have another man. He'd show her.

When he'd stumbled to the bathroom that awful night to inspect himself in the mirror…to see… When there hadn't been anyone in the mirror, he'd begun to quake and then to claw the mirror in an attempt to make his reflection reappear. When it hadn't, he'd begun to weep and pound the mirror with bare fists.

The same thing had happened when he was a little boy. He'd been very, very bad—so bad, mirrors had been empty when he'd tried to see himself. After his father's death, his mother had been so frightened, she'd sent him away to boarding school. For a long time he'd felt powerless, as if he'd simply ceased to exist.

The night Georgina had left him, he'd broken the mirror with his bare hands. Then he'd scrawled Georgina's name on the white bathroom tile floor with his own blood. The last thing he'd heard before he'd collapsed was a siren.

She must have called the ambulance as soon as she'd known she was safe because when he'd awakened, he'd been in a trauma unit and they'd been praising his famous, beautiful wife to the skies.

Where was she, the famous Georgina, they'd wanted to know? Why wasn't she with him? Their unspoken question had been, if she wasn't with him, who was she with?

He'd known what he had to do.

Find her. Teach her. Retrain her…as he had in the beginning when she'd been a young bride. The wages of sin…

Like a cat, he'd toy with her awhile. He'd tie her up with bloodred satin ribbons like before. He'd…

He got hard just thinking about how her husky voice would sound when she begged him to kill her.

"Say, 'Please,'" he'd whisper. "Say, 'Please, Sir.' Kiss me down there and say you love me.

He touched himself, gently, very gently, just like he'd taught her to.

Just the thought of her lips there had him hard as a rock. Then he came, wetting all over his suit.

See what you made me do?

She would pay for that, too.

BOOK ONE

*When we look into the mirror
we see the mask. What is
hidden behind the mask?*

DIANE MARIECHILD

One

*C*ampbell never forgot a face. Never.

Joe Campbell's posh law offices with their sweeping views of the high bridge, port and bay were meant to impress and intimidate. The tall ceilings, the starkly modern ebony furniture, the blond hardwood floors and the Oriental rugs reeked of money and power and social prestige—all of which were vital to a man with Campbell's ambitions. Not that he was thinking about anything other than the exquisite woman he was supposed to be deposing.

The case had been dull, routine; until she'd walked in. She was beautiful and sweet and warm—and scared witless of him.

This should be good. He rapped his fingers on his desk and tightened them into a fist that made his knuckles ache.

The minx had him running around in circles like a bloodhound that had lost a hot scent. His ears were dragging the ground, his wet nose snuffling dirt.

Minutes before the deposition, Bob Africa, one of the partners and a former classmate at UT Law School, had strutted through his door as if he owned the place—which he practically did. Bob specialized in class-action lawsuits and had just won big, having collected more than two million dollars in legal fees from a cereal company for a food additive.

There hadn't been a shred of evidence any consumer had been injured. Africa's fee had come to $2,000 an hour. Consumers had received a coupon for a free box of cereal.

Campbell was jealous as hell.

All smiles as usual this afternoon, a triumphant Bob had slapped him on the back and ordered him to win this one—or else. Salt in the wound—after the Crocker loss.

"I went out on a limb for you, buddy. I told the other partners you just had a run of bad luck in Houston and got a rotten hand here with that medical case."

"Thanks." Campbell hadn't reminded Africa that he'd been the man who'd rammed that loser Crocker down his "buddy's" throat and then he'd kept the more promising cases for himself.

Bob had smiled his wolverine smile and slapped his back again. "You're the best, buddy. But, we don't pay you to lose—"

Lose. Campbell had felt the blood rising in his face. Hell, at least Africa hadn't reminded him about the death threats all the partners had been receiving ever since Campbell had lost the case. Hell, the incompetent quack had won. What was he so mad about? Crocker's wife, Kay, maybe? She'd made a play for Campbell, a helluva play.

Today a letter from some crackpot, who said he was praying for Campbell, had arrived. The letter was in the same loopy handwriting as the death threats.

Strangely, somehow it was even scarier. Mrs. Crocker had called three times this week, too.

But it was the woman across from Campbell who had him rigid with tension. He had to beat her—or else.

Her face was damnably familiar. Her husky voice was so exquisite and raw, it tugged at Campbell on some deep, man-woman level.

He hated her for her easy power over him even as his cold lawyer's mind told him she was a fake. This was a staged performance. There was definitely something too deliberate and practiced about her lazy, luscious drawl.

To buy time he played with his shirt cuff. He'd asked dozens of questions and had gotten nowhere. She was a liar, and if it was the last thing he did, he would expose her.

"I—I swear I knew nothing, absolutely nothing about mo-o-old in the O'Connors' house," she repeated for the tenth time.

I think the lady doth protest too much.

When he shot her his most engaging smile and leaned toward her as if the deposition were over, she jumped. Her lovely, long fingers and unpolished nails twisted in her lap so violently, she almost dropped the damning photographs he'd jammed into her hands a few seconds earlier.

"I—I swear...no mold," she pleaded.

Then why won't you look me in the eye?

"*Toxic* mo-o-old," Campbell drawled, pleased his *o* lasted even longer than hers. His mocking gaze drilled her.

She shook her dark head like a true innocent and began flipping through the photographs he'd made of the black muck growing inside the walls of the O'Connors' mansion.

"There has to be a mistake," she whispered.

No, you little liar. No mistake.

Campbell's long, lean form remained sprawled negligently behind his sleek ebony desk. His beige silk suit was expensive. So was his vivid yellow tie.

Hannah Smith, her knees together beneath her full white skirt, sat on the edge of the black leather chair opposite him. Flanking her was the attorney from her insurance company, a mediocre, colorless little stick of a man. Hunkered low in his chair in an ill-fitting undertaker's suit wearing smudged, gold-rimmed glasses Tom Davis looked about as dangerous as a terrified rabbit.

"No mistake," Campbell said. "The O'Connors had to abandon their home. It'll cost more to remediate it than they paid for it, which was a substantial sum—"

"More than a mill… But it's not my fault!" she protested. "I was only the Realtor. I thought smart lawyers like you only sued rich people…."

Didn't she get it? The deep pocket here was her insurance company. Not her. So, why was she working herself into a sweat?

"Mold was not in your clients' disclosure statement," he said.

"There was no mold!" Her voice shaking, she began a boring repeat of her defense.

"Maybe you didn't realize mold is a very serious issue on the Texas Gulf."

"Because lawyers like you have made it into a billion-dollar industry?"

"I'm supposed to be asking the questions. And you are liable—"

She opened her pretty mouth and gulped for a breath.

Hannah Smith was lying. And she wasn't all that damn good at it, either.

And yet he liked her.

This was bad.

Joe Campbell, or rather just plain Campbell, as he was known to most people, at least to those with whom he was on speaking terms, and there were fewer and fewer of those in this town since his line of work tended to alienate a lot of people, had been a trial lawyer too long not to be able to smell a liar a mile away.

He'd been screwed, glued and tattooed by the best liars in the universe—his ex-wife and his former best friend and boss had taken him to the cleaners.

Here we go again. The pretty little con artist across from him smelled warm and sweet. And thanks to his air-conditioning register that wafted her light fragrance Campbell's way, he was too aware of that fact.

Chanel. He frowned, shifting his long legs under his desk as another unwelcome buzz of man-woman excitement rushed through him. By now he should have boxed her in. She was scared and pretty, and he should have had her on the run. And yet...she had him oddly off balance.

Her nervous fingers shuffled and reshuffled the photographs of the O'Connors' estate. He caught glimpses of the abandoned pool, the empty hot tub, and the red brick path that wound through the straw-like remnants of formerly showy flower beds. Her slim, graceful hands trembled so badly when she came to his damning shots of the mold, she nearly dropped the whole bunch.

"Think how those images will affect a sympathetic jury, Mrs. Smith."

"That's not a question," her lawyer said. "You don't have to answer."

Deliberately, she licked her lips with her pink tongue. "I'm sorry Mr. O'Connor's sick, but..."

Hell. She sounded sorry. A jury would believe her, too. He almost believed her. When she began talking faster and faster, swallowing, and glancing everywhere but at him, Campbell found himself studying her wide, wet lips with obsessive interest.

Sexy voice, intoxicating scent...and that delectable mouth... Everything about her seemed soft and vulnerable and likable. She was too damned likable. Not like him.

Suddenly Campbell wanted her to shut up and just look at him, and that scared the hell out of him. His big house was lonely and empty, his footsteps echoed when he finally made it home and climbed the stairs to his bedroom alone every night.

Was anything about her for real? Was she sucking him in...as Carol had?

Mrs. Smith was damned attractive, too damned attractive, despite that shapeless white sack that concealed her figure, despite thick, inky bangs and huge dark glasses that masked her face. Her legs were long and shapely, her ankles slim…even though those low-heeled, stained canvas shoes did nothing for her calves.

Yes, she was pretty despite the fact that she'd gone to a lot of trouble not to be. Why had she done that? Most women liked to add *pretty* to their arsenal of weapons when they went up against him or a jury. For an instant, he remembered Mrs. Crocker's slit skirts and shapely legs. She'd been built like a gymnast.

"Call me Kay," she'd said the day Campbell had lost. "Better, call me…anytime."

He'd been angry because he'd lost. "I don't mess around with married women."

"So, my husband's wrong about you," she'd purred. "You do have a principle or two. I like that."

"No principle. I just don't want to get shot by a jealous husband."

"My husband's a good shot, too. He's a hunter."

"This lawsuit wasn't personal, you know."

"So, why are you so sore you lost?"

"I'm sore about a lot of things."

"So am I." Her eyes had sparked.

Forget Kay. Concentrate on Mrs. Smith. Campbell ran a tanned hand through his jet-black hair and yawned, pretending he was bored by what Mrs. Smith was saying. Bored by her. If only he was, maybe he could concentrate on the O'Connors' case and finish her off.

She was tall. From the moment she'd glided into

his office, he'd been riveted by her exquisite lightness of being. Something sweet and vulnerable screamed look at me, love me, please. Her every gesture—her quick, nervous smiles at Tom—hell, even the frightened glances *he* got both charmed and maddened him.

A jury would be equally charmed.

Then there was the way she couldn't seem to catch her breath when he got too close. She was playing the role of damsel in distress with a vengeance that should have infuriated him. And yet... Her fear felt so real and palpable, he wanted to protect her.

Damn it, he *had* to get her. Africa had made it clear, his ass was on the line.

If her accent was fake, he'd bet a year's salary her black hair came out of a bottle. The harsh color was wrong for her fair complexion, the style too severe for her narrow face. He kept eyeing the thick, glossy mass, longing to undo the cheap plastic clip.

Hell, what were those white bits of dust that clung to her bangs? What had she been doing before she'd dashed late to his office.

"If the O'Connors are so concerned, why aren't they here today?" she finished in that velvet undertone that undid him.

"They hired me to represent them." His voice cut like ice.

"You mean to do their dirty work?" she finished, glancing out his windows like a trapped animal.

Damn it, Campbell felt sorry for her. Then Tom put a cautionary hand over hers, and Campbell felt a wild, really scary emotion.

"What's all that stuff in your hair?" Campbell growled, wanting to rip Tom's hand away.

"Oh!" Her eyes flew self-consciously to his. She gulped in another big breath, and he felt like the air between them sizzled.

This was bad.

She stirred her fingers through the mess of her purse and finally plucked out an elegant, gold-framed mirror. When she saw herself she wrinkled her nose. Quickly, she yanked at the hideous clip and shook out her long, thick hair.

When lots of little white bits showered onto his gray carpet, she smiled, revealing deep dimples, and he felt that damn buzz again. Despite a bad haircut, she was way sexier with her hair down. She studied herself in her mirror and wrinkled her nose again.

Campbell squirmed in his leather chair. He didn't need this.

"Bits of Sheetrock," she explained airily. Lifting her triangular chin, she shot him a pious look. "I was inspecting one of the waterfront properties I represent. For mold, Mr. Campbell."

"Just call me Campbell...."

"There was a suspicious stain on the ceiling.... I wanted to be sure...."

She and Tom exchanged self-righteous glances.

"My expert didn't find any," she said.

Touché, Campbell thought grimly, even as some part of him cheered for her.

Again, her hands fluttered prettily as she reclipped her hair. She didn't wear a wedding ring. For no rea-

son at all he longed to remove those huge glasses that
hid her eyes.

Were they dazzling blue or soft velvet brown? Or
fiery black? He wanted to sweep her hair back, get a
good look at her. Maybe then he'd remember where
the hell he'd seen her.

Damn it. He grabbed one of the mold photographs
from his own duplicate pile and forced himself to focus on *his* clients and *their* toxic-mold problem.

"Paul O'Connor is in the hospital barely able to
breathe or think," Campbell said.

"I'm so sorry he's ill."

*You don't give a damn about Paul and you know
it.*

And yet again, her face paled, and her voice went
soft with husky concern that turned Campbell to
mush.

Destroy her. Unnerve her.

Campbell fumbled awkwardly with the disclosure
sheets of the sales contract. Then he rustled through
his list of questions he'd deliberately structured to entrap her.

Somehow he had to get this smooth-talking actress
to admit that she'd known all along about the mold
and hadn't disclosed it. Her shaky voice and hands
meant she was highly agitated. Maybe if he got her
really mad, she'd snap. He was famous for his Perry
Mason moments.

"Back to this mold situation at the O'Connors',"
he murmured in a tight, low tone. "It was an old
house on the water—"

"There was no mold." She glanced at her watch

and out the window again. "The Tylers were diligent about maintaining their home. They repaired leaks, cleaned air-conditioning ducts. Besides, we had it tested for mold."

"By an unreliable agent."

"Just because your man, whom you no doubt paid to lie…three months later—"

Tom wagged a warning finger at his client, but she was too flushed with excitement to heed him.

Campbell almost grinned when she attacked her own attorney.

"Mr. Davis, I thought you were my lawyer."

Campbell noted that there wasn't a hint of that lazy drawl now. Just for a second he caught a couple of syllables that sounded crisp and elite…almost foreign. East Coast? No, that cut-glass accent wasn't American.

"How can you defend this…this pirate?" she was saying.

"Please, Hannah…"

"It's all right, Davis. I've been called worse." Campbell faked a scowl.

"A pirate…who…who cunningly plasters his handsome, ruthless face on every billboard and phone book cover his money can buy?"

Handsome? Campbell's perverse mind got stuck on the word.

"He's a fake, pretending he's some Robin Hood defending the poor. How can you defend such a rude, crude ambulance chaser?"

Ambulance chaser? The day of any accident, the

*insurance lawyers are there, lady! But do you criti-
cize them?*

"Mr. Campbell has repeatedly called me and
threatened—"

"I was merely trying to set up an appointment for
this deposition," Campbell said in the same reasonable, sympathetic tone he used to persuade juries.

"Don't talk down to me! You have no right to sue
me."

"This is America, Mrs. Smith. *Texas,* America.
The Wild West. Anybody can sue anybody."

"There was no mold when I sold the O'Connors
that house."

Campbell leaned toward her, automatically
straightening his bold tie. "My clients say there
was."

She sank lower in her chair and gasped in a breath.

"Slimy. Greenish." Campbell warmed to his subject as if she were a juror. "Black. Fungus. Toxic
mold. Aspergillus, to be exact. Mr. O'Connor is a
very sick man. Take a look at those photographs."

"I'm sorry if he's sick, but Mr. O'Connor doesn't
have anything that a green poultice won't fix," she
said softly.

"That's an old joke. I won't sit here while you
disparage innocent—" Deliberately Campbell leaned
back in his chair.

"Innocent? They're not innocent! I am! I told you
there are such things as evil homeowners who…
who…"

"Who what?" Campbell sprang forward again.

"Who don't want to be taken advantage of by Realtors like you?"

She opened her mouth wide and strained to get a breath. "Homeowners, who...who get up on the roofs with hoses and pour gallons of water into cracks between the walls!"

Her words hit him like a swift punch in the gut. To cover his fear that his clients had lied and he was on the wrong side again, he sprang to his feet. "I'm more interested in evil Realtors, Mrs. Smith, who misrepresent properties to make a quick sale."

She stood up, too. "Don't accuse me of your dirty games—"

Campbell smiled. "And what kind of dirty games do you play, Mrs. Smith?" His sensual gaze swept her from head to toe.

What the hell did she look like naked?

A hot crimson flush stained her cheeks. With a startled gasp, she sank back down in her chair.

Buying time, he stalked around to his desk and sat down, too.

"I think you're vile," she whispered.

"Who, me?" he murmured. "Vile?"

"Tom told me to save these for later," she rasped. "But I'm too furious."

She plunged her hand into her shapeless beige purse again and shook out three lipsticks, the gold mirror, wadded bits of paper and a photograph, which she slapped onto his desk.

"You're not the only one with a camera! That's your Mr. O'Connor on the roof."

All Campbell saw were thighs to die for and masses of long golden hair.

"Wow!" he whispered, finally recognizing her. "You look much better naked than I imagined—well, half-naked."

"Naked?" When she saw the snapshot, her cheeks caught fire. "Give me that!"

"Are you trying to distract me with sex, Mrs. Smith?"

"You low-down—"

Campbell laughed appreciatively. When she tried to snatch the picture back, he held it away from her.

The subjects in the photograph were a gorgeous blonde in a thong bikini and a blond little girl in a pink playsuit. The kid was about four. But the woman—

Wow. Bombshell. Wet dream.

Incredible breasts bulged out of slippery red material, and yes, she most definitely had thighs to die for. Mother and child were patting turrets of a sandcastle. There was a big house on a tall cliff in the background. The woman was staring at the little girl with a look of utter adoration.

He looked up at Mrs. Smith and grinned like a cat that had just munched a turtledove and found the repast delicious.

Well, now I can guess what you look like naked.

"I like you better blond.... And the less you wear, the better you look!"

With a wild guttural cry of sheer rage, she lunged for the picture.

"Wrong picture," she said icily, when he released it.

Thrusting it back in her purse, she came up with two dog-eared photographs and slapped them onto his desk. "There!"

"I like the shot of you in a bikini better."

"Concentrate. See that hose? Mr. O'Connor doesn't look sick to me. I have a video of him, too, and I'm sending them to my insurance company. He deliberately created that mold to get an insurance settlement to pay for his remodeling. You're not going to destroy my good name."

Campbell went cold. Somehow he forced a warm smile, his best lawyer smile. "Pictures like this won't make any difference."

"If they don't, it's because the entire legal system...is bought off by corrupt, rich lawyers like you. Since I've been in Texas..."

"Since you've been in Texas?" he repeated. He stood up, and she struggled for her next breath. "Where were you before Texas? Why did you dye your hair...?"

She went absolutely still.

He stared at her hard and then let it drop. "You're taking this lawsuit way too personally," he murmured.

"Oh, I am, am I? Well, for your information, being sued for more money than I'll ever make if I live to be a hundred feels personal!" She walked back to her chair and sat back down and turned to Tom. "Oh, what's the use of even trying to talk to someone as low as he is? I can't take any more of his questions or accusations. Not today.''

"Low…'' How in the hell could her ridiculous insult hurt? Or was it that she'd turned to Tom, when *he* wanted all of her attention?

Low.

"I…I've read things about you, Mr. Campbell,'' she whispered, rallying.

"Such as, Mrs. Smith?''

"You stole money, ruined your best friend's company, and your brokenhearted wife divorced you.''

"Ah, my wife…'' Icy despair seeped through Campbell. He didn't give a damn about his wife. Still, he had to clench his hand into a fist to hold on to his control.

"And I don't blame her one bit.''

"So, you've researched me—''

"She got your mansion in River Oaks—''

As if that was what had made him bitter and filled him with hate.…

He remembered the way Carol had curled against his body every night and felt sweet and soft and warm during those first months of marriage.

His black eyes narrowed. He'd believed her when she'd told him she loved him. He'd adored her, worshiped her and believed in her. For the first time in his life, he'd almost felt…human.

"You had to leave Houston because you're so corrupt people there despise you. Your best friend's wife killed herself because of—''

Campbell's face turned to stone. His mouth tasted like ashes. "Is that so? Do go on.''

"You...why, you're such a terrible father your son won't have anything to do with you."

His son. Every nerve in his body buzzed.

"And *you're* such a good mother," he murmured so cuttingly she gulped in a breath.

"The state even tried to disbar you because you are such a bad lawyer. You...you solicited clients improperly after that awful two-plane collision in east Texas where those little children—"

"You don't know a damn thing about me!" he shouted, banging his fist on his desk. "I'm not on trial. I'm deposing *you.*"

Davis stared wide-eyed. It was Campbell's turn to gulp in a savage breath. If it were the last thing he did, Campbell had to get control of this exchange and finish off her and her wimp of an attorney once and for all.

"One corrupt judge tried to have me disbarred. And failed, Mrs. Smith. Just as you will fail, if you fight me with these ridiculous, rigged photographs." Getting up, he tore her pictures in two.

She stood up, too. She was tall, but he was taller. When she shuddered, he realized his massive size intimidated her. Good. Using his body as a weapon, he moved closer.

"I—I've got more," she whispered, backing away from him.

"So do I," he thundered.

"And...and they aren't rigged. I'm not like you. I wouldn't rig—" She tore his pictures into zillions of pieces and tossed them onto his rug. She was almost to the door. "Goodbye, Mr. Campbell."

"I'm not finished with you yet. You think I don't know about you? Well, I do. I've done my research, too!"

She paled.

"Everything about you is a damned lie, Mrs. Smith." He backed her against the door. "Where the hell is Mr. Smith? Or is there a Mr. Smith? What's your real name, honey?"

"Please... I—I'm sorry.... I shouldn't have said...any of those horrible personal things. I—I was upset."

Her apology seemed sincere. She was white and shaking, cowering from him, but he was too furious now to care.

"Too bad you got personal." His mouth thinned. "I intend to win this, Mrs. Smith." *He had to win this. Africa, the ruthless son of a bitch had said so.* "Now I'm more determined than ever to expose you."

He ripped her sunglasses off.

Her eyes were blue. Huge vivid irises were ringed with inky black lashes. She looked young and vulnerable and very scared—of him.

"Who are you really?" he rasped.

"You're the last man I'd ever tell," she whispered.

Spunk. He liked her spunk. And those thighs she had— She'd looked so loving in that picture.

Relationships. He was no damn good at relationships. And even if he was, they were off to a bad start.

With a shaking hand she grabbed her glasses and

jammed them clumsily back onto her narrow, white face. "Please... Just let me go...."

When he grabbed her hand, it was as cold as ice. With his huge body, he drew her toward him and blocked the door.

"What are you so afraid of...besides me?" he whispered.

She gave a little cry and yanked herself loose.

He had the strangest compulsion to reach for her, but he knew that would only scare her more. With a curt nod, he stepped aside.

As if she considered him some sort of devil, she crossed herself and ran.

Campbell sank back into his chair exhausted. He loosened his collar and his bright yellow tie.

When Campbell heard Tom reassuring her outside in the hall, his mood blackened and he swiped his arm across his desk, knocking all the papers and files that dealt with the O'Connor lawsuit onto the floor.

Maybe she was a liar, but the O'Connors had lied to him, too. Clients had a bad habit of telling their lawyers only one side of a story—their side.

He opened a lower desk drawer and took out the bottle of Glenlivet he kept hidden there. Hating himself, he took a quick pull. Then he wiped his mouth with the back of his hand. He kept seeing that picture of her. She'd been smiling at that kid so sweetly, and he couldn't forget her thighs.

He'd better forget them. His job was to search and destroy—to expose Mrs. Smith; to do whatever he had to do to hurt her, to win for the O'Connors.

The thought of hurting so much as a single dyed

hair on her inky head caused a sick, queasy feeling in the pit of his stomach.

Who the hell was she?

Whoever she was, it was his job to find out and destroy her.

He rapped his fingers on his desk. With some difficulty, he squashed his guilt and dialed Chuck.

The detective picked up on the fourth ring and sounded grumpy and half stoned. "Yeah—"

"How's it going?" Campbell began, really cringing now at the thought of siccing his old pal, the Charger, on the frightened Mrs. Smith.

Chuck groaned or, rather, bellowed in the middle of a yawn and some other noisy, repulsive body function, "What the hell time is it, anyway?"

"What the hell's wrong with you? I know not to call you till noon—"

"Ooh…" Chuck paused. "Bad night." Another groan that pierced Campbell's eardrum. "Hangover. Vicious little hammers pounding in my brain. Not to mention—"

"What'd you do—"

"Got into a little…er…altercation…." The Charger let the statement hang.

"You got drunk again and picked a fight—"

"No, man, this bastard insulted my bike. I took serious issue. Nobody says shit like that about the Charger's bike. The ape was wearing steel-toed boots, and he had more friends than I did. They had chains. Every muscle in my body feels like he kicked it. I've gotta black eye that's as purple as a plum and a tooth that's hanging by a pink thread."

"Your big mouth is going to be the end of you yet." Campbell talked tough, but he felt affection. "Got something I want you to check out. A *lady*." He told him everything he knew about Hannah Smith. He finished by saying he'd have Muriel fax key information from her file.

"What's she done?"

"Just find out who she really is—ASAP. And no rough stuff."

Chuck was six feet four inches, three hundred pounds of flab and muscle. Just a glance at the Charger, and the average Joe Blow thought—*thug,* if not worse things. He had massive arms, shoulder-length red hair, a gold loop in his right ear and a beer belly with a death head tattooed on it. He rode a Harley, which was as immaculate as he was unkempt. Not that he was as tough as he looked.

The Charger had strong convictions, which got stronger when he was drunk and forgot he was a coward. He'd been on the wrong side of trouble a time or two. Campbell had bailed him out more times than he could count. Nevertheless, after years of brawling, the Charger had found a niche of sorts. He was a top-notch detective and a whiz on the computer, not that he let on to any of his biker buddies.

"Hannah Smith, huh. Mystery lady? No rough stuff? You got the hots for this mama or something?"

Campbell suppressed a vision of her in the bikini. "Just find out who she is. And don't let her see you. She's scared of her own shadow. One whiff of you…and she'd run like a rabbit."

"You *do* have the hots." The Charger laughed.

"Scare the hell out of her if you want to, for all I care!" Campbell slammed the phone down and ordered pizza. He did not give a damn about Mrs. Smith. He didn't.

Speaking of the hots, Muriel came in and told him Mrs. Crocker had called four more times.

"Call her back. Tell her I'm gone for the day."

Shuffling through the stacked files on his desk, he saw the name Guy James on one of the labels and remembered he was supposed to make a decision as to whether or not to hire the kid as a law clerk. The kid was taking a year off from law school because his little brother was sick and getting sicker. Guy was raw and young and smart. He'd needed a job so badly he'd really pressed Campbell.

Impressed as Campbell was by the kid, he was in no mood to call him. Later.

Shoving James's file aside, he eyed the rest of the stacked files and wondered how much he could get done if he worked until midnight. No reason to go home; there was nobody there. He was opening the top folder on his stack when Bob Africa buzzed him.

"I want to know how the deposition went. My office. Ten minutes? Okay?"

Not okay. Campbell hated stacks and wanted to get to work.

"Sure." Campbell's low voice was mild, but he spoke through his teeth and slammed the folder shut.

Hell.

Two

When the big metal door clanged shut behind her, Hannah stood in the dark beneath the burned-out light in the shadowy parking garage. For once she didn't really register she was alone in the kind of place she was terrified of.

No, she was still shaking all over from the intensity of Joe Campbell's attack, still too upset by the dark fury scrawled on his handsome, piratical face when he'd ripped off her glasses and stared at her with those black, deadly eyes that had stripped her to the bone while he threatened to expose her.

His wife had divorced him. Lucky woman.

Clasping her throat, where a large hand had once pulled red satin ribbons too tight, Hannah shivered, feeling sick to her stomach. *Are you somebody else's woman? Admit it. You'd better admit it because I've been watching you.* Then the ribbons had squeezed off her breath.

Behind closed doors Mr. Campbell was probably a dangerous, violent and pathetically sick man.

She'd dreamed about this deposition, dreamed about him, had nightmares about him. But he had been worse than her nightmares. Every slick question, every pretty-boy white smile, every sympathetic stare when she'd tried to tell him what had really happened had been meant to trick or entrap her. And the way he'd kept looking at her, and looking through her, had thrown her totally off balance.

Naive fool that she still was, she'd wanted to be honest, but with a predator of his ruthless reputation, she'd known the foolhardiness of that tactic. So— knowing what kind of man he was, suspecting he was even worse in private, she'd deliberately baited him and made him so mad that he really was out to get her now. Why had she done that?

Because his black, deadly eyes had made her feel trapped and scared. She'd felt that if she'd attacked him, maybe he'd let up on her. But, of course his kind never backed off. She should know.

Oh, why hadn't she just stuck to her plan to be careful and not to say anything that he could use against her?

Now he'd really be gunning for her. He'd called her a fake and threatened to expose her. Her stomach heaved queasily.

Oh, if only she could go somewhere, have a cup of tea or something, get over the awful encounter…maybe catch her breath, even.

She wanted to sit alone in a café where she could calm down and have time to digest what had happened, maybe think of a new game plan to appease him. Maybe she could ask Tom to settle on the mold issue so Joe Campbell wouldn't threaten her entire life and the safety of her little girl.

She glanced fearfully at her watch. No time for tea. As usual, she was late to pick up her darling Georgia.

Late! It was never smart to keep Georgia waiting. No telling what mischief her dynamo might get into.

Hannah heard the rumble of wheels on concrete and the soft purr of a finely tuned engine several floors below. Suddenly, it struck her that she was all alone in a place that terrified her. Why hadn't she thought to have Tom walk her to her car?

As she moved away from the door to find her Mercedes, the ninth floor of the parking garage seemed to be bathed in an eerie, shadow-filled light. The air felt dank and thick and way too warm. She gasped for breath, for air itself.

Enclosed places. Hot spaces. Not her thing. Especially since she'd been stalked.

She swallowed and inhaled another little breath. Something was wrong—she could feel it. Turning her head, she peered into the darkness, but nobody seemed to be there. And yet, she felt a presence, as if someone was watching her. Naturally, she thought of the man who used to track her every move, the man who'd professed undying love for her.

He isn't here. He can't be. Crossing herself, she tilted her chin upward. Then she forced herself to pad silently in the direction of her ancient Mercedes, which she'd parked by the up ramp.

Why hadn't she just parked on the street? Why?

Because it was important not to give in to every fear or whim, or pretty soon her whole life would be dictated by them.

Because being afraid was no way to live.

Don't go there, she thought. Don't think of *him.*

Lately, she'd been dreaming about him. Instead of

reliving the dark, horrible memories of their marriage like she used to, she'd been dreaming he'd found her. That he was here, that he was only waiting, that he was playing one of his cat-and-mouse games again before he pounced on her.

"Did I ever tell you hide-and-seek was my favorite game when I was growing up?" he'd whispered lovingly one night.

Walking faster, she began rummaging in her catch-all of a purse for her car key.

At last she saw her Mercedes. She'd parked it in Joe Campbell's spot because it had been the only empty space—and to defy him.

Only something was wrong. Her silver-blue sedan looked off balance somehow.

"Oh dear...." The front right tire was flat. *He* used to flatten her tires.

From somewhere on the same floor, she heard hushed male laughter and then slow, deliberate steps. Then something moved toward her from the shadows.

A man? *Him?*

Black wings hurtled out of the ceiling struts straight at her. When a feather brushed her cheek, she screamed.

It was only a bird she'd startled. Not that that knowledge slowed her down any. Without investigating the tire, she skittered back toward the door that led to Joe Campbell's offices as fast as she could run. Only when she got to the door, it was locked. When she jiggled the metal knob and yanked at it, and the door wouldn't open from the outside, she beat on it, screaming. There was a keypad by the door, but she was too hysterical to remember the combination Muriel, Mr. Campbell's beautiful, efficient secretary, had given her.

Her mind darted about wildly. She'd written it down, but it was lost in the scramble of scraps of paper in her purse somewhere. No use to even look for it. Not now.

As she pounded, the heavy footsteps behind her reverberated through the concrete parking garage.

He'd found her. Her dreams had been right once again.

If *he* killed her this time, what would happen to Georgia? Would he hurt her daughter as he'd threatened? And what about her mother?

Frantic, she beat on the door and screamed Campbell's name.

To her surprise, the door was suddenly thrust open by a powerful arm. When a tall, dark man flung himself into the dark garage like a warrior on the rampage, she fell back, gasping.

Gold cuff links flashed when he held his hand up as a shield against the glare from the slanting sun behind her. His tie was lurid yellow. Coal-black eyes regarded her with intense hostility as he held a raised golf club.

"Campbell?"

He nodded, lowering the golf club. "Who'd you expect? You were yelling my name at the top of your lungs. You in trouble?" He was panting as if he'd run the whole way from his offices just to save her.

She tried to deny that she'd called for him, but her throat was dry, and her lips seemed completely paralyzed.

He looked exhausted. No! He couldn't have found the deposition as draining as she. And he hadn't run all the way to save anybody. Least of all—her. Joe Campbell was the devil. Nobody could have eyes so deadly and cold and not at least be a red-horned disciple. And yet, somehow he seemed human. The terrible truth was she'd never been so glad to see anybody in her whole life.

"You? You again?" he muttered, recognizing her in the gloom. "I thought you'd left."

When she just stared at him, he crossed his arms. "What's wrong? Did you forget something? Don't just stand there staring at me like I'm the devil incarnate."

She couldn't seem to stop looking at him, and suddenly she felt slightly ashamed she'd compared him to the devil. Yes, his hair was midnight black. It was so long it brushed his crisp, white collar and curled against his ears. But he had a cowlick that made her want to run her fingers through his hair and smooth it. And he was handsome. More importantly, he'd come when she called.

"I have a flat. I don't know how to change—"

"A flat? Hell! Why didn't you say so, woman? That's nothing to get so upset about and scream like somebody's murdering you. Why don't you call a car service or something instead of yelling my name to kingdom come?"

It galled her to think he was probably never scared of anything, that he got to do all the scaring. And yet she was glad he was here. Fiercely glad.

"So, who's upset?" she said. "I'm fine."

"You look scared, a lot more scared than you did in my office." He voice matched his eyes and was almost human. "What are you so frightened of? Tell me—damn it."

"Nothing." But she swallowed.

"You're not a very good liar."

"Maybe I need lessons from you."

"Anytime," he whispered in a silky voice. "Did you know that the fact that you're a lousy liar was the first thing I figured out about you?"

"W-we were talking about my flat."

"Right. So, do you have a towing service?"

"Yes, but I—I don't want to wait in the garage...all alone."

"See, you are scared."

She bit her lip.

"I...I could stay and wait with you." He stared at her, or rather through her, and made her heart skitter. "Would that help?" he asked.

She shouldn't spend an extra second with him. "Y-yes."

"So, where's your car?"

Reluctantly, she led the way. Which was a mistake—she was parked in his spot. Worse, he stayed behind her and watched the way her hips moved when she walked.

When he laughed, she whirled on him. "Do you have to drill holes through me?"

His gaze shot sparks. "Do you have to walk like *that?*"

"Like what?"

"You know."

She put her hands on her hips and glared at him. "I don't have the energy or time for this. I'm exhausted, okay?"

He drew a long breath and nodded.

They walked the rest of the way to her Mercedes in silence.

When they reached the front of her car, she pushed her hands in her pockets. "I'm late to pick up my little girl."

"Georgia?"

"How did—"

"Old car," he said.

"New tires," she countered. "I maintain it."

"My parking spot."

"Sorry. Look, I'm in a hurry."

"If you don't want to wait for a wrecker, I have a can of something that blows air and a sealant into a tire. It's only a temporary fix, but it should get you where you're going."

"I'll pay you for the can."

She pressed her lips together and stared into the corners of the shadowy garage.

"Follow me," he murmured, watching her too intently. "The can is in my car."

His brand-new, gleaming black Porsche was parked on an upper floor. Quickly, he opened the trunk and pulled out a spray can. They walked back down the stairs to her car together. Then he knelt beside her front tire and began twisting something before he attached the can to her tire.

"Muriel should have told you not to park so near the ramp and definitely not in my spot when she was giving you instructions how to get here," he muttered as he punched the nozzle that sprayed air and goo into her tire.

"She did. I—I think."

And she'd told Muriel she probably wouldn't park in the garage, anyway.

"Every summer, the street kids like to skateboard in the garage," he said. "They flatten the tires of any car that parks near the ramp where they make their turns."

He was frowning, and she had the distinct impression that he was leaving some vital piece of information out.

"Why don't you stop them?"

"We've tried everything. But what we eventually learned is that if we don't want to come out to a flat tire, we don't park near the ramps."

"I'd think a building full of lawyers could best a bunch of kids."

"Street kids are a dangerous breed." He spoke with the authority of one who knew.

"Were you a street kid?"

He didn't answer.

It should have been difficult to imagine him as a little boy, but the image of a tough little guy in a tougher neighborhood sprang full-blown in her mind. She saw a red sky and an industrial neighborhood peopled with young thugs that beat him on a regular basis.

The kid in her vision was brown and dirty and had a permanent scowl. The other kids his age refused to play ball with him. Bullies chased him.

"Kids used to beat you up when you walked home from school, didn't they?" she said.

A muscle flexed in his jaw, and he nodded. "But not every day. Back then I could run like a greased jackrabbit. I had this fat friend—the Charger. He wasn't as fast as me, so they usually caught him and beat him up. He was big, so it took about five of them."

"And you just ran off and left him?"

His mouth quirked.

"So, where's the Charger now?"

"Around." The skin above his white collar flushed and he focused on filling her tire. When her tire was full of air, he stood up.

Nervously she backed away from him but not without glancing around the garage. "I—I guess I'd better go—"

"Just say thank you. Thank you for fixing my flat, Campbell. That will suffice."

"Thank you," she whispered, "for fixing my flat."

"I could follow you," he offered, catching her frightened glance when she turned back to him.

"Oh… No… I'd rather you didn't," she said, plunging her hands into the pockets of her jumper so he wouldn't know how violently they were shaking.

"Just to make sure your tire doesn't go flat before you reach your destination," he offered.

"As I said…" She paused and made her eyes and voice firmer. "I'd rather you…didn't."

He flushed and set his jaw. "Right." He drew in a deep breath. "I could give you another can."

"That's not really necessary."

"Hopefully not." His tone was clipped now. "But just in case, I don't want you stranded somewhere."

As though you care.

As they walked upstairs to his car again, their footsteps echoed in the concrete stairwell. She glanced around nervously, keeping close to Campbell. When they reached his car, he opened his trunk again and pulled out another can.

"At least let me follow you out of the garage."

"No. You have to know you're the last person I would have asked for help if…"

"If there had been anybody else with a golf club handy."

"Just so we understand each other."

Again he flushed, his dark eyes so haunted, he almost looked human.

As if he were a gentleman, he followed her down the stairs. Anxious to pick up Georgia, she ran down them as rapidly as possible.

When they reached her car, he opened her door.

"Who the hell are you really?" he muttered as she got in. "What the hell are you so afraid of?"

She looked up. "I'm sorry I kept you. Thank you."

In a panic to get to Georgia's school, she rolled her windows up and started her car before the glow plugs had a chance to warm up. When he shouted at her to wait, she raced quickly away.

Every mile she put between herself and the parking garage calmed her until she got to Georgia's school and saw his gleaming black Porsche parked in front of the school. She gasped when she recognized Joe Campbell, of all people, sitting under the wide ash trees right beside her own darling, innocent, unsuspecting, little Georgia and the elementary school principal. The two men were chatting as if they were old friends.

Coincidence? She didn't think so.

Georgia was reading out of a storybook. Her golden hair shone. Her pose was unusually still. The book had to be wonderful. Usually Georgia was such a live wire, her teachers complained.

When Campbell glanced down at the little girl, he looked sweet and fatherly. Hannah's throat tightened. He wasn't a nice man. She had to remember that. He had no business here. Still, for nine years, she had dreamed of Georgia having a father to dote on her. She'd kept hoping that Dom... The thought of Dom terrified her.

Shoving her car door open, Hannah got out of her Mercedes. Georgia didn't look up until Hannah called her. Then her rambunctious, little darling jumped up and skipped down the sidewalk toward her, avoiding every crack.

"Mommy, what took you so long?" Georgia's smile was so trusting, Hannah forgot Campbell and smiled, too.

When Georgia hugged her, Campbell shook hands with the principal and started toward them as if he'd been waiting for her the whole time.

Georgia turned her head and beamed at him shyly.

"Sweetheart, get in the car," Hannah said before turning to face Campbell.

Three

The sun was streaming through the trees, making shadows dance across his target's dark, carved face as teachers streamed out of the building on all sides of him and the little girl.

Mothers were double-parked in their cars, and the air reeked with exhaust fumes.

Damn.

One minute he had him in the scope and the next he was blinking at a bright disk of white glare.

Campbell's Porsche was parked directly in front of the school. A few students loitered, teasing one another, laughing, talking and shoving one another. The watcher smiled grimly as the barrel of his rifle roamed from the chain-link fence surrounding the schoolyard, from the crossing guards, the teachers, to the kids carrying armloads of books.

Bang. Bang.

The watcher itched to blow them all away.

You're not here to play games.

It took a second or two to pick Campbell out of the crowd and sight him in with the scope again. One glance at that arrogant face in his crosshairs, and the shooter's finger twitched. Sweat beaded his brow. It was so damn hot one wondered why the dry brown grasses on the playground didn't burst into flame.

His gut twisted as he zeroed in on his target, dead center. His eyes blurred. His temple throbbed. Soon the pain in his head was intense, electric, explosive. He had his target; he had the right weapon, a Sako .270 mounted with a Nikon scope.

He was thinking how easy it would be to take Mr. J. Campbell out. So, easy. Then a woman with black hair, fine-boned features and pale, creamy skin got in his way.

Move your cute ass, bitch.

He shifted the gun to the unsmiling woman. She seemed to be scolding a blond little girl.

The woman moved toward Campbell. She was angry. All of a sudden the watcher felt a nagging sense of familiarity.

His trigger finger shook again. No way to miss. Not at this range; not with a gun like this. With difficulty he set the gun down and wiped his sweaty cheek on his shoulder.

To do this right, he had to eliminate his emotions. With difficulty he suppressed his hatred and distrust for the legal system and for his intended victim and watched him through his scope.

Lowering the gun, the watcher stared at Campbell and the woman. They seemed like players on a stage as they stood perfectly still, their gazes fixed on each other.

Shoot him. Blow him away. What have you got to lose?

* * *

"Yes, why did it take you so long to get here?" Campbell demanded, his eyes hard and intent on Hannah's face.

Frowning at him, Hannah turned to Georgia. "*Darling*, I said get in the car."

"But...but this nice man, Mr. Campbell, is a friend of Mr. Brayfield's."

"I thought I told you never to talk to strangers."

"Besides, Mummy...er...*Mommy*, you were late. And he isn't a stranger. He gave a speech to our school. He's a friend of the principal."

Campbell smiled at her. Hannah's stomach writhed.

"I have something to say to our friend, then," Hannah muttered through her teeth.

"Mummy—"

"Georgia!"

Now, for the first time, Hannah wished Georgia was an easy child.

"Please, Georgia..."

Georgia recognized that low tone in her mother's voice that meant business and hastily hopped into the Mercedes.

Hannah strode up to him and put both hands squarely on her hips. "I asked you not to follow me."

He shrugged. "I didn't. I took a shortcut."

"Stay away from my little girl. Stay away from me."

"You were scared in the parking lot...hysterical."

As though you care!

"I was not!" Her voice was so shrill two young teachers turned to stare. Campbell's sable hair glinted in the sunlight as he smiled at them. Annoyed even more, Hannah flushed when the women smiled back.

"Keep your voice down," he advised. "And for the record, I *was* worried about you."

"Why don't I believe you."

He forced another of those broad white smiles, which he no doubt knew made him ten times more handsome.

"You won't tell me who you really are, or what you're afraid of," he said in a mild tone. "So, on a hunch, I got here as fast as I could…just in case…you were being followed and your daughter was at risk."

"You are not, let me repeat, not a Good Samaritan. You keep a string of pneumatic blondes on the—"

His face darkened. "I never heard that word before."

She paled. "I do not believe you have even one drop of decency in your blood."

"I think you're running scared…which makes you vulnerable—"

"What would it take to get you out of my life?" she whispered.

"You could settle with the O'Connors."

"Never in a million years."

"You're going to regret that decision," he said.

"No, you're going to regret getting high-handed with me."

"If you go to trial, there's a chance some juror might find your face familiar, too. His memory might prove better than mine." She trembled when he looked directly into her eyes. "Who are you? Why did you dye your hair? Who the hell are you running from?''

She felt faint. His face blurred. She couldn't endure another moment of this. ''Nobody.''

"Mrs. Smith?" He smiled. ''Like I said, you're one lousy liar.'' His expression was intense. ''You're from the UK.''

Somehow she found her voice. ''What?''

''Your daughter has the accent. You can hide it. She can't.''

Hannah felt light-headed as he slid a brown hand into his hip pocket and took out his wallet.

Her mother and grandmother were both Americans. So was Georgia's real father. Hannah was good at accents and was careful about vocabulary. How difficult was it to change *lift* to *elevator* or *bonnet* to *hood* or *loo* to *rest room?*

Quickly, he handed her his card. ''Call me if you change your mind about settling.''

Mute with too many out-of-control emotions, all she could do was glare at him.

''And something else you might want to consider—if you settle, I'll make sure nothing about the case makes the papers.'' His uncanny black gaze focused on her lips.

''The papers?''

''You must be new here. Big settlements are news. And if this case makes the papers here, the news just might reach London.''

She winced, remembering too well what it was like to live in the blinding glare of paparazzi.

''Mommy!'' Georgia began honking the horn.

"Who the hell are you running from?" he repeated softly.

"At the moment—you."

"I've seen your face somewhere. I've got a detective doing research...."

"You what..."

"You heard me. It's in your best interest to settle—fast."

She blanched. "Stay away from me and my little girl or you'll be sorry."

"Is that a threat, *Mrs. Smith?*"

"Absolutely."

He laughed. She threw herself inside her car, slammed the door, jammed her fists down onto the door locks.

He leaned down. Because she was curious, she lowered her window.

"I'd like to follow you home. That tire might—"

"Not your problem."

"I could be held liable since I fixed—"

"Good—then I'll get to sue you!"

"I'd settle in a heartbeat." The bright afternoon sun slanted into the garage and made a golden aura around his black head and broad shoulders. He was handsome, but he'd made her so angry she was shaking.

"Move, before I back over your toes."

She turned around to make sure Georgia had her seat belt on. Then crossing herself, she stomped on her accelerator so hard, thick black fumes plumed out of her tailpipe, as she sped away.

Georgia and she drove in silence for a while.

Settle? Hannah was so upset, she forgot her fear. *I'll be damned before I make one more bargain with the devil.*

Georgia's clear, piping voice from the back seat suddenly broke into Hannah's thoughts. "Mummy, me hungwee."

Georgia had begun reverting to baby talk when they'd moved to Texas.

"Mommy, remember? And no baby talk, darling."

The Big Burger sign winked invitingly from the next corner.

"I said me hungwee."

Hannah's heart softened. Because she felt guilty for having dragged Georgia halfway around the world, she pulled into Big Burger way too often.

With a show of determination she kept driving. "Remember, darling, last night, how we made that vow—no more burgers, that we'd try that new salad bar on the island, the one Taz likes...." Taz was their next-door neighbor. They were supposed to go to dinner with Taz tonight.

Hannah could see Georgia's head whip around in the rearview mirror when they passed the Big Burger sign.

"I want a big burger and double fries. But...but after tonight...after tonight..." Her coaxing voice was sly. "Then I'll promise...to eat with Taz."

"Darling—Mommy said no."

It was a word she'd said numerous times that day.

Not wanting to alarm Hannah Smith, the watcher held back, keeping her ancient Mercedes barely in sight until she headed onto the causeway that went out to the offshore island where she lived. Soon lines of orange barrels and flashing lights narrowed the road to two lanes. Traffic soon slowed to a slug's pace.

Concrete walls hemmed her in. On one side of the roadway lapped the gray waters of the Laguna Madre. The bay was to the left. Extra-tall telephone poles marched beside the causeway toward the intercoastal canal. The tide was so low, clusters of white pelicans walked about in the water wade-fishing. The exposed mudflats and oyster reefs made the air reek with the stench of rotting sea vegetation.

When she crossed the bridge over the intercoastal canal, his bloodshot eyes lifted to his rearview mirror. *That same white car that had been behind him since he'd left Campbell's parking garage was still there.*

The big Harley roared onto the causeway. A few miles later, the Mercedes made a quick left onto Mustang Island. So did he. So did the car behind him, even though the light had turned red.

The big Harley spun on its side and made the turn, too.

What the hell is this—a lousy parade?

He followed her ten miles through a moonscape of white dunes to Port Aransas, where she made a right turn on one of the roads that led to the beach.

He glanced into his rearview mirror. The white car was still behind him.

And so was the Harley.

What the hell was going on?

Four

The first thing Hannah had done when she got home was to race to her bedroom, rip off her ugly jumper and toss it onto her bedroom floor on top of everything else she'd worn that week. Okay, so she was a lousy housekeeper—

Stripping off her panty hose, she pulled on a worn pair of hip-hugger, button-fly jeans and a T-shirt that didn't reach her navel.

When Georgia ran into her bedroom with her nail polish and begged her to paint their toenails orange, Hannah was in no mood for company. She wanted to tell Georgia she was too young for orange nail polish. But since Georgia had no friends her age here to play with, she smiled and gently said, "Sure, darling, let's go for it."

Georgia squealed and squatted on the floor in front of Hannah's bare feet. "I'll paint yours first and then you paint mine!"

"Don't forget to stay inside the lines."

Georgia laughed and did her best, but her best left a lot to be desired. Soon orange nail polish was on Hannah's heel and dribbling between her toes onto the oak floor.

"Sorry, Mommy."

"Oh, well, a little nail polish will wash off." When Georgia skipped off to her room after she was done, Hannah found a rag to clean the floor and hollered after her, "Put the polish back where it belongs, love."

Georgia's door slammed. Without bothering to wait until her orange toenails dried, Hannah slipped into a pair of tall platform sandals and returned to the kitchen to enjoy a glass of wine by herself while Georgia played on her computer.

Big Burger wrappings littered the kitchen counter. Georgia had only had to plead thirty seconds before winning the Big Burger battle hands down. Hannah was too tired tonight to feel too guilty about indulging her.

The phone rang, and she picked it up before she checked the caller ID. If she'd checked, she would have put Katherine Rosner off until she was back in her office. The woman came on a little too strong, which was natural since Katherine's doctor husband was divorcing her. The woman was feeling desperate at the thought of having to move to a smaller place and go back into nursing. Hannah sympathized, but she was tired tonight.

"It's me. Do you have a minute?" Katherine's soft, sexy voice was highly charged.

Tiny redheaded woman. Huge aura. Something about Katherine bothered Hannah. She moved with the grace of a leopard, fast and swift and silent, so you didn't always know she was coming. Then there she was, her ferocious eyes flashing as she made some demand or launched into a rant about her grievances—the main one being her husband.

Hannah had spent eight hours showing Katherine houses the day before.

"Hi, Katherine, I was wondering what you'd decided."

"I still can't make up my mind. The house in Country Club needs too much work. Besides, it's owned by a lousy personal injury attorney. I'm not going to feed one of those sharks by buying a house from him."

Translation: the house in Country Club was way more than Katherine could afford without her doctor husband's salary.

Hannah sighed. "You never mentioned you had it in for attorneys."

"Just the personal injury guys."

Hannah thought about Joe Campbell. Katherine did have a point.

"Then we'll keep looking," Hannah said.

"You are so sweet."

"Yesterday was fun." That wasn't totally true.

"I was feeling so depressed after you left, so I went out for a drive. I saw a sign on Ocean. Darling house. There was a blue heron on the pier."

Katherine probably wouldn't qualify for a loan on a house on Ocean Drive. "Do you really need a pier? I mean do you fish or anything? And a seawall costs a lot to maintain."

"I grew up in the country. Four brothers. I fish, hunt... So, can we see it together tomorrow? Nine? Your office?"

Hannah jotted down the address and agreed to meet her though she knew it was a waste of time.

Katherine was a sleek, elegant doctor's wife on the wrong side of forty, who worked hard not to look it. She had a good body. When she wore skirts, she showed a lot of leg.

From what Katherine had told her, Hannah had gathered she'd been the other woman in the doctor's nasty divorce ten years earlier and didn't want to be blindsided by a younger, hotter version of herself.

"So, is he leaving you for another woman?" Hannah had asked when they'd been touring the garden of the house in Country Club.

"No, he said he just doesn't look forward to coming home to me at night anymore."

"Oh, Katherine…"

"It's so unfair. He's no prince. He's overweight, older. He has nose hairs. He's always clipping them when he follows me around yapping at me. And he's no big deal in bed."

"Then maybe he's doing you a favor."

"He's leaving me!" Katherine had shrieked. "I'll be all alone…again. He makes *money*. I was a lousy nurse before…"

After the phone call Hannah tried to unwind again, but Katherine's restless energy had infected her. Hannah felt as uprooted as Katherine. She didn't belong in Texas, but she couldn't go home. The window over the sink was cracked an inch, so the roar of the surf and the smell of muggy, salt air and pungent, rotting sea things permeated the tiny kitchen—alien scents.

She was used to grass and trees, to big-city life, to a cooler, softer climate. To glamour. To horror.

Hannah clenched her fingers. Who was she to judge Katherine? There was a big hole in her own life. Huge. Only her problems weren't as simple as Katherine's. Hannah couldn't fix them by a divorce. If only Dom would give her a divorce.

They say if a frog hops into a kettle of water and you light a fire under it, the frog won't jump out as the water warms up. He'll die.

That had happened to Hannah twice before with men.

Sometimes she felt like she was that frog, dying, little by little. For nine months she'd been in exile, living, if you could call it living, while she waited for a miracle. Away from her friends, Georgia had become increasingly bored and unhappy, and that made Hannah feel guilty.

But you're still alive, and Georgia's alive.

If you want things to change, you have to do something, kiddo.

I ran away—that's something!

Now it's time to do more!

She opened her newspaper and recoiled when Joe Campbell's avid white grin gleamed at her from the front page. Billboards, telephone book and now the newspaper! His black eyes burned through her defenses and made her feel totally vulnerable. Worst of all, he looked a little like Dom.

The article that ran beneath Campbell's picture had to do with large medical malpractice awards in the county attracting big names like him to the city. The good news was that he'd just lost a big medical case to a Dr. Albert Crocker. The press about Campbell was unflattering, and neither he nor the partners of his firm had agreed to be interviewed for the article.

Beneath his story ran a headline, Neurosurgeons in Short Supply.

"Due to soaring malpractice insurance rates, doctors and insurance companies are fleeing Texas...."

She was in no mood to read further. There was another story on mold litigation. Mold claims were paying off big in Texas, too. Homeowners' insurance rates were soaring. Lots of people could no longer afford to insure their homes.

Hannah wadded up the paper. Then she unwadded it and snipped out *his* picture. Not knowing why she did that, she flung the rest of the newspaper aside and rushed to her refrigerator, where she eyed her half-full bottle of chardonnay on the lower shelf for several minutes before removing a milk carton. She couldn't let Mr. Billboard and his hot eyes and the litigation-crazy world she was forced to do business in drive her to drinking alone.

Not that she was alone. The beach house was so small and the walls so thin she could hear Georgia in her room, her fingers tapping on her computer keyboard.

Georgia being home only makes it worse, and you know it.

How many more long, lonely and sometimes terrifying evenings without the intelligent companionship or solace of another adult could she endure?

Then there were the nights when she couldn't sleep, and worse, those when she could and had nightmares.

When her cupboard proved empty of clean glasses, she splashed milk into a white cup with little blue seagulls on it. She loved her dishes. After a sip, she went out to the mailbox. Again, there was no mail. That had been happening a lot lately. Which was odd. Not that it mattered, really. Almost nobody from her real life knew where she was, so there wouldn't have been anything but bills and junk mail, flyers to pitch in the trash along with the newspaper and the brightly colored Big Burger wrappings.

Finishing her milk, Hannah stuffed the cup into her sink, which was overflowing with dirty dishes. She should cook and clean house, go downstairs to the washing machines with a load of clothes, maybe. But where to begin?

How ill prepared she was for ordinary, middle-class life. She was used to a man doing the heavy work, to a maid and a nanny, to long glamorous dinners with family and friends, not to tasteless fast food or house-work in a remote beach house at the end of a long day. Oh, how she missed her beautiful things, her social life.

But there were things she did not miss.

At least, while here, she got to live on the gulf. Maybe the fragile barrier island was a thirty-minute commute from downtown Corpus and Georgia's private school, but as soon as she'd seen the For Rent sign on the gray beach house at the edge of the dunes, the house had spoken to her.

When she was frightened or lonely, all she had to

do was step outside to breathe in the smell of the gulf and to hear the seabirds, which she'd come to love...especially the brown pelicans and blue herons. Tonight there would even be a full moon. She would look up at the stars and know how small and tiny she and her problems were. The island with its rustic beach houses built on pilings and the glamorous high-rise condos and looser ambience attracted all kinds of people—tourists from all over the world, artists, rebels, runaways...like her.

She ran a damp rag across the counter to clean off the hamburger bun crumbs and headed toward the sink with the wet grit. She sighed. Then her thoughts turned to home again. Was her mother all right? *He* wouldn't hurt her mother, would he?

He never had before.

You never left him before.

Her mother was famous. Even if she were impaired now, people would notice if Claudia Hayes had an accident. The story would make the papers. Hannah would know if her mother wasn't all right.

Hannah glanced toward her phone and felt almost desperate enough to dial the home where her mother resided. But the roar of a motorcycle in the drive and then the sound of light footsteps and the jingling of tiny bells on her stairs saved her. Then she remembered. Taz still thought they were going to dinner.

"Knock, knock," rang a cheery, determined voice.

Hannah started silently for the door.

"You're supposed to say who's there," the voice jeered.

For once Hannah was almost glad she had a pushy, overly friendly neighbor.

A plump dark arm pushed the door open, and Hannah gave a little shriek of delight when she saw the wild creature gilded in her doorway by the fiery sunshine.

"Taz, is that you?"

"Sister Tasmania!"

The short black woman in her late twenties looked older than she was and tougher, too, but in a good way. People took Taz seriously in spite of her tendency to be flamboyant.

Tonight Taz had bells on her gold, strappy sandals, so she jingled when she pranced across the threshold. "Don't you dare say you're too busy to go out and eat again!"

Taz whirled to a chorus of more tinkling bells. "How do you like the new me?" Taz shot her a hot white smile. Waist-length black braids danced about her wide, golden face. She barely came up to Hannah's shoulders; still, she exuded the presence of a woman ten times her size. Unlike Katherine, she wasn't scary or intimidating. Taz was plump and inviting, and men of all ages, classes and races threw themselves at her.

"Not that any of them have ever been someone I can take home to my grandmother," Taz had confided to Hannah one afternoon when Taz's phone hadn't quit ringing. Like Hannah, Taz had a weakness for bad boys.

"Whoa. What did you do to your hair?" Hannah asked.

At least a hundred braids fell about Tasmania's vo-
luptuous shoulders. A pleated gown that made her
look Egyptian swirled around her hips as she danced
about the kitchen.

"You definitely got carried away this time."

"I told my man to take a hike. Then I got me a
massage and a makeover." She wiggled a foot and
showed off painted green toenails.

"You don't look much like a high school principal."

"Don't want to, either. Not tonight, anyway." Taz
laughed.

"Tinkerbell with Egyptian braids."

"Who rides a motorcycle, too." She pushed past
Hannah and slapped a hot pink card onto the counter.
"Got my new business cards. You got a beer?"

"Just chardonnay."

Taz frowned. "How did your deposition with Mr.
Billboard go?"

Hannah's eyebrows furrowed.

"Bad, huh? Well, you got to him. A friend of mine
who works for the handsome no-good told me. He
was so upset after you left, he kicked a door."

Hannah beamed. "He fixed my flat, too."

"Better watch yourself, girl. He definitely wants
you in bed."

Hannah shrugged. "He *is* handsome."

"No man ever does the slightest thing to help you
if he isn't enticed."

Hannah rolled her eyes and guzzled a big sip of
wine.

"Test my hypothesis some time. You'll see I'm

right. But I want to talk about this lawsuit stuff. Did I tell you—I'm being sued, too?''

''What? Why?''

''As if you need a why in south Texas. But... okay...you want the details. You know I broke up with Sid.''

''Right.''

''Well, the night before we broke up, we'd had some pretty raucous sex. Sid was hungry, so I nuked him a leftover hamburger. The damn pickle fell out of the bun and burned his...er...member. The man did carry on. He turned beet red. I'm afraid I started laughing and couldn't stop.''

''You burned his pickle with a pickle and laughed and then you dumped him?''

''Yeah. 'Cause he got so mad when I laughed. I can't stand a man with no sense of humor.''

''You shouldn't have laughed.''

''You should have heard the mean things he called me. It wasn't fair. If he wouldn't have been talking and eating at the same time the hot pickle wouldn't have... So, it's his fault! But his lawyer, he says it's my fault Sid can't make love to his new woman.''

''If you go to court, lose the braids.''

''Hell, now I wished I'd bobbed his pink pickle or something. Then he wouldn't be worried he can't put it where he shouldn't.''

''You are mad.''

''I got served with a bunch of legal stuff at school today. What I need is to go out and distract myself. Where are we going to supper? What about a bar, too?''

Hannah opened the fridge and got out the bottle of wine. Then she sifted through her sink and washed two wineglasses.

"Don't bother drying." Taz grabbed a wet glass and poured. She took a sip and choked. Then she emptied a teaspoon of sugar into her wineglass and swirled it.

Hannah read Taz's new hot-pink business card. "Let Sister Tasmania make your wishes come true. Defeat your enemies. And your rivals. If you have a problem with the past, present, future, marriage, business, finance or health, Sister will help you out. There is no burden too great for her to lift from your heavy heart. She succeeds where others fail." Hannah set the card down and laughed. "You're supposed to be a school principal."

"Not for long. That was my grandmother's dream. I'm opening myself a little business on the side, something more spiritual, so I have more time to stay in touch with whatever's out there."

Hannah lifted the pink card again. "Oh, boy, do I have a burden."

"Mr. Billboard?"

"He's one problem, yes."

"You want him off the case? Jump his bones. The man has a weakness for the ladies. Get him on your side."

"I loathe him."

"Baby, don't you know that'll just make the sex better? I hated Sid half the nights we did it."

"I'm not like that," Hannah said. "I want to love the next man."

"You're one hot lady. I can tell that about you."
Taz pursed her lips. "Even with sugar, your wine is
so-o dry. It doesn't quench my thirst at all."

"Sugar! I can't believe you put sugar in—"

"Let's go out for a beer. And no salad bar! I could
do with something tasty like a burger, too."

"No more burgers." Hannah crossed her heart. "I
made a vow. Besides, after your hot-pickle adventure,
I wouldn't think you'd want—"

"I blame Sid—not burgers!"

With a shake of her head, Hannah pointed toward
the back of the house. "I'm sorry Taz. We already
ate. You know I can't go because Georgia's—"

"You ate already? That's just like you. Since I've
known you, you have never gone out. Not once.
You're going to go crazy if you don't get out of the
house at night at least once. You're going to snap.
I've seen it happen."

Hannah could almost feel it happening.

"I'm really sorry, Taz."

"I have a girlfriend with some kids two houses
down who'll sit."

"Taz, no—" Just the thought of leaving Georgia
alone with a stranger at night scared her.

The phone rang before Hannah could say no again.
She covered the phone and mouthed to Taz that it
was Zoë. "I've got to schedule an appointment with
her."

"Zoë?" Tasmania's eyebrows arched as Hannah
rummaged through her purse for her calendar. "The
doctor's wife?"

Hannah shook her head.

"Oh, right, the new client...the shady lady from Shady Lomas, who's here looking for a house in town, Veronica Holiday's editor? She's here? Now?"

Hannah nodded as she pulled out her calendar. "In that new beach hotel."

"Ask her to meet us at the bar in her hotel."

Hannah covered the mouthpiece. "I'm not going out. Besides, she's married and pregnant."

"All the more reason for her to get out—before the baby comes and ties her down. This is fate."

Hannah sighed. "You're hopeless."

She flipped her dog-eared calendar to the right page and jumped. Stuck between the pages was that darn picture of her in the thong bikini that she'd accidentally given Joe Campbell.

"Tell her we're going out," Taz insisted. "This feels destined. Besides, we had a date."

Why had she ever mentioned Zoë to Taz? As a Realtor, Hannah was alone with her clients in her car long hours. While they drove or walked through empty houses, people tended to share their most intimate secrets. Zoë had told her most of her incredible story the first thirty minutes they'd known each other.

Then this afternoon while they'd checked for mold on a waterfront house, Zoë had filled in the last gaps in her tale. Not that Hannah had paid as much attention as usual since the deposition had been looming over her.

The scene replayed itself in her mind. Her most trusted carpenter, a retired navy guy with a bad knee, Tommy Thompson, had been on a short, wobbly ladder sawing a hole in the ceiling. Zoë had chattered underneath him about her new husband, Tony, a rancher, who'd been her high school sweetheart. Their ranch was sixty miles south on the outskirts of a gossipy town called Shady Lomas. Apparently, they'd had a lovers' quarrel as teenagers. To get revenge, Zoë had gone to a pig race at a rodeo, and Tony's scandalous Uncle Duncan had gotten her drunk there. Uncle Duncan had had his own plane, and when Zoë had awakened in Vegas the next morning, she'd had a ring on her finger and was married to the old reprobate.

Zoë had been in the middle of her tale of woe when a hunk of drywall had fallen out of the ceiling and shattered, spraying both women with white bits of wallboard. Tommy had yelled "no mold," triumphantly, and Hannah had grabbed his ladder to steady it.

"I'll make an offer tomorrow," Zoë had said, clapping.

"Everybody ready to go? I'm late," Hannah had said.

"The deposition?" Zoë had asked.

"Joe Campbell is like an ax hanging over my head."

On the way to Zoë's beachfront hotel, Zoë hadn't stopped talking. "Duncan knew he was dying all along. He married me so he'd go out with a bang."

"For this reason he ruined your life?"

"No, he was sweet." She'd paused. "He died a few weeks after the wedding and left me everything. Unfortunately, the inheritance included the ranch

Tony leased and believed should have been his. Then
Duncan's daughters sued me, too.''

By the time Hannah and Zoë reached the hotel,
Hannah was thirty minutes late, and Zoë was still
talking about the gossip, lawsuits and spite that had
driven her from Shady Lomas and the man she'd really loved to Manhattan, where she'd become an editor.

''Not a very good one, though, I'm afraid, and I
was so lonely,'' Zoë had admitted sadly. ''My only
claim to fame is that I discovered Veronica Holiday
and edit her books.''

''*The* Veronica Holiday? I've read all her books.
She's fabulous.''

''Well, I'll tell her I met a fan. She's here, you
know. At this hotel. On tour…and…writing.''

''What?''

''Thought I'd kill two birds…. Shop for a house
and help her…. Long story.''

Still, Zoë hadn't gotten out. ''Oh, I almost forgot—
the adoption papers on Noah came through.''

The entire conversation flashed in Hannah's mind
as she jotted 2:00 p.m. on her calendar for tomorrow.

Zoë needed a house in town because the schools in
Shady Lomas didn't challenge Noah, her nine-year-
old stepson.

Never one to be left out of a conversation for long,
Taz punched the speaker phone button while Hannah
slid her calendar back into her purse.

''So how did your deposition go?'' Zoë's voice
blared into the kitchen.

"He's got the hots for her," Taz said. "He fixed her flat."

"Who's this?" Zoë sounded both surprised and curious to hear a new voice.

"Joe Campbell does not have the hots for me!"

"I'm her next-door neighbor—Taz. Her spiritual adviser. She's trying to stand me up for supper."

"Did he or did he not hit on you, Hannah?"

Flushing, Hannah glared at Taz.

"The…the only thing he tempts me to do is murder—"

"Lawyers. The only good lawyer is a dead lawyer," Taz said.

Zoë laughed. "Joe Campbell's partner, Bob Africa, is suing me."

"What?"

"Tony called me about it today. Bob Africa had Tony served today. Apparently, my stepdaughters hired Bob. They've gone through all the money I gave them when we settled the first lawsuit. Now they say I suckered their lonely old father into marriage and killed him for his money. People have stopped speaking to Tony and me. Tony hung up so tense *he* would barely speak to me. I've been crying ever since."

"What kind of lowlife sues a pregnant lady?" Taz began. Then she told Zoë she was being sued, too.

Zoë giggled after she'd heard the story. "He's going to tell the judge he's mad because a hot pickle burned his pink pickle?"

Everybody laughed.

Zoë said, "We've got too many lawyers, or at least the wrong kind. In South Texas, anyway."

Taz chugged a second glass of wine. "Hey—I say we adjourn to your hotel bar and have a serious discussion about this issue...."

"No," Hannah said.

"Yes! And the more the merrier," Tasmania persisted. "I've just been dying to meet the shady lady of Shady Lomas."

"I'd love to meet you, too, but this is sort of a work night. I'm with a writer. She's here on tour for her latest book, *Four Wishes,* but her work-in-progress is late. And she's blocked. And when she's blocked she gets so crazy there's no telling what she'll do. Tomorrow, she's got a television show and a book signing, and she's publicity shy. I promised her tonight I'd play Muse."

"Sounds like you both could use a break," Tasmania persisted. "Besides, I swear I'll inspire her. Have you been to that great bar in your hotel that overlooks the beach?"

"I can hear the music all the way up here. Okay, if you really want to come...but just for a little while." Zoë gave them her room number.

"No way am I driving back to town," Hannah began.

But Zoë and Taz had already hung up.

"I'll drive then," Taz said. "A writer," she mused. "This is great. She's got to have a creative mind. She'll know just what to do about Mr. Billboard and Mr. Hot Pickle whose pickle wasn't all that hot if you want the truth."

"Murder," Hannah suggested.

"But how? Honey, we need specifics...a plot."

"It doesn't take a genius to shoot a guy in his parts, grind him into hamburger meat and sell it to Big Burger to feed the natives," Hannah said. "How's that for specifics?"

"Honey, I know you're off burgers and mad as all get out, but, please, don't ruin my appetite. I'm dying for a burger, cut the pickles, please, even if every bite decides to live on my thighs. Besides," Taz said, "Joey boy is too cute to shoot, and you don't have a gun."

"That's no problem in Texas."

BOOK TWO

The world of reality has its limits; the world of imagination is boundless.

JEAN-JACQUES ROUSSEAU

Five

Campbell's head pounded as he wheeled into the nursing home parking lot so fast he spun gravel. His headache got worse as he parked his gleaming black Porsche near the front doors of the red brick building. Twice a month he came here, and he hated every minute of it, even as he hated himself for being such a sap as to come.

A group of old men and women, their wheelchairs jammed together in a tight little semicircle, were smoking and telling stories until they saw him. Every one of them set his cigarette aside and stared at him blankly—as if he were someone interesting.

Campbell cut the ignition and got out of the car. Poor devils, didn't they have anything better to do? No, they were out here every time he came to visit. He smiled and they smiled back, just like always. Hell, at least they had one another. Who the hell did he have?

When he got nearer, they waved and he waved to each one, scanning each wrinkled face. But his father never left his room.

His mood darkened as he headed inside, striding down a long hall past limp, corpselike figures in recliners on wheels, past the nurses' station, where the head nurse eyed him warily.

He wasn't the most popular visitor. Too many lawyers had won huge judgments in Texas against nursing homes by charging neglect for bad results that were nothing more than the natural consequences of old age. Not that Campbell ever took such cases, but the old battle-ax didn't know that.

He stalked down the hall and into his father's room. As always, the shades were drawn. Still, he made out two beds squashed together in the gray light. The bed nearest the door was empty, yet the floor and bed linens and chairs reeked of old man and dried urine and pine-scented disinfectant. Vaguely he wondered what had happened to the old fellow who'd been here last week.

When a thin stick figure with grizzled hair and a wizened face that somehow still resembled his own stirred in the bed by the window, Campbell snapped on the light.

"Dad?"

The old man hadn't been washed or shaved that day. He blinked a couple of times and then held up a thin hand that was spotted with age.

At the sight of Campbell, the old man's expression darkened just like it used to. "Turn out the damn light and get out of my sight! Nobody invited you. You ain't no son of mine."

Campbell shrank from him just like he had when he'd been a boy.

"I came by to see if you needed anything."

His father snorted. "As if you give a damn."

The harsh words hurt way more than they should have. Campbell couldn't account for it, didn't want to account for it. He'd never known anything but pain from his father.

"I know we didn't get along in the past—but you're sick now. Maybe you need somebody."

Maybe I do, too. Did they have to hate each other forever? Then he remembered his mother. Yeah, maybe they did.

"Are you deaf? And crazy, too?" His father picked up a bedpan and threw it at him.

Campbell ducked as he hadn't been able to duck as a kid, and the pan whizzed past him out into the hall.

"Get the hell out of here," the old man said.

When Campbell hurled himself outside into the brightly lit hall a dozen patients stared blankly at him and the bedpan.

"You killed her. Remember that. Just like you're killing me. Don't come back."

Campbell told the nurse the old man smelled bad and needed a bath. She told him three orderlies had tried, but he'd fought them so hard, they'd given up.

Campbell walked down the hall, his spirits lifting, but only a little, when he saw the exit sign.

The trouble with old people in nursing homes waiting to die was they slammed you into your own mortality. Campbell couldn't come here without taking a long, cold look at himself.

What the hell was he doing with his own life? Would anybody care if he died tomorrow?

Yes, they would. A lot of people would be glad.

* * *

War Party.

The red neon letters of the hotel sign flickered like flares against the red sky and bay. In the distance a lone sailboat rode the waves. Not that Hannah noticed the yacht. She was too busy wondering why she'd let Taz talk her into this.

One glance at that hotel sign had her pulse in overdrive. The huge motorcycles gleaming in the red sunlight in the jammed parking lot didn't help her mood, either.

"Taz, let's go home."

"We just got here, girl. Georgia's fine. Lilly's a great sitter."

When Taz wheeled into the lot, a burly pair of bikers in black vests with chains belted around their waists hooted, "Women—over here!"

Grinning at Taz, they gunned their engines and then rolled their big chopped hogs out of a parking space beside the hotel entrance.

The bikers' burly arms had tattoo "sleeves."

"Taz, I want to go home."

With a jaunty smile Taz zoomed into the empty spot. "Jesus, I wish we were on my bike."

Hannah buried her face in her hands.

Taz laughed. "You need this recharge way more than I do. Your life is too bo-oring."

"Which is exactly the way I want it."

"Why?"

Because I want to be safe. Because I want Georgia safe. Because I've learned lessons I never wanted to learn.

Not that she could tell Taz any of her story. Not about her crazy, superfamous parents or their highly publicized squabbles. Not about the wall between their two houses. Not about her little-girl dream of wanting them to simply be happy. Not about her own fame at too early an age. Not about her own need to rescue bad handsome men, either. Not about the terrible experiences her husband had had in boarding school.

She'd loved the wrong men with a big open heart. She'd paid a huge price for her naiveté. And so had Georgia. No more. For Georgia's sake, if not her own, she had to make more prudent decisions.

Inside the hotel, Hannah had barely had one long slim foot with badly painted orange toenails across the threshold of the jammed bar, before she knew for sure she was in the wrong place at the wrong time again.

Then Veronica showed up in a hot pink miniskirt and a revealing blouse looking wild beside a radiantly pregnant Zoë.

Every outlaw in the smoke-filled din lifted a beer and saluted the four women in the doorway.

"Three cheers for the Hot Ladies."

Veronica laughed as if oblivious to the undercurrents in the room.

"Doesn't look like there's a table for four," Hannah blurted. "Taz, let's go."

Taz grabbed her by the elbow and held her fast. "Looky— Over there— By the pool tables— Four gentlemen—"

"Not exactly," Hannah murmured as four guys in

tight, greasy jeans and dark wraparound glasses shot
clumsily off their stools, knocking a couple over as
they pointed at the table and beckoned them.

Taz's braids shook as she laughed in delight.
"What did I tell you? Bikers—my kind of guys. Is
this place great or what?"

Zoë and Hannah rolled their eyes.

"Are you crazy?" Hannah asked.

"It's my makeover that's got 'em so wild."

*Don't forget Veronica with her platinum hair and
low-cut outfit.*

"You're a high school principal," Hannah said.

"Don't remind me."

"Maybe you should do volunteer work at an all-
male prison," Hannah suggested as she clutched her
purse against her nipples, which were standing at attention in sheer terror. Then, like a duck following
her mama into a deep pool, she stayed glued to Taz's
ample hips as her friend plowed through the men and
the haze of cigarette smoke to their table.

Why had she worn a white T-shirt that glowed blue
and clung to her flesh like shrink wrap? Hannah wondered. Better question—why hadn't she at least worn
a bra and a blousy shirt that hid her belly button?

"Table or not, I still want to go home," Hannah
repeated as the women squeezed themselves onto four
short stools and Taz signaled a waitress and ordered
four beers.

"No beer! I—I want a diet cola," Hannah blurted,
but the waitress had already left. "Taz, this is a mistake. These guys are in lust."

"We just got here," Taz said. "Chill. Okay? I can

handle the situation. Like you said, I'm a principal. And where I grew up, girl, these guys would be pussies.'' Taz smiled her huge smile and began to clap and writhe along with Veronica to the jungle beat.

Since Taz, her ride, seemed hell-bent on staying, Hannah turned to Zoë. ''Why didn't you tell me the hotel was overrun with a motorcycle gang?''

''It's some kind of convention. The manager says they do this every year. I'm sure they're all dentists and doctors and lawyers. Veronica met one of them on the beach earlier. He said he was a stockbroker. She even had a beer with him and a doctor.''

Veronica did not strike Hannah as a reliable judge of men's characters.

Veronica laughed. ''Mr. Moneybags is over there trying to be invisible. We may get together…later.''

Veronica waved at her new friend, who was long and lean and slouching in the darkest corner of the bar.

''You said you were going to write…later,'' Zoë reminded her.

Hannah eyed the bar's denizens uneasily. ''Dentists? Doctors? You're kidding.''

Veronica nodded and fluffed her puffy white hair.

''Right,'' Hannah said. ''The three-hundred-pound Goliath over there with the grizzled eyebrows, swollen black eye, potbelly, long red hair and the golden loop in his right ear is a dentist? He's staring holes through my T-shirt every time I lower my purse—and you're telling me the big bear does root canals for a living?''

"Well, maybe not him," Veronica admitted. "It's your fault. You should have worn a bra."

The ape adjusted his yellow bandanna as he leered at Zoë. There was a gap in his crooked smile.

"Don't encourage him, Zoë." In desperation Hannah lowered her lashes, clutched her purse tighter against her chest for coverage and sipped from her mug. The beer felt cold and tart going down, but it heated her blood and calmed her a bit. For the first time all day she relaxed a little.

Good stuff. Too good. Hannah swigged some more. Then she wet her napkin, tore off little bits, wadded them up to use as earplugs and stuffed them into her ears.

"You pointed Goliath out to me," Zoë reminded Hannah.

"Forget I said anything. Just quit looking at him."

"He's cute," Taz said. Lifting her beer, she smiled at him. "Cheers, everybody."

"I really think we should go," Hannah began again.

"Relax," Taz growled. "Shoot some darts or something. Drink. Hey, I brought you a target."

"No way am I getting up and making a spectacle of myself before this wolf pack."

Before Hannah could stop her, Taz waved Goliath over. "We want to shoot some darts…er… What's your name, big boy?"

"The Charger," he purred. "What's yours, hot lady?"

She gave him a look. "Okay, Charger, can you get us some darts and pin up this target…?"

When he glanced at the newspaper picture, the biker looked a little startled.

"You got a problem, big boy?" Taz asked.

"No problem, hot lady." His broad hand slapped the clipping of Joe Campbell against the dartboard, pinning it there with four darts.

"Draw a circle around his crotch," Taz ordered. "Here—use my lipstick."

She handed the Charger a tube of the stuff, and he drew crude red genitals instead of a circle. The bikers roared approval.

"First guy to hit the big red pickle where it hurts standing from behind me gets to dance with the Egyptian hot lady here," Taz yelled. "On my table!"

The men nearest Taz got off a few earsplitting yells. A squabble broke out and a table was turned over before the issue of who got to throw the first dart was resolved.

A guy in a black vest with a scorpion tattooed on his arm and a patch over one eye went first. When he hit Campbell in the eye, everybody booed. The next guy got a turn. The dart hit the mark but bounced off without even tearing the paper. Hannah hid her face in her hands and said a prayer.

"Me—I go for men with balls of steel," Veronica mused, winking at her friend in the dark corner. He lifted his hand and signaled her to come over. When she didn't jump up, Hannah felt his hostile gaze fix her, and she shivered. Not that she could really see him. But she could *feel* him. And he gave her a bad feeling like she'd had in the garage.

The next biker took his turn and missed as well. The mood in the bar turned brutal.

Goliath had the deadliest aim. A few darts thrown from his meaty arm put a gaping hole where Campbell's lipstick-smeared pickle had been.

"Ouch," Taz said as she climbed up onto a table to dance and beckoned the Charger.

Hips undulating, the Egyptian hot lady and her gap-toothed Hun from Hell put on a show to a loud song with a wild beat. He stomped; she wiggled and twisted and ate him with her dark eyes, showing caramel-colored legs every time she twirled. Their dance was pure raw sex, and she stirred the men to a frenzy. When they were done, every man in the bar rushed over to help Taz down from the table. They were all clamoring to dance with her when the Charger told them she was his and asked her to dance with her again.

"I ain't nobody's," Taz said.

He was climbing back onto the table, when she crossed her arms and said *no* in her loud, school principal voice. He glared down at her in surprise. Since he was on the table, and she was short, she barely came to the tops of his muddy motorcycle boots.

The silence grew tense. His bottom lip bloated sullenly, and he flushed purple. Hannah half expected Charger to grab Taz and tear her apart, or to at least kiss her to thrill their gaping audience, but he merely growled good-naturedly, "You heard her. The lady, she said no."

Hannah couldn't believe it when he jumped off the table with a resounding thud and swaggered heavily to the dartboard and ripped Campbell's picture off the wall. Then he yelled, "No more dancing. No cussin', either. We got ladies present." Then his eyes locked on Taz's face with respect and shy affection.

Taz beamed at him.

There were grumbles as the men sat and resumed their drinking, but the Charger hovered nearby their table, a silent hulk making sure the other beasts left his lady friends alone.

Heck, maybe the Charger *did* do root canals for a living. During the table dance, Hannah had drained her mug, and when another was placed in front of her, she sipped from it, too. Maybe it was the beer that eased the tension in her. Instead of pleading to go, she relaxed and began to chat with her friends in their dark corner.

"So, you're Veronica Holiday," Tasmania said. "Hannah was telling me you were here. I've read your books."

"If I'd known I was going to meet a fan, I would have worn my glasses and tried to look intelligent."

Taz laughed. "I'm not disappointed."

Veronica didn't look like the sophisticated woman in her publicity stills. In those photographs, she wore power suits and demure shades of makeup.

"Zoë said you were being sued, too," Tasmania said.

Hannah frowned as she sipped more beer. "So, who's suing you, Veronica?"

The music was so loud they had to yell to be heard.

"This thief, this idiot from my hometown, who's been jealous of me since I sold my first book. Her name's Camille. She married *my* old boyfriend right out from under me when we were kids. Then she ran me out of town. Now she has the gall to say I stole her body and wrote the story of her life. Her life! *In her dreams.*''

Tasmania's black eyes gleamed. ''Stole her body?''

''I had a boob job. We're the same bra size now.''

Tasmania snorted. ''Give me a break. Did Zoë tell you I'm being sued because of damage to a man's eenie weenie done by a pickle I nuked?''

''This could be your next novel,'' Zoë said.

''If I wrote about it, Camille would really sue.''

Hannah looked up. ''So how can we stop these frivolous lawsuits? In this city, all the judges are bought off.''

''It's called—campaign contributions,'' Zoë screamed over the music. ''It costs a lot to run for office. Politicians and judges don't make much.''

''Under the table they do,'' Taz said.

''You don't know that for sure,'' Zoë countered.

''What planet do you live on?'' Holding her mug up, Taz eyed the waitress and tapped her mug and held up four fingers. ''They make huge contributions to political action committees, PACs they call them. Wouldn't it be fun to turn the tables on these jerks?''

''But how?'' Hannah asked.

When more beers arrived, the four women were about to raise their mugs and clink them when the fight started.

''But I want to dance with a hot lady!'' a biker yelled. ''You danced with her! Why the hell can't—''

''This is why the hell why, you son of a—''

The Charger let a beefy fist fly, and it landed smack, square in the loudmouth's jaw. As if a bomb had gone off, the bar erupted. Cigarettes were squashed out on the floor. Everybody started shouting and ramming one another with their heads. Tables and chairs crashed to the floor. Beer bottles smashed as they rolled off tables.

"Let's go!" Hannah screamed, ducking.

"We could do room service in my suite," Veronica yelled.

"Sounds like a winner," Taz agreed, keeping low, running after them.

"Why can't we just go home?" Hannah pleaded.

Not that Taz or anybody else paid the least bit of attention to her.

Six

The wave loomed over Campbell's bowsprit like a solid brown wall. "Hold tight for a sec, Paul—"

Campbell jammed his cell phone into the pocket of his windbreaker fast. Instead of slamming into the wave, *Victory* surfed up its side with the gathering speed of a roller-coaster car.

Foam sprayed across the bow. Water frothed the length of the yacht. Charged to the max, Campbell wanted to yell.

With a grim smile, he swiped the burning salt water out of his eyes. Blinking, he studied the roiling swells for a calm patch and then jammed the phone to his ear again.

"Still there, Paul?"

"Settle with that Smith bitch? Whose side are you on?"

Campbell remembered her smile and the way she'd looked at her kid on the beach.

Paul couldn't stop screaming. "You out of your mind? You saw those mold pictures! You visited me in the hospital—"

When Campbell made no reply, O'Connor burst into a stream of profanity that was so abusive, Campbell stuffed his cell phone back into his pocket.

"Are you there?" The thunder and venom of O'Connor's voice was mostly smothered now. "What's all that noise?"

"The wind," Campbell replied in a mild tone. "It's pretty raucous out here."

"I thought you were driving home. Where the hell are you?"

"Told you. On *Victory.*"

"If you'd stay off that boat, you might have more time for my case."

"Yacht," Campbell corrected. "Thirty-six feet of lean, mean sailing machine."

Victory was his main mistress, his therapist—his salvation most nights. Not that O'Connor gave a damn.

Still, Campbell tried to explain. "New sail came. Had to try it."

"I don't give a f—"

Campbell slid the phone back into his pocket and let the wind whip his black hair. When O'Connor kept yelling swearwords, Campbell took a long pull of Glenlivet straight from the bottle.

"If you use language like that on the stand, we're finished," Campbell said when he finally lifted the phone back to his ear.

The western sky over the city was bloodred. A huge orange sun squatted on his roof like a Halloween pumpkin and blinked flames at him. The luxury condo high-rise beside his house looked dark and sinister.

He'd been on the water an hour. Long enough to know the new Kevlar foresail was sheer magic.

"Damn it! I'm trying to get your attention," O'Connor said.

The breeze screamed across Campbell's stern. He was running dead downwind, which was a risky tack in these winds. But the danger of it was a rush. Campbell felt exhilarated as he flew toward his private marina and mansion and the high-rise building beside them.

"I'm hanging on every word." Campbell frowned when he saw his jib begin to ripple at the mainstay. *Wind change? Maybe.*

He decided not to alter course. "Paul, she has pictures and a video of you on the roof with a hose—"

"That bitch! I don't give a good goddamn what she showed you—"

"A jury will."

A wave hit the bow wrong. The big foresail crackled noisily, and Campbell plunged to his haunches a microsecond before the boom slammed across the cockpit.

"What's going on?" Paul demanded.

"Not much." With one hand, Campbell winched in the jib. *Victory* rode up another wild wave, seesawed crazily at the crest and then hurtled down it at a crazy angle.

"You're fired," O'Connor said.

Waves sloshed over the bow. Another broke across the bowsprit, splattering the deck and washing into the cockpit.

"Come up with a reasonable figure you can live with, and I'll call her—"

"A million—"

Victory was wallowing in a trough, her bow pitching.

"The key word is *reasonable*. Call me at home in an hour."

"To hell with you—"

"Call me when you cool off."

"Whose side are you on, you ass—"

Campbell hung up.

Victory rode up another wave, which was even higher than the last one. Which meant she fell harder. Trailing waves slung her stern wildly to starboard. The bow dived under a wave. The wheel spun out of Campbell's grip. Then the boom whipped across the cockpit again in another accidental jibe, zinging mere inches above Campbell's scalp.

Close.

For a long moment the yacht lay on her side. Water sloshed around his knees as Campbell struggled to right her.

He held his breath. When she finally righted herself like a porpoise surfacing, Campbell burst into wild laughter. Being on the water felt good after the office and nursing home. After O'Connor.

He pointed the bow at his red-tiled roofline and the high-rise and flew down the next coffee-dark wave.

"Thank you for taking ten years off my life," Hannah said to Taz when all four women had made it safely out of the bar into the hotel lobby.

"You do look younger," Taz replied with a mischievous smile.

"That's not what I meant."

"Are those sirens?" Veronica said. "Follow me. My room! I don't want to do my interview tomorrow from a jail cell."

"Are you sure? That might be just the trick to jump-start your sales," Zoë teased. "Especially if you wear that same outfit."

Half an hour later the four of them were out on Veronica's balcony staring at the moonlit bay as they drank beer and ate cashews and chips. Beneath them the bar was quiet, the bikers bedded down somewhere, and all the cops gone. Hannah had called Lilly and felt less worried about Georgia.

There had been quite a bit of excitement for a while after the police showed up, but things had calmed down fast. It was still early. Not even ten.

Now there was only the sound of the surf and a lone jogger in black on the beach, who'd stopped and was staring up at the hotel with an intensity that made the hair on the back of Hannah's neck stand up. Hannah had *that* feeling she'd had in the garage suddenly.

Dom used to follow her around London when she didn't know he was there. The first time he'd slipped into their conversation the things she'd done when she'd gone out shopping, she'd tried to tell herself it was just a charming quirk of his.

"You bought those little sparkly clips for your hair on the second floor at Fortnum & Mason, didn't you?" he'd said maybe a month after she'd gone to that store. They'd been eating Italian on Piccadilly. His tone had been light, caressing. He'd even smiled his beautiful smile. "Second floor. I like them." He'd touched her hair, and she'd shivered. "Just the right touch. Classy."

"You looked at a scarf trimmed with ermine. On your way out, you took two of those little chocolate bonbons out of the free candy dish. Naughty girl. Then you rode a bus to Piccadilly. You ate here, by yourself. That corner seat over there."

She'd felt slightly guilty that she'd minded his following her so much, but she'd tried to hide it. "Why did you follow me?"

He'd been rearranging his silverware on the table, replacing the knife and the fork over and over again. "Waiters these days... Why can't anybody set a decent table?" He'd frowned at her angrily. "Did I ever tell you how I loved to play hide-and-seek?"

She'd picked up his fork and his grin had gone cold, scary. "Dom, why—"

He'd shoved his chair back. "Do you ever wish you were a fly on the wall? That you could really know somebody? The real person." His eyes had drilled her. "People only tell you so much...what they want you to know. I want to know the real you."

She'd try to tell herself that he loved her *that* much.

"Next time just come with me."

"It wouldn't be the same."

The beach beneath her was almost deserted. Who was the jogger? Could he see them or hear them talking?

Maybe. Maybe not. They were a few floors up, sitting down, clumped around a low table, and they had the radio turned down low. Still, she hunkered lower in her chair, feeling strangely exposed. The jog-

ger had moved deeper into the shadows, but he was
still there, watching their balcony—she was sure of
it.

Don't think about Dom. Not tonight.

They'd kicked off their shoes, and their hair was
blowing in the damp, salty air. Hannah forced her
thoughts away from the jogger and Dom. Leaning
down, she scraped bits of orange polish off the skin
of her toes.

"If you ask me, this suing thing is just one more
stupid game men like to play," Tasmania said as she
finished her burger and the side order of pickles she'd
ordered from room service and put on Veronica's bill,
which Veronica had said was actually her publisher's
bill.

"Suing is like football, tennis, golf, pool, even
darts...." Taz laughed, biting the tip off a pickle.

The other three women blinked.

"Golf?" The sport seemed innocent and dull to
Hannah's way of thinking, but why argue?

"Archery. Ball games. Guys can't get over this
sperm thing," Tasmania continued, wadding up the
tissue her burger had come in and pushing her plate
away.

"Sperm?" Hannah let out an incredulous gasp.
"We were on lawsuits and then golf. How'd we get
onto sex so fast?"

"It's a man thing." She bit into a pickle. "Just
listen. On some level men are all into sperm hitting
the egg. Getting there fast. Winning the race. Zeroing
in on the target. They're a desperate, competitive

bunch. They never get over that race to fertilize the egg. Scoring. You get my drift?''

"The hole in one...is actually guys raping and pillaging golf courses?'' Veronica furnished brightly as she stood up, leaned over her railing and stared down at the jogger in black.

"Guns and bullets?'' Tasmania suggested, licking and then biting into another pickle. "Same thing.''

"Spermatozoon,'' Veronica offered helpfully.

"What about war?'' Hannah had to throw that in as she eyed her watch, wondering if she'd ever get home to Georgia.

"War? Guys having an orgy.'' Tasmania shot them her most superior smile. "Car chases in movies? It's all about sperm. The problem is, as women, we're their natural target. Their prey.''

Veronica leaned closer. "I met this guy today.''

"The stockbroker?'' Zoë queried.

"No, the doctor with him. He was sued. He won, but it cost him a lot of money and time and worry to win. It nearly broke up his marriage, and even after he won, he's still obsessing about being sued. He says it's time the citizens rose up and did something. Time we took the country back from the lawyers. He wants to form a vigilante lawyer-killing club.''

"Catchy,'' Hannah said.

"He's pretty grim about his experience, and so are a lot of his colleagues. Doctors' insurance premiums are soaring. Especially those in high-risk specialties like heart surgery or neurosurgery. He got me thinking. We're being sued. Maybe we should start a fantasy ladies' murder club.''

"What?"

"We've got to get this lawyer stuff off our minds, so we don't obsess like that doctor. I mean, we don't want this to keep damaging our psyche. That guy was a real nutcase. He says he still follows the lawyer who sued him. Follows his friends, too. And he always carries a gun just in case he might get the perfect shot."

"What was his name?" Zoë asked.

"Being a hot lady, I was more interested in his hot friend, so I didn't ask."

"I got stuck on the damaging-our-psyche thing," Hannah said.

"Writer talk," Zoë supplied. "Don't worry about it."

"Well, for me writing is therapy," Veronica said. "Writers turn their worst moments into pages. It sort of empowers us. I say we form this pretend murder-the-son-of-a-gun-suing-us club, write down everything we'd do to these jerks…if we could get away with it. Express our worst fantasies-come-true on paper. And then…we let it go and get on with our lives."

"I love it!" Taz said. "Especially what you said about empowerment."

Hannah watched her pick up her knife and chop the leftovers of her pickle into tinier and tinier slivers.

"Can't we just go home?" Hannah asked again.

"Spoilsport," Taz said, not looking up from her mincing operation.

"Sooner or later your battery has to run down."

Taz laughed. "When it does, I'll be out like a light."

"Okay. We make them suffer, and then we kill them one at a time," Veronica continued. "Once we get this written down, maybe we will have exorcised their power over us. Then we'll all go out and beat them in court."

Zoë smiled. "I feel better already."

Hannah yawned. Hopefully, Georgia was sound asleep. If she wasn't, there'd be hell to pay tomorrow.

Veronica had a notebook on a knee and was looking for a pen. "I wish I had one of those darts, so I could get this down in blood."

Suddenly Hannah threw her arms up as if to embrace the full moon. "I feel good, or almost good," she said in amazement. "So good, I'm almost glad I came out."

"Nothing like a change of scene and companions." Taz shot her an I-told-you-so look.

Hannah's new mood felt instantaneous. She took a deep breath. "Good for the first time in a long time. You wouldn't believe the day I had."

Tasmania laughed. "It's either the beer or thoughts of murdering Mr. Billboard."

Hannah sighed.

"We need a title...I mean a name for our club. What about the Hot Ladies Murder Club?" Veronica suggested.

"Not bad," Taz said.

All four women held up open palms and gave each other a high five.

"I need a pen," Veronica said.

Hannah pulled out a tube of lipstick. "Use this."

Veronica raised her head after she'd written the name of the club down. "Who are we putting on our bad-lawyer hit list?"

"That's easy. For starters Mr. Billboard and his partner, Bob Africa," Zoë replied.

"And Harry Woods," Tasmania said.

"Don't forget Camille's lawyer, Mitch Kirk," Veronica added. "He's a real jerk."

"Okay—we know who we're killing. So—how do we do it?" Taz asked.

"I want Africa to suffer," Zoë said.

"We should choose the way that would hurt them the worst," Veronica said. "As a writer, I always think about my worst fears and then do that to my characters."

"Hannah wants to shoot off Campbell's testicles and turn him into hamburger meat," Tasmania said.

Veronica frowned.

"No, I don't," Hannah blurted, surprised that the thought of hurting Campbell held absolutely no appeal.

Veronica rolled the bright red lipstick out further and began to scribble, saying each lawyer's name aloud as she finished it. "Joe Campbell. Bob Africa. Mitch Kirk. Harry Woods. So—what's next?"

"Okay, so I'll tie a bomb to his pink pickle and blow him up," Tasmania said. "There's a new building going up downtown. I'd stick his body in wet concrete and bury him for good."

Veronica wrote swiftly.

"I'll go next," Zoë said. "I'm scared of water, so

I want my guy to drown. Maybe I take him out on a sailboat, wrap him in chains and push him into the bay. He sinks to the bottom and that's the last of Bob Africa.''

"We've got a shallow bay," Taz pointed out. "Somebody already did that and the body rolled to shore."

"Okay, then I take mine out in the gulf."

"The doctor I met in the bar told me I could concoct a little cocktail of nitroglycerin. I could get him hot, and he'd die in my arms," Veronica said.

"That's good," Taz said.

"She's a writer," Zoë said.

"Like I said, I had some help doing the research earlier this afternoon." When Veronica was done writing, everybody turned to Hannah, who yawned sleepily.

"I'm stuck. I—I guess I don't really want to kill anybody."

"This is only a fantasy. We writers kill characters all the time."

"Characters you make up. Not real people."

"Trust me. They're always based on real people. So, what's your worst fear?" Veronica persisted.

"I'm claustrophobic," Hannah admitted. "And I'm not too crazy about heights, either."

"Okay, so how about closing Campbell up in a tight, dark place...hey, an elevator? Top floor. The door jams, a cable snaps, and we drop the jerk twenty floors. He screams. Then there's this sickening thud."

Hannah was too sleepy to object, so Veronica scribbled in red. "Now, do we all feel better?"

Everybody except Hannah fixed one another with bright smiles and gave one another a high five.

Hannah yawned. She was so sleepy, nothing seemed real. The moon came in and out of focus. So did her friends' faces. "This is our secret, right?" she whispered groggily.

"Right," Veronica said.

"It's just our private little joke," Hannah persisted. "Nobody gets shut in an elevator—"

"Right. Scout's honor," Veronica said. "Not that I was ever a Scout. I flunked out of Brownies. But seriously, we're just playing around."

"Okay. Can we go home now?" Hannah said.

"I motion that we adjourn the first session of the Hot Ladies Murder Club," Taz announced.

At last.

"Second," somebody said as Hannah drifted off.

The balmy damp breeze felt good in her hair. Not saying anything to the rest of them as they chatted for a while longer, she just lay back in her chair and longed for home.

And it came to her as ideas do when one finds a still moment, what she had to do about Joe Campbell.

It was simple really.

Campbell didn't let himself think about O'Connor or Bob Africa until he had *Victory* tied in her slip. But, as always, sailing was only a temporary escape.

Boat shoes in hand, he trudged up the steep, grassy bluff to his house, which looked like a Mediterranean castle. The windows were dark, so it seemed more forbidding that usual. Suddenly he almost preferred dwelling on what Bob had said before he'd left the office, which had so infuriated him he'd left the office early.

Bob hadn't wanted to see the O'Connor files. "Like I told you—you have to win—for the firm," he'd said from behind his messy desk.

The public parts of the firm's office, those rooms clients saw, were far more plush than the working offices, like the one Africa had been holed up in. Africa had had files strewn on every square inch of gray carpet, carpet that hadn't seen a vacuum cleaner in probably a year.

"Okay, Campbell, so *your* clients are lying. So, this isn't the case of the century. So, the broad gives you a hard-on. Clients always lie. Broads always give you a hard-on."

Campbell had begun rapping his fingers on the arm of his chair.

"So what?" Africa had said. "You said *she* was lying, too. So, get her. Screw her." Bob's eyes had gleamed with envy as he twisted his wedding ring. "And I don't mean just in bed…although I envy you that part. Nice ass. She moves like a model…like she's expensive…like she's made of ice…until you get her in the sack and turn on the heat. I bet she melts all over you then."

Screw her. The sex remarks had penetrated Campbell's brain like the repeated stabbings of an ice pick. Maybe because he'd been able to see it all just as vividly as Africa had described it.

"She's not like that," he'd muttered, clenching his fists so tightly his knuckles had turned white. He'd tossed the pieces of the pictures Hannah had made of Paul on the roof with a hose onto Bob's desk and pieced them together.

Bob didn't even glance at them. His raptorlike gaze focused on Campbell. "She's not like that. What's that supposed to mean? What is she to you?"

Campbell hissed in a savage breath. "She's got a videotape, too."

Bob had arched his brows quizzically. Then his face had lit with his wolverine smile.

"No. I haven't seen it—*yet.*"

Bob pitched the photographs into the trash. "Find out what she's hiding. Go for her jugular when you're done sucking her tits. Like I told you—this is your chance to prove yourself to the firm, buddy."

"My big chance, huh?"

"If you don't scare something out of her, you're in big trouble— *We're* in—" He paused. "You're good at scaring women. That's your specialty, isn't it?"

"Gottcha." Campbell spoke through his teeth.

"Trust me, this is no time to get creative. We're in this together, buddy—"

"Togetherness. You and me."

"Where's your idealism, buddy? Have you forgotten that only entrepreneurially motivated trial lawyers can protect ordinary people against bad treatment by doctors…and bad Realtors like your Mrs. Smith?"

"Right." Campbell threw his boat shoes down beside the patio doors and hosed them off with fresh water. He ripped off his shirt and hosed himself off, too. The fresh water felt good against his skin after the salt spray.

Grabbing the clean, fluffy towel he'd left by the door, he dried off before letting himself inside. The towel felt good too until he opened the door and got an icy blast of air-conditioning against his wet skin.

God! The house was a refrigerator. His maid, Rebecca, had hot flashes. Because of all the media hype on the subject, she refused to take hormones.

Campbell walked slowly across the slick, freshly waxed, hand-laid Saltillo floors, not really caring that he left a trail of puddles. The big rooms with their vaulted ceilings were so dark, he could barely make out the shadowy silhouettes of his overstuffed couches, chairs, lamps and artwork. He'd had a decorator, but the place wasn't him. At least, when he was barefoot, the cavernous tomb didn't echo.

He was halfway up the stairs and freezing his ass off when the phone rang. He had to run the rest of the way to catch it.

O'Connor must've had a cussing session with somebody with brains because he grumpily spat out a reasonable figure.

"I'll run it by her," Campbell said.

Campbell took a long, hot shower, changed into faded jeans and a T-shirt before heading down to his refrigerator. As usual, Rebecca had left several plates covered in plastic that he had to reheat.

Tamales and chili. Frijoles—her staple. And carrots! No matter what he told her, she had a thing about carrots. Said they were good for the eyes or something. What was he—a rabbit? He pitched the vegetables in the trash and warmed up the heavy, meaty stuff.

He turned on the TV just for noise. The first program that came on was a family-oriented sitcom. One shot of the perfect dad and the perfect mom and the perfect kid and the cozy house had him jabbing at the remote. He stuck with a show about a macho idiot swimming with crocodiles and shoveled a forkful of tamale that was ice-cold in the middle into his mouth.

He spat it out, remembering Houston and sitting down to dinner with Carol. She'd been a good cook. She hadn't allowed television during dinner. Dinner had been served in the dining room to classical music.

He'd had the perfect wife, the perfect house, the perfect son. Then his career and marriage had blown up in his face, and he'd realized none of it had ever been as perfect as he'd told himself.

Remembering made him get up and splash Glenlivet into a glass. He gulped down the tamales, barely tasting them.

Dinner alone. And after dinner…the hours loomed. He wished he'd stayed at the office.

He could go out…to a bar, maybe. Or to his yacht club. He had a little black book with lots of names in it. He could get laid.

He thought of Carol again. She'd always thought up fun things to do at night. One of the perks of marriage was having an available woman around. A man could just do it without a phone call or an expensive dinner or having to make polite, idiotic conversation.

Damn it. Carol had been shallow and spoiled. Not

his type. She hadn't understood that everything they'd had had been because he'd worked his ass off eighteen hours a day.

"You're never home" was all she'd said.

That was her excuse for bedding his best friend. Nobody had blamed her, but everybody had blamed him for Sheryl.

He stalked into the den and opened his briefcase. Removing a couple of files dealing with the O'Connor case, he reached for his gold ballpoint pen and wrote down the figure he and Paul had agreed upon. Then he scribbled Hannah's home phone number beside it.

Not that he needed to write it down. He had her number memorized. Why? Hell, he had a lot of things about her memorized.

He remembered how cute she'd looked in that snapshot. She was pale and fragile, fine-boned and graceful. And that deep, throaty voice. Even her smell turned him on. Not to mention her huge blue eyes ringed with black, or the way they'd devoured him when she was afraid. She needed someone to look after her. He was a sucker for that kind of situation. Carol had used it on him...on Rod, too. He sensed that Hannah was alone and lonely—just like he was.

Which was no way to live.

God. He *had* thought about Hannah Smith a lot. Too much. His mood darkened as he studied her phone number. How would she react when she heard his voice? Remembering the way she'd slammed her door and driven off at Georgia's school, he took another pull from the bottle. He was more than a little buzzed by the time he got around to dialing Hannah.

Her machine answered. At the sound of her low, sexy voice, his brown hand clenched the receiver.

"We're not at home right now, but we really want to talk to you, so leave us…"

Like hell. He slammed the phone down and took another long pull from the bottle.

Disassociated from his surroundings, he stared at the picture of himself on the telephone book without really seeing his own carved dark features and the blatant advertising beneath it.

Was she out with some man? In bed with him maybe? He imagined her naked in bed…. What she did was none of his business, he reminded himself.

His mood blackening, he opened a drawer and got out his little black book and flipped through it. He really needed to get laid. He read the names and phone numbers. He'd scribbled in descriptions of the women, things they'd talked about. Because they were all so forgettable, he always had to read his notes before he dialed one of them.

Jamie Thomas. Rabbits. All over her apartment. Brass rabbits. Pottery rabbits.

He slammed the book shut, bored at the thought of the women he knew, and lost himself in his big-screened television for more than an hour, switching channels—not really seeing anything or thinking about anything—except *her.*

Scare something out of her, Bob had said.

Why couldn't he forget how loudly Hannah had screamed his name and how hard she'd pounded on the door of his parking garage? He'd been in the hall, talking to Daniel Gannon, who'd been leaving to play nine holes of golf. He'd grabbed a club and run the whole way. Who was after her? Why the hell did he care so much?

You're good at scaring women. That's your specialty, isn't it?

Campbell winced. In the garage her face had been as white and transparent as sea foam, and she'd been trembling.

He wanted to get the O'Connors off her back. And then he wanted...

He was about to take another pull, but the big room began to tighten and spin around him. He set the bottle down. The voices on his television sounded like the jabber of a foreign language.

What the hell did he want from Hannah Smith, really?

His head began to pound as he pictured her face and remembered the way her voice lit him up on the inside. And her eyes. He wanted to sleep with her. Damn it, that had better be all this was.

She'd looked at her kid with such adoration. And the kid was a handful. Not meek and wimpy like Joey.

You're a damn fool, Campbell.

Seven

"Taz! Slow down!"

Hannah pointed at a large two-story house with shadowy galleries and immense, dark windows. A hodgepodge of palms, oleander and bougainvillea lined the wide circular driveway. Despite the vegetation there was something cold about the mansion that was set high upon its commanding bluff. A sleek sailboat was docked in a private marina. Beyond, the rough bay glistened like hammered silver beneath the glitter of a full moon.

"You can't talk to him tonight!"

Hannah read the numbers of the address. "Holy cow. So this is Campbell's. Stop!"

"Well, no wonder!" Taz muttered, obeying Hannah for the first time all night.

"What?"

"Mr. Billboard's got to win a lot of cases to make the payments on this sucker. Okay. You ready to go?"

"I guess. No...maybe..." Hannah fingered her door latch. "Why can't I go up to his door and just try to talk to him?"

"Don't you even think about ringing his doorbell at this hour."

"Now you're the one in a hurry to get home."

"It's nearly midnight. A mean guy like him— He's probably licensed to carry a handgun. He might shoot—"

"I'll be back in the morning, then—"

"Girl, you're drunk."

"I know, and I feel brave enough to do anything. If he and I just sit down and discuss—"

A light flashed on downstairs. With a shriek of wild laughter, Taz stepped on the gas. "We were just joking about murdering…those guys…even Campbell…. Weren't we?"

Hannah laughed. "Maybe you were." When Taz looked worried, Hannah said, "Of course we were joking. We did the pretend murder club. My anger toward the man's completely out of my system."

"Great."

But when Taz zoomed away, Hannah watched his house and the dark high-rise condo building beside it until she couldn't see them anymore. Then she called Lilly, who reassured her Georgia was fine.

It was getting really late, and Campbell still hadn't gotten through to Hannah Smith. How come every time he lifted the phone to call her, his palms got sweaty?

He dialed. Once again, her sexy message came on. This time he left his own message.

"This is Campbell." He sucked in a breath. "The O'Connors want to settle. Call me back…whenever you get in."

He waited an hour and called her again. She still

didn't answer. He left all his numbers—his unlisted home phone, his cell phone, hell, even his pager number. Furious at himself, he slammed the phone down.

You're insane, Campbell.

He shut off the television and let the silence and the loneliness of his immense house with its soaring ceiling engulf him as he took another pull of Glenlivet straight from the bottle. At some point he called her again. His voice was deeper, gruffer, and more slurred from the whiskey.

As if by rote, he repeated everything he'd said before. And then suddenly, his voice broke on a raw note, and he croaked, "Look, I'm sorry for the way I behaved." *Oh, God.* "I wish…I wish we'd met under different circumstances.… Because I like you. Hell…"

Damn. What was he saying? He didn't even know her. He felt himself go weak in the gut as if all the blood in his body had drained out of some gaping wound.

He slammed the phone down and jumped away from it as if it were a snake that might sink a poisoned fang into him if he so much as touched it again.

This is your chance to prove yourself to the firm, buddy.

Campbell called her back an hour later and hung up as soon as her message came on.

Was it only a year ago that Campbell had presided over a team of twenty-five lawyers for Rod's energy business in Houston? That the transactions he'd overseen had been heralded as the epitome of ingenuity? When a major energy firm had toppled, the government had taken a closer look at the little guys in the same field, guys like Rod. Then the transactions that had been common practice had become suspect. The company's stock had plummeted. He'd been made a scapegoat.

Campbell lifted the Glenlivet bottle and drained it. For a long moment he studied the line he'd penciled on the Glenlivet label two days ago, so he could keep up with his drinking. Not that drawing the line had slowed him down any. Still, it was a reality check.

He pitched the empty bottle into the trash and dropped his arms onto his desk. He lowered his black head but didn't close his eyes. His thoughts were such a muddle, he got up and lurched toward the stairs that led up to his bedroom.

He never made it.

Desire sparked through Veronica when she recognized his tall, lean body. He was waiting for her in the cabana near the pool after Zoë and the others had gone home—just like he'd promised.

Mr. Moneybags? *If you're a stockbroker, I'm a virgin.*

She'd changed into stretch pants and a tight black T-shirt. When he saw her he removed his mirrored glasses, and his black eyes burned as she moved toward him, her hips undulating. Odd. The man looked a little like Hannah's Mr. Billboard. Excitement pulsed in Veronica's blood, and she stopped when she got near him.

Music thrummed from the outdoor speakers, so she

swayed to the heavy rock beat. She raised a finger and beckoned him to join her.

Instead he lifted his beer bottle and saluted her. "I like to watch—hot lady."

"Kinky," she murmured without a trace of her earlier coyness as she oozed into a chair beside him. "You were down there watching us, weren't you?"

"I thought they'd never leave."

"We started a club. You'll like this. The Hot Ladies Murder Club. It's a secret, though."

He laughed. "Some secret. I wondered what you were doing. Who are you planning to kill?"

"Lawyers."

"As long as it isn't me."

It was her turn to laugh. "We made a list."

"A hit list. Did you write it down?"

"In murder-red lipstick."

"You're worse than that lousy doctor who hates lawyers. But I don't want to talk about lawyers anymore."

She smiled.

"So you like to watch? What else do you like to do?"

"Lots of things."

"An enthusiastic lover, then?"

"I haven't had any complaints." His eyes glowed when she took his bottle and sipped from it.

"You've got an accent. Where—"

"You ready to get the hell out of here, hot lady?" His voice was crisp and hard, the accent gone. His tone chilled her even though it was eager, and she wanted eager.

"Anytime." She laid her hotel key on the table beside him. When his big, dark hand closed over it, she shivered. Then he did an odd thing. He pulled a pair of latex gloves out of his pants pocket and put them on.

Five minutes later he locked them both inside her room. In the next moment he grabbed her, roughed her and had her against the door. The more she struggled, the tighter he held her.

He was tall, his hairless body well built. His long black hair was shot with gold. His skin was dark. He was the most handsome man she'd ever seen even if his mouth and eyes were too cruel.

He yanked her T-shirt off and her stretch pants down. He was fully aroused and rock hard when he positioned himself and shoved himself inside her. His mouth reeked of beer; his body was sweaty. He moved faster and faster, but right before she began to shudder in ecstasy he pulled out.

"Put it back," she screamed.

"Get on the bed, Georgina."

"I'm not—"

He was holding a scarlet ribbon. "Tonight you're whoever I say you are, *hot lady,* and you'll do whatever I'll tell you."

Suddenly she didn't want to do this, but something told her not to argue. The gloves scared her. For some reason he didn't want to leave fingerprints.

His face spun in the dark. He ripped off his shirt, and she saw that he had a dragon tattoo on his right arm. Blood pounded in her head as red satin wound too tightly around her throat. Then he yanked her toward him hard. She could hardly breathe as he groped her breasts.

"You'll do whatever I say."

When she didn't answer, the ribbon tightened.

"Y-yes..."

"Say 'Please, Sir'..."

Then he was inside her, and everything changed. He was big. He felt good. She wanted him to go on and on, no matter how much he scared her.

"Don't stop. Don't stop."

"That's not what I told you to say. Say 'Please, Sir'...."

"Please, Sir."

He laughed at her with contempt. "Who do you want to murder now, hot lady?"

"Dawk," Georgia wailed as Hannah fumbled for the beach house key while the two of them stood on her balcony with the damp, salty wind whipping their hair.

The poor darling sounded so lost and frightened, Hannah's arms tightened around her as she unlocked the door.

Why had she left Georgia with a sitter? It seemed brutal to wake her up in the middle of the night. Georgia had cried the short distance home because she was afraid of the dark. Thank goodness it was only ten minutes from the sitter's house, because it unnerved Hannah to hear her daughter cry. Which was one of the reasons Georgia could seem so spoiled and high-strung, or so the teachers told her.

"The porch light's just burned out, darling. I'll put a new one in in the morning," she soothed.

"Do it now. Dawk... Now!"

Georgia was so sleepy, her speech was slurred.

"Okay. Okay. Hush. And I will."

Hannah's answering machine was beeping as she led Georgia, who was practically sleepwalking through the kitchen and living room of their shadowy beach house.

"Dawk..."

"No. See, the night-lights are on."

There were dozens and dozens of little square aqua lights, in every socket nearly. Still, Georgia stumbled into the couch.

"Mummy—"

Hannah didn't correct her.

"Turn on the light—"

Hannah switched on a lamp on a low table, and Georgia squealed, covering her eyes with her hands.

"Sleepy."

"Me, too."

With a yawn, Hannah soon had Georgia tucked into her bed along with several teddy bears and dolls. Hannah felt guilty for not bothering to make her brush her teeth or even put on her nightgown. Kissing her darling on her brow beneath her golden bangs, Georgia closed her eyes and smiled serenely. Hannah stared down at her little angel for a long moment. When she was awake, Georgia rarely looked so peaceful or contented. Finally, she got up and pulled her daughter's door until it was almost closed, but not quite. Like her mother, Georgia couldn't stand to be locked in.

The answering machine beeped, which was annoying at this hour when Hannah felt so tired and guilty to have gone out, and apprehensive because it wasn't long until she had to get up and drive back to town for her appointment with Katherine. She went into her bedroom and grabbed her bathrobe.

Why did I buy a machine that beeped? Because you ignore blinking lights, and beeps drive you crazy.

Realtors, especially Realtors who were relatively new in town, had to make themselves available. It was a downside to the job. She had a pager, but she'd left it on the kitchen counter.

Removing her gold earrings, she punched the button on the machine to retrieve her phone messages. Then she stripped down to her leopard-print uplift bra and matching leopard-print thong panties.

The first message was a hang-up. The caller hung on, breathing. Hannah had been getting a lot of those lately, even at work.

The second message was a hang-up, too. Only this time whoever it was slammed the receiver down so hard, the noise hurt her ears. Alarm prickled down her spine, and she thought about her missing mail and then of her premonition about Dom.

Curious, she checked her caller ID. The first call had come in as unavailable, but the second was from Joe Campbell.

Five times, he'd called. She sighed with relief as she pulled on her red bathrobe. With a twinge of remorse she remembered the bikers shooting all those darts at his lipstick-smeared crotch.

When she punched Play again to hear the rest of her messages, Campbell said her name.

"Mrs. Smith…"

The low, husky voice created a furor in her senses. *Campbell.* She experienced a full-body flush when he struggled to speak to her as if he were some shy, tongue-tied schoolboy with a crush on a girl.

Slam the phone down. Go to bed. You don't care what that scoundrel has to say.

"I really wish you'd call me," he finally said. "I have an offer that might interest you." He left several phone numbers.

His picture was on the cover of her phone book. He'd used the same photo for his telephone ad as the one that was on all the billboards. Good picture. It caught his scary quality, but it caught his charisma, too. She stared at his black hair and eyes, trembling a little even as she registered how arrogant he was.

In the next message the low voice was different, deeper, raspier. His words were more slurred and yet edgy, too. He sounded all too human and every bit as lonely as she was.

The next call really got to her. His voice actually broke.

"Look, I'm sorry for the way I behaved. I wish… I wish we'd met under different circumstances.… Because I like you. Hell…"

She hung on the line, wanting more. When he slammed the phone down, she recoiled as if he'd slapped her.

When she couldn't stop thinking about him, she ripped his picture off the cover of her phone book. Crumpling it, she pitched it into her trash can. Then she slumped onto her couch, only to hate herself when she played his last message again.

And then again.

And again.

Was that was a low sob of sheer desperation before he spoke those final words? *Because I like you.*

A dangerous buzz of excitement was humming inside her when she finally punched Stop. She left the receiver off the hook and laid her head back and listened to the surf.

He lived on the bay. Why? Did he love the water as she did? Or did he live there just to impress people?

He'd apologized. He'd sound so sincere...almost nice. He'd fixed her flat tire. He said he'd gone to Georgia's school because he'd worried about her. He'd said he wished they'd met under different circumstances. Was he lying? Was he just coming on to her?

Because I like you. Over and over, his low, almost inaudible voice kept repeating those words in her head like a broken record.

She didn't care about him. She couldn't. She pounded a sofa cushion.

Stupid, he's suing you, remember?

I wish we'd met under different circumstances.

Every time she'd listened to him say that, her body had ached with loss and desolation and loneliness. With an effort, she thought about her mother. Then she forced herself to remember she had to protect Georgia. She couldn't make any more mistakes.

Hannah knew she should get up from the couch and go to bed. In fact, she fell asleep thinking exactly that. And what she could avoid thinking about during the day, overcame her while she slept.

She dreamed of *him*. And at first it was like a fairy tale. Campbell was Prince Charming and she was Cinderella, but like the ball, the happy moments were tinged with some desperate knowledge their happiness, no matter how thrilling, was doomed. One moment they were dancing in a golden room with golden people. Then suddenly, the walls of the ballroom became elevators. They were on the top floor of a very tall building, and Campbell had to go down on an errand.

He said to wait for him, and she told him no....

Then he was stepping into an elevator trimmed in gold and red leather, and somehow she was able to see through walls and doors and watch him in that gilded box as the cable snapped, and it hurtled downward endlessly.

Magically she flew to the bottom and was there when he hit. The doors opened, and he was dead on the slate floor. Only now he wore the loud yellow tie he'd worn at his office. She threw her arms around him and kissed him on the lips. They were still warm. His eyes opened, and she felt a flood tide of joy.

Then the red walls seemed to spin. He smiled malevolently, and slowly, terribly, his face seemed to melt like wax and reshape itself into that other breathtakingly handsome face of the man she'd once loved.

She saw long dark hair shot with gold. She saw a tanned arm ornamented with a dragon tattoo.

"Dom…"

Dom's smile was sweet, but his eyes were cold. "Yes, it's me, Georgina. Your husband. Say please, sir."

She woke up screaming.

Shaking, Hannah rushed down the hall to Georgia, who was sound asleep, her smile as serene as ever, her slim arms draped around a golden doll that was dressed like a ballerina.

Some time later, when Hannah was calmer, she went back to the living room and punched Play on her answering machine, just so she wouldn't feel so alone and afraid.

"Look, I'm sorry for the way I behaved. I wish…. I wish we'd met under different circumstances…. Because I like you. Hell…"

She experienced an intense awareness of Campbell as a man, and a profound joy that he was alive. For an instant she felt almost safe. Then fury closed over her heart at her gullibility, but she stabbed the button again, anyway.

Because I like you. Hell… Because I like you. Hell…

Over and over, she listened to it, and that mixed-up emotion that drove her to be so stupid about an awful lawyer after all she'd been through turned her anger at herself into something ferocious.

Why can't I ever learn? Finally, something broke inside her, and she began to cry for the dreamy girl who'd grown up in big houses with servants, who'd felt she didn't deserve what she had. Her famous

American mother had told her she should be rich and famous, too, or marry someone who was, that it was perfectly possible to marry a prince and live like people did in fairy tales—happily ever after. Only the princes who'd wooed her had been princes of the dark, men she'd wanted to bring into the light and make part of her very own fairy tale.

It had all been too easy, at first. Her handsome, dark, bad-boy prince. He'd been so in love with her, so in need of salvation. She should have known it couldn't last. And it hadn't. She'd had her baby girl. She'd been so crazy about her little darling. Georgia's handsome father had left her. Then Dom had come along and saved her....

Joe Campbell was yet another dark prince. She should walk away, leave him alone, but when her tears and rage at herself subsided, what did she do? Like an idiot, she punched Play again.

Because I like you.

She made a fist and brushed the tears from her eyes. *You can't let yourself want him. You can't save him. You can't save anybody. Haven't you learned anything?*

Frantically, she dug the phone book advertisement that had his picture on it out of her trash can, smoothed it out and lost another piece of her soul the second she glanced into his fierce, predatory black eyes.

Because I like you.

Joe Campbell was a lost soul. Just thinking about him made defeat slump her shoulders.

"I think I could like you, too," she whispered. "But don't you dare tell anybody."

Eight

The awful words Mr. Moneybags had called her burned Veronica like acid.

Why? Why did I—

At the first timid knock on the door, Veronica twisted wildly at the ribbons. She didn't want to be found like this. Naked, gagged and spread-eagled on the bed, she mouthed words that came out like gurgles.

Red satin ribbons tied her hands and ankles to the corners of the bed frame. A red satin bow was looped dangerously tight around her throat. Every muscle in her body ached. But her heart hurt worst of all.

When the faint tapping at her door resumed, she jerked at the ribbons. The bastard had left the curtains open so anybody walking by outside could see her. He'd wanted to humiliate her. Thank God it was raining, or rather, pouring in torrents, a real semitropical outburst, so nobody was out and about.

"Veronica—"

"Zoë—" Thank goodness it was only Zoë…. But how could she ever explain…?

Go away. Go away.

Despite the rain, the sky was such a bright shade of white, Veronica blinked. Thick bubbles of condensation misted the windows, blurring the view of the bay and the rain, blurring her to whoever might happen by, too. Water streamed from the eaves, slashing the sides of the hotel in such great violent sobs that Veronica barely heard Zoë's knocks.

The air conditioner vent blasted Veronica's bare skin. Why did everybody in Texas want to live in an icebox in the summer? She had a throbbing headache and was sniveling and shivering violently.

When the knocking ceased, the room was too still.

Don't leave me, Zoë. What if he comes back?

Desperation overwhelmed Veronica, and she screamed into her gag.

"I know you're in there," Zoë said gently. "I'm going to get a key—"

Thank God.

Last night after he'd gotten high, there'd been a moment when his large, strong hands had closed around her throat and his eyes had blazed like bits of fire. When he'd knotted the ribbon, she'd almost thought he'd kill her. Then he'd laughed and told her to take him in her mouth. She'd lain awake most of the night shaking and weeping. Just the memory of all the things he'd done to her and made her do caused more hot tears of fresh humiliation to leak from her eyelids.

Why? Why? Why do you do these crazy things? With men you don't even know? With men you don't want to know?

He was sick. So are you.

This time when the uncertain knocking resumed along with Zoë's pleading voice, the doorknob jiggled. Then Zoë flew inside, only to stop and cover her mouth when she saw Veronica.

"Oh, my God! What happened to you? Who did this…?"

Veronica flushed a deep shade of red. Shutting the door, Zoë rushed to the bed and loosened the gag and brushed Veronica's tangled hair back from her face. Then she pulled up the sheet covering Veronica's nakedness and began frantically trying to untie her wrists. But the knots were too tight.

"I have a pocketknife in my suitcase. Right side," Veronica squeaked. "And…and shut the drapes, so nobody else will see—"

"Who did this to you? That guy in the dark corner? The stockbroker?"

Veronica shrank deeper into the covers and hid her face in her pillow. "Water," she whispered in a shamed, broken rasp.

Big-eyed and concerned, Zoë brought a full glass and sat on the edge of the bed and patted Veronica's shoulder while she gulped like a thirsty animal until the glass was empty. Then they stared at each other, neither knowing what to say.

Finally, Veronica said, "I'm sorry you had to witness this."

"Did he rape you?"

Maybe. Maybe not. Veronica had been too afraid to say no to anything he'd wanted. Her body shuddered.

"I—I don't want to think about it…much less talk about it."

Zoë went to the bathroom for more water. Three

glasses later, Veronica still couldn't talk about it. Or him.

"Oh, Zoë. What's wrong with me?"

"I thought your therapist told you no dating."

"Last night wasn't…a date."

"I mean—I—I meant…"

"I don't need a lecture," Veronica croaked, her eyes darting about the room.

"What about a doctor?"

A sense of inevitability was swamping her. "I just want to be by myself."

"But the book…do you need me?"

"Forget the book. For now. Just go. This… I—I…"

"But what about your television interview?"

"For now, I just need to be alone."

Wrapping herself in a sheet, Veronica got up and stumbled on legs that felt rubbery at the knees across the suite, trailing bed linens. She opened the door for Zoë and then hid behind it so no one passing in the hall would see her. "Thank you for coming by. I'll call. Soon—"

"What about something to eat?"

Veronica frowned and shook her head.

"You really should see a doctor. What if he had a disease or—"

"Just go."

After Zoë hugged her and left, Veronica sagged against the door. Time passed as the memories swept her. If only she could just punch Delete like she did on her computer and blank her mind. But the awful things he'd said to her kept repeating themselves in her mind.

To keep from going crazy, Veronica searched the room, rummaging through her drawers, purse, suitcase and computer case, to see if he'd stolen anything, and sighed in relief when he hadn't.

Then she went into the bathroom and took a long, hot bath without turning on the light. She scrubbed her skin vigorously with a rough washrag. Somehow she felt safer, lying in the dark with the moist steam rising out of the water like a warm caress. When the water cooled, she slathered body lotion all over herself. She got dressed and searched the room again to make sure nothing was missing. Dimly she remembered him typing on her computer with latex gloves while she'd screamed into her gag.

After her bath she sat down at her laptop and felt thankful when she discovered none of her files were missing. Still, she was very shaken. Despite her long bath, she still felt dirty and abused and very, very scared.

Just like she used to as a little girl.

Where had that thought come from?

Tears were streaming down her face when she began to type.

The first blush of dawn was so bright and fierce, it set the gulf on fire. Shielding her eyes, Hannah got up from the couch slowly. For a second or two she thought she was home, safe, and that everything was as wonderful as she'd believed it was on her wedding day when she'd married Dom and had been so sure they were each rescuing the other. Then she saw the receiver off the hook and Campbell's phone book picture, and the homesickness seeped inside her. She remembered Campbell's phone calls and Dom's hate-filled, golden gaze in her dream.

Rubbing her eyes, she stumbled down the hall to check on Georgia before making coffee. Her little girl was still asleep and as serene and beautiful as an angel, so while the pot brewed, Hannah tiptoed outside.

The wooden planks of the deck flooring felt cool and gritty with windblown sand, which stuck to her toes. She kept seeing Campbell on the elevator floor. As she knelt over him, she heard his deep voice. "I wish we'd met under different circumstances."

Then his face changed to Dom's.

Dom wouldn't give up—ever. She'd always known that. He would find her—even here. He would come. Maybe he was already here.

Outside, she saw angry black clouds hanging over the city in the direction she had to drive later. She groaned. She hated driving in bad weather, especially when the causeway was under construction.

When Georgia got up, she was grumpy from lack of sleep, or maybe because the sitter had let her eat sugar. They fell into their usual bickering routine— Georgia refusing to hurry or do anything unless she was nagged. Only, Georgia was more high-tempered and stubborn than usual. Every chance she got, she turned on the television and watched cartoons.

Hannah lacked her usual patience as she told Georgia to eat her cereal and brush her teeth and comb her hair and to turn off the television. One of Georgia's favorite pink sneakers was missing. After a ten-minute search and tantrum, Georgia agreed that, yes, maybe she could wear her old pair. But instead of putting them on, she put on her toe shoes and then said they were too tight. Finally, Hannah found the missing sneaker on the windowsill in Georgia's room behind the shutters.

Hannah couldn't stop thinking about all Campbell's phone calls and how lonely he'd sounded. When she heard Georgia turn on the television in her bedroom, she decided to call him at his house...to discuss the settlement...to set up a time to meet.

His phone rang and rang. When she got his answering machine and heard his deep voice, she shivered and quickly hung up without leaving a message.

The alarm on Campbell's wristwatch went off at 6:00 a.m. sharp. He jerked awake only to find himself sprawled on the cold Saltillo tiles of his den floor.

It wasn't the first time.

He had one helluva hangover. His head pounded, his mouth was dry, and his stomach was queasy. Every muscle in his body ached as he pushed himself up from the floor and all but crawled up the stairs to shower and dress for work.

Look, I'm sorry for way I behaved. I wish... I wish we'd met under different circumstances.... Because...

"Hell."

He'd made a fool of himself last night over a pretty little liar who...

It wouldn't happen again. He had a book full of beautiful women who would leap at the chance to go out with him.

He didn't give a damn what Hannah Smith thought or did. Or if she was scared of her own shadow. He didn't.

Hannah and Georgia were in the Mercedes, which was parked beneath the pilings of the beach house. The sky was nearly black toward town. The wipers were slashing back and forth because the windshield was covered with salt spray. Hannah was wearing a clingy white knit dress and a blue blazer.

"Mommy, stop! I forgot my lunch pail."

"We're late. I've got a nine o'clock—"

"It's on the counter—" Georgia unsnapped her seat belt.

"I said *no*." Hannah handed her white purse over the front seat and kept backing up. "Dig some lunch money out of—"

Georgia burst into tears.

Hannah hit the brakes. "Darling, please—"

"Me hate living here. Why can't we go home?"

Gulping in a breath, Hannah said, "I hate living here, too, darling. And please…no baby talk."

They stared at each other for a long moment, each assessing the other's level of misery.

Her big blue eyes huge with hurt, Georgia sniffed back a final tear. "I'm sorry, Mummy." To Hannah's immense relief, Georgia began to pick quarters out of Hannah's change purse.

"I'm sorry, too, sweetheart."

Hannah was almost out of her driveway when to her dismay, she heard her snoopy landlady's dachshund, Matilda, yapping wildly. Next she saw her snowy-haired, red-faced landlady dragging the sausage-shaped creature through the sand to reach Hannah before she got out of her driveway.

Taz had said the reason Mrs. Truman was so bossy was because she was a retired principal. ''She used to have a whole school to boss. Now she only has us.''

Mrs. T. was an avid mystery reader, too. She kept a pair of binoculars, a book and a container of cookies on her windowsill.

''Mrs. Smith, thank goodness I caught you.''

Hannah's temple began to throb. She had no time for a chat about Matilda's various talents.

''A man came by to see you on a motorcycle last night. He followed you and Taz when you left.''

Hannah sat up straighter. ''Oh?''

''He was as big as a bear. Long red hair.''

Hannah expelled a sigh of relief. ''I don't know anybody like that.'' Then she thought of Taz dancing with Goliath, but decided the description had to be a coincidence.

''Thanks, Mrs. Truman. Keep me posted if you see him again.''

Mrs. Truman backed away from the car. It had started to sprinkle, and Matilda had begun to bark again.

''You'll have to come over for a cup of tea some time,'' Hannah said.

Hannah was on the causeway, halfway to town, when the road narrowed to one lane, and it really began to pour. The rain was so thick all she could do was inch along beside the orange barrels, straining to see as her wipers slapped back and forth. By the time she reached the outskirts of the city, the streets were like rivers. Nervous, she inched along. Newer cars than hers were stalled everywhere.

No sooner had she dropped Georgia at school than Katherine Rosner called her cell and said the water was so high she couldn't leave her house. From her office, Hannah rang Campbell's cell again.

When his phone was answered by the same recording of his deep voice, her fingers tightened around the telephone cord before she hung up.

When she called his office, Muriel said she wasn't sure where he was but she'd have him return her call first thing. She also informed her the O'Connors would settle for a reasonable amount. Hannah hung up, feeling restless and unable to concentrate on work.

She knew where he lived. On the off chance he was there, maybe she just go over and hash it out with him. His house wasn't far from a new listing she needed to inspect. The sooner she talked to him and got him out of her life for good—the better.

Say 'Please, Sir'—

Even though her lower back was killing her, Veronica sat hunched over her computer typing like a madwoman.

Maybe she'd nearly died last night, but this morning she had her ending. As always, once her book popped, she was in a creative panic to get it down. When her stomach growled, she kept her rear firmly planted in the most uncomfortable chair in the universe and ignored it. When the maids came, she told them to leave clean towels and scram. She penciled the time of her television interview onto a sticky-note and stuck it onto her computer screen and kept writing.

Time stopped. The terror of last night gave her some kind of weird energy. Maybe her real life was so bad, she just wanted to escape.

Words flowed. In her panic she hardly knew what she wrote. Soon it was as if Veronica herself ceased to exist. She was Susana Blackfeather living in a white birch house in the woods on the East Coast. The house was surrounded by terrorists. It was fall, and the leaves were as crunchy as cornflakes underfoot. Susana had a gun, but she didn't know how to jack in the clip. There was no way out, and she was a coward. But a determined coward. The bad guy had her little girl. The hero had betrayed her.

Veronica typed most of the morning. In her books, her characters always vanquished their demons. Veronica preferred living in her books to her own life, glamorous as she tried to make herself appear to those who couldn't see the scared, insecure wretch she really was.

She had less than an hour to get ready for the interview when she finally typed *The End*. Then she backed up the draft of her final chapters on a floppy disk and punched Print. Only as the pages began stacking up in her printer tray did she realize that she had a headache and was so exhausted, she felt absolutely drained. She was ravenous, too, but she couldn't face last night's memories or the thought of meeting strangers in a restaurant.

He was out there somewhere. What if he watched her on television? What if he wanted her again?

She refused to think about him or what he'd gotten her to do in bed because if she did, she'd go crazy. Besides, she'd gotten most of it down in her book.

She took another long bath, but no matter how vigorously she scrubbed every place he'd touched her with his mouth or those latex gloves, she still felt filthy. The water was cooling off, and she was shivering again, when she finally dragged herself out of the tub. She wrapped her body in a fresh towel and began perusing the room service menu. As she was picking up the phone to order a hamburger, the phone buzzed.

Afraid it was him, she froze.

With a shaking hand, she lifted the receiver to her ear.

"What? You're still in your room?" Jackie burst out.

Veronica clutched her towel around herself at the frenzied energy in her publicist's voice. "I was just leaving," she croaked guiltily.

"What are you—sick? You sound like a frog. Are you okay? Can you do the interview?"

Veronica felt like some sea creature that wanted to curl itself in the depths of its shell and sink to the bottom of the bay.

"I finished the book," she said.

"This is great! But what about the interview?"

Veronica twisted the phone cord and tried not to feel pressured as she looked at the messy bed and her haggard face in the mirror across the room. She saw red ribbons, undulating bodies. She felt the cool latex gloves sliding around her throat.

There was a long pause as she gripped the phone, remembering how furious he'd gotten when she'd watched what they were doing in that mirror.

What are you looking at?

Us.

Describe us.

Can't you see for yourself?

He'd slapped her hard. "Open your mouth, I'm about to come. Beg me! Say 'Please…Sir'.…"

"Look, I won't keep you," Jackie said. "I'm faxing you the rest of your tour schedule to make sure you're all right with the dates."

Veronica went cold. She hated tours. Meeting strangers, doing interviews, acting as if she was a real writer terrified her. Like today—how would she ever pull herself together to answer questions on television? When *he* might be out there—watching her? "Great," she said, but with no energy.

"What? No complaints? You must be having the time of your life in Corpus Christi."

Veronica's head ached. So did other parts that had been stretched too painfully. She felt like she was two people—one sane; one insane.

"Last night I went to a bar with three other ladies and we formed this little club called the Hot Ladies Murder Club."

"What?"

Veronica was halfway through telling her about the hit list when she broke off in a panic. *The list! Where was the list? He'd been so interested in it.* She hadn't seen it when she'd searched the room and her purse to see if he'd taken anything. She began to tremble when she remembered he'd been there when the doctor had been banging the table and ranting about the need to create his kill-a-lawyer club. El sicko had wanted to know who Hannah had wanted to kill. The question had confused her.

"All four of us are being sued," Veronica explained shakily. "Lawsuits are big in Texas."

"They're big everywhere. If they weren't, would we have so many rich lawyers?"

Veronica's brain began to churn. She distinctly remembered putting the list in her wallet.

"I love this murder club idea. Four hot ladies on the rampage. Maybe we could use it with some of your promotion for—"

Use it— "Oh Jackie—no. I forgot…. The club's a secret."

She'd told him, though.

"A secret! Even better!" Jackie exuded, more turned on by the idea than before. "I'd better hang up and see if I can pitch this to the television hostess down there this afternoon to play off your book, *Four Wishes.*"

"I said no."

"Secrets sell big."

"No."

"So do sex and murder. Knowing you, you'd probably sleep with your guy before you'd kill him."

Images of writhing bodies, wrists and ankles bound with red ribbons came alive in Veronica's mind. She

saw a tongue between her thighs in the mirror. The
latex gloves had felt like snake scales.

"Jackie, no! We were drunk, joking around.
Haven't you ever done something stupid when you
were drunk that you don't want anybody to know
about?"

"Not in recent history. I envy you."

"You wouldn't if you knew."

Jackie laughed. "Write about it, okay? And read
my fax. And get to that interview! I'm going to call
the producer—"

"I said no—"

"Don't forget to get back to me if you want to
change any dates."

Veronica wasn't really listening. She had turned
her purse upside down and dumped everything onto
the bed. Next she shook out her wallet.

All her crumpled bills and change, her tubes of
lipstick, her sterling compact and lots of credit cards
and receipts were there. Slowly she replaced her medical insurance card into the pocket in her wallet where
it belonged.

The only thing missing was the Hot Ladies Murder
Club hit list.

The sick bastard must have taken it.

BOOK THREE

Trust that still small voice that says, "This might work and I'll try it."

DIANE MARIECHILD

Nine

Campbell had no idea how long he'd been seated alone in his dark office behind his desk, staring at the massive stacks of legal documents and deeds to be signed. Rain slashed against his floor-to-ceiling windows. He'd been a fool to call Hannah Smith when he was drunk. Why the hell had he opened up to her the way he had? On the phone? On the damn phone?

Suddenly the skin on the back of his neck prickled. He knew somebody was there even before he whirled his soft leather chair around and spotted Guy James slouched in his doorway. The kid was thin and tall—his face and rangy frame seemed all bones in the shadowy, early-morning light.

"Law clerk job, right? How'd you get in? What the hell…what do you want…at this hour?"

The kid shrugged insolently. His handsome mouth twisted. "The doors were open. You said you'd call. You didn't—"

"It was my move to make—not yours."

James jammed his bony hands in the pockets of his faded jeans. "Right—your move." He balled his hands into fists, stretching bleached denim. "Your move—sir."

Impatience—the trait was good and bad. He should know. The silence between them lengthened.

"I was in the neighborhood," James said at last.

How the hell had he gotten past security? "I haven't quite made up my mind about you yet."

"Guy James," the kid said as he ran a hand through his wet blond hair.

The lock of gold just fell back over his high, carved brow into his eyes. The kid looked like a thug.

"You could do with a haircut."

The boy's chin jutted out, but he didn't say anything.

He probably couldn't afford a haircut, Campbell realized, remembering his own lean days. James reminded Campbell too much of himself at the same age. *Scary.* He'd even grown up in a tough refinery neighborhood near the Houston Ship Channel adjacent to the one where Campbell had grown up.

"You'd have to learn to dress if you worked here, James."

Guy shifted uneasily. He was tall and too thin for his big-boned frame, which contributed to his raw, edgy, dangerous aura. A thin black T-shirt stretched across his broad shoulders.

"I could borrow a pair of slacks and a dress shirt from a friend till the first paycheck. Maybe you could loan me one of your flashy ties."

Self-consciously Campbell fingered the knot of his hot-pink tie. "You're mighty sure you'll get the job."

Guy glanced at Campbell and the plush office and then he glanced away. The kid's long body coiled in on itself. He was ready to bolt—not sure he'd fit in here after all. But he stood his ground. Campbell liked that. He remembered how intimidated he'd been of other lawyers in the beginning, how afraid he'd been of being patronized by all the high-class snots with East Coast degrees until he'd learned the worst were just hoods in suits. Not so different from the bullying thugs from his old neighborhood. Slicker, but not better.

"Why don't you have a seat and we'll get this over with—"

"Now?" The kid's eyes flashed with fear and then with wide-eyed bewilderment when Campbell nodded, but he scampered across the room like a jackrabbit, only to slouch down in the stiff leather chair opposite Campbell as he flipped through the kid's résumé.

"Great LSAT…but your grades… Hell, you dropped out."

The kid flushed an ugly shade of crimson and scrambled to sit up straighter. "My grades suck…er…stink. I could have done better." His blue eyes were laser bright. His pupils looked like tiny pinpricks. The kid was sharp. "Way better," he was saying as he leaned forward. "The courses were easy, but I had a full-time job. Had to—because of my brother. He was sick then, too. M.S. Between working, school and taking care of him, there wasn't much time to study. That's why I dropped out for a year."

Campbell snapped his file folder shut.

"If you give me a chance, sir, I'll work hard. This will be different from school. Because I'll get paid…and my family needs… I sure could use the job and a steady paycheck…*sir.*"

"So, you want to be a lawyer—"

"I want to help people in trouble."

"That's what I thought…when I started out. But the legal game is a rough business sometimes. It's not what—"

"Am I hired?"

"There will be a probationary period."

The kid's face lit up. He slouched again and looked away to hide his eagerness. "You won't be sorry," he muttered.

The kid was so thrilled, Campbell felt uncomfortable. "It's just a job."

"Maybe to you."

"I'm not the easiest guy to work with—"

Hannah's tires whirred in the wet as she braked sharply at the far end of Campbell's circular driveway, driving no closer than she absolutely had to to his house. When she shut off her engine, the dark mansion seemed to glare at her out of the bright wetness of the day. To the south the high-rise condo building rose like a glass tower above his property line.

Palm fronds rustled raucously near the car. Bits of pink, what was left of fluffy oleander blossoms ravaged by the thunderstorm, littered the wet cement.

She swallowed at the thought of seeing him again. But if she could settle this thing…if he were reasonable…if she could get this over with… If she could get Joe Campbell out of her life…

Because I like you—

Her heart raced.

Staring at his big house, she thrummed her fingers on the steering wheel. His apology meant nothing. She knotted her fists against her heart. *The O'Connors want to settle. Concentrate on that—period. He doesn't matter.*

Before she lost her nerve, she shrugged out of her blue blazer, threw her door open and dashed blindly for his front porch. She was smoothing her fitted bodice and so intent on practicing the little speech she intended to blurt as soon as she saw him that she didn't notice the white Lincoln off to the right. She didn't even see the slight, shadowy figure hunched behind the dark blue wicker chair at the far end of Campbell's gallery. Nor did she see the suitcases piled beside the front door until she stumbled against them and one toppled onto her big toe.

"Ouch!"

Pressing her lips together and taking a deep breath as she hopped on one foot, she jammed a fist on Campbell's doorbell. Then she crossed herself and waited. When he didn't come, she rang the bell a second time.

Had venting with Taz last night about Campbell appeased her? Or had watching the bikers throw darts at his lipstick-smeared crotch and putting him on top of the murder club hit list dulled Hannah's rage against him? Or was it the dangerous vulnerability in his slurred voice on her answering machine that had softened her?

Whatever the cause, she was in the mood to work with him this morning.

Problems didn't solve themselves. One had to think about solutions and then work out steps to achieve the solution. Step number one was to at least try to have a rational conversation with Joe Campbell. She gulped in a big bite of air and hit the bell again.

A cat meowed, and she whirled and stared at the cage sitting on the dark blue wicker chair.

"He…he isn't there," said a soft, timid voice from behind the chair.

Slowly a little boy with big, solemn black eyes and inky hair that needed to have a comb run through it rose to his full height and peeped over the back of the chair at her. He had a cowlick just like Joe Campbell's, and he picked up the pet carrier and clutched it against his chest as if he were terrified she'd try to steal it.

"Who are you?" she asked.

"Joey, his kid…I guess."

"You only guess?"

When she walked toward him, he shrank behind the chair again. "Don't be afraid. Not of me. I—I have a little girl. She wants to be a ballerina when she grows up."

"What's her name?"

"Georgia." She paused. "How old are you?"

Shyly he held up nine fingers. "I want to be a fireman."

"The same age as my Georgia."

His slim shoulders hunched, the big eyes lowered now, he edged out from behind the chair.

"Do you have a cat in that cage?"

"His name is Patches. I can't let him out or he'll run away."

"So, what are you and Patches doing on your father's front porch?"

"He doesn't like me.... He doesn't want me. Or Patches."

"Of course he likes you. He's your father. Are these suitcases yours?"

"He thinks I'm sissy...'cause I'm allergic." He sneezed.

A car door slammed out in the drive. Four-inch heels tapped like spikes being driven into concrete.

The boy started at those sounds, then stared from Hannah to the suitcases against the wall before crouching behind the chair again with his cat.

A tall, busty blonde in a red silk top and hip-hugger jeans that were too tight pranced jauntily up the wet drive.

"So, do all these suitcases belong to you?" Hannah asked the boy again.

"Yes, they do," the blonde snapped. "I knew if I waited long enough somebody would show up."

Hannah turned. "And you would be—who... whom?"

The woman appeared to be on the wrong side of thirty. She would have looked great with less makeup, a softer haircut and more conservative attire.

"Where's Joe?" the woman demanded.

Hannah stiffened. "At work, I guess."

"This early?"

"I asked you who you were."

"As if old Joe hasn't bad-mouthed me enough for you to guess."

When Hannah said nothing, the woman sighed impatiently. "I'm Carol. His *ex!* And proud of it!"

Not knowing what to say, Hannah punched Campbell's doorbell again.

"If you think the bastard's going to answer, you're way dumber than you look. Probably saw the kid or recognized Rod's car. Hell, maybe he saw me. Or you!"

Hannah shot Joey a worried glance.

"You're not his usual type, honey."

"His what?"

"Well, a word of advice—you'd better wise up and get used to his lies and cheating. He's a louse, okay? Good in bed. Good at making money, too. Women love him. But he's a real creep. Lousy husband. Never home. I should know. At least I didn't kill myself."

A horn blasted impatiently from the direction of the white Town Car. Looking bored suddenly, Carol shrugged. "Hey, I've got to go. Give him this for me, will you? And tell him I wish him the best." Her eyes narrowed. "Ha!"

Carol stuffed a long envelope into her fingers. "You tell him he can have Joey here for now, maybe for keeps. I'm getting remarried. Tell him I'm marrying Rod Brown." She laughed. "Rod doesn't want Campbell's son around his two little girls, see. Joe's a real skirt-chaser. Rod says genes are everything. Joey looks more like his daddy every day." She paused.

When the woman turned to go, the timid, dark-haired little boy found his courage and sprang from his hiding place and ran after her just as it started to rain lightly again.

"I—I don't want to stay here," he pleaded. "I don't know her. I—I hate him...."

"He's your father—"

"Ma'am..." Hannah raced after them. "You can't leave him here. Not with me. I hardly know your ex—"

"Lucky you." Carol turned her back on her son and Hannah. Getting into the Lincoln, she slammed the door. Then the man at the wheel hit the gas.

Joey ran along the edge of the grass after their car. Was the woman for real?

Feeling for the little fellow, Hannah sank down in the wicker chair and waited until the poor dear gave up and returned. He stood on the curb for a long time—waiting, hoping his mother would change her mind and the big white car would come back. It took him nearly ten minutes to give up and walk slowly back to Hannah, his eyes lowered to the wet driveway, his thin shoulders hunched.

By the time he reached the porch, his eyes were dry, and he was quiet and very self-controlled. Dangerously so, Hannah thought.

His black hair sticking up at his cowlick, the little boy came as far as the bottom step and stared up at Hannah. His enormous dark eyes were huge pools of pain that tugged at her heart. Still, something about his stiff, proud posture reminded her so very much of the rougher-cut Campbell.

"She woke me up in the middle of the night," he said.

Hannah got up and went to him. "Don't be scared." Kneeling, she hugged his rigid little body close. She'd always had troubles doing photo shoots in Third World countries because of the fierce need in so many of the street children's eyes.

With a feeling of inevitability, she took his little hand in hers. His fingers were cold and lifeless; his hand was so much smaller than Georgia's.

She knelt. "We'll find your father. He's not so bad...once you get to know him."

She crossed herself. *Please. Please. Let that be true.*

His bottom lip trembled.

She ran her fingers through his thick black hair, trying in vain to smooth down his cowlick. "We're going to leave your suitcases here."

"Not Patches."

"Not Patches," she agreed.

"Mom doesn't want me anymore." His voice was filled with bleak despair.

What kind of jerk threw her own darling little boy away? "Of course she does."

"She wouldn't let me bring my toys, either. Only Patches. 'Cause she doesn't like him, either." When he held up the cat cage, there was a pungent odor of urine, the mad scrape of claws against plastic and a frantic meow.

"He hasn't had any food or water since Houston."

"Sometimes grown-ups are all mixed up...just like

kids. We'll buy some cat food and cat litter first thing.''

He didn't reply, but he didn't resist when she took him by the hand and led him to her Mercedes.

On the way to Campbell's office, Hannah did a double take after Joey pointed at a billboard and then innocently asked, ''Who shot the hole in Daddy's sign?''

''What?'' Hannah glanced up at the billboard and froze. Instead of Joe Campbell's crotch, she saw blue sky.

Guilt stabbed her as she remembered putting him on the hit list.

Joey raced across the polished pink granite floors of the lobby so fast he knocked down a huge yellow sign that had been propped in front of one of the elevators. Boy and sign slid across the slick floor.

As Hannah ran to pick him up, he started crying. Even before the screams from the elevator shaft drowned out the boy's weeping, she felt sick to her stomach. Hugging him close, she stared at the elevator doors and realized her imagination was working overtime. There were no screams.

''You're all right,'' she whispered, helping him to his feet.

She picked up the sign. Bold black letters read ''Out of Order.''

She remembered her nightmare about Campbell falling in the elevator, so when Joey headed toward the broken elevator, she tugged at his hand.

''Not that one, darling,'' she managed gently.

Holding on to him firmly, she led him to the elevators on the opposite wall. Slowly, her sensation of dread lessened.

Vaguely she remembered Veronica teasingly joking that since she was afraid of closed-in places and heights they should let Campbell fall to his death in an elevator. If she'd stopped Veronica then, maybe then she wouldn't have had her nightmare about it or feel so guilty every time she was reminded of it.

The doors shut them into the elevator, and Hannah experienced a momentary sensation of panic. Then Joey was so wild to push the up button, she let him. Indeed, instead of punching only their floor, he punched all the floors, grinning as each one lit up and then clapping when the doors opened at every floor. Each time the doors opened, she felt better, less shut in. Other than a few frowns from impatient passengers, they reached Campbell's floor without further incident.

Campbell's office was so busy, his clients spilled into the hallway like drinkers at popular London pubs on Thursday night. People in wheelchairs and on crutches were lined up outside his office. Holding Joey's hand, Hannah said at least a dozen excuse-me's before they squeezed inside the door.

If anything, the mahogany reception area was more densely packed than usual. Men in neck braces and women and children, their arms and legs swathed in bandages and slings, occupied every chair. An old man with an eye patch stumbled into Hannah as she made her way toward the receptionist.

"You tripped me!" he said, shaking his cane at her rather too vigorously for a blind cripple.

"I'm sorry," Hannah whispered gently as she helped him get his balance. Joey's attention was caught by a pretty girl missing a leg, whose eyes were downcast, and he squeezed Hannah's hand.

"Don't worry. Your father's a nice man. He's going to help these people."

"Will she get a new leg?"

"Shh."

Muriel, the same secretary she'd met yesterday, had impressive pointed breasts and stiletto heels. Today she looked harried. Pushing a strand of gold out of her eyes she asked Hannah whom she wanted to see.

"If you'll just take his son and give Mr. Campbell this note from his wife—"

"He had a family emergency and got here late," Muriel said. The phone rang and she held up her hand. When she finished, she jotted a quick note before looking up at Hannah again. "Oh? You're still here? Do you have an appointment?"

"No, but I have to see Mr. Campbell."

"I'm sorry, but he's swamped. These people all have appointments. He couldn't possibly work anybody else into his schedule."

"Not even his son?" Hannah clutched Joey's hand.

"Mr. Campbell doesn't have a son."

"His ex-wife says he does. She left this little boy on his doorstep this morning."

"She what?"

"His son." Hannah tapped the long white envelope on the counter. "Maybe you'd better give your boss his wife's note."

Harold was damn sure full of himself this morning. Campbell sat behind his desk, his hands steepled as he waited patiently for his pompous client to come to the point.

"The only reason I'm hiring you, Campbell, is because business demands doing unto others *before* they do unto you."

"I'm hardly a lethal weapon, Harold. I'm just a dull, boring lawyer, a drone who works too hard."

"Ha! Not according to your billboard ads. You know what everybody calls you—the intimidator."

Campbell felt his face heat. "I'll write the letter first thing. My secretary will fax you a—"

Guy James came to the door and Campbell waved him away. James shut the door softly and vanished.

"Scare the hell out of them," Harold said. "Hey, I couldn't help but notice on my way in here that some bastard shot holes in your—"

When his office door opened again, Harold clammed up. Frowning, Campbell said, "I'm with a client, Muriel."

"I wouldn't interrupt, sir. I know how busy…if…but…really, I wouldn't— If I didn't think… It's sort of…an emergency…a highly irregular…and, well, we don't want her to go and just leave the child without asking you first."

"Leave the child?" Harold's heavy voice was more than curious.

"The little boy. *Joey,*" Muriel said. "He does have a cowlick like—"

Joey? Joey was here.

Campbell's temper and guilt were on the rise, but he never argued with his staff in front of a client. He forced a smile as Muriel's five-inch heels clicked across the hardwood floors and she blurted out still more incoherent gibberish about a note from Carol.

Campbell glanced at his client. At least Harold, who was extremely self-centered, was more curious about the interruption and turned-on by Muriel than annoyed. Indeed, his gaze was glued to Muriel's tight red jersey blouse that was stretched to the max across her breasts.

With a flourish Muriel set a small envelope with Campbell's name scrawled on it down on his desk and then pivoted on her impossible heels and ran out of the room. Swiftly Campbell stuffed the envelope into a drawer. Whatever Carol had to say could damn sure wait until he was finished with Harold.

"Well? What's this about a boy about to be dumped? Aren't you going to open it—"

"With your permission, sir."

The banker nodded.

Campbell pulled the letter out of the drawer. His lips barely moved as he read the short note followed by the swirl of his ex-wife's unreadable signature.

Bloody hell.

Joe, I'm marrying Rod. As you know he's stuck raising his young daughters because poor, spineless Sheryl killed herself when you caused him to lose his company. Or was there more to it? Rod said she mentioned you in her note.

Campbell did a slow burn. Then old ghosts rose to haunt him.

Well, he doesn't want Joey around the girls, and I can't say I blame him. They are not a good mix, and three children would be more than I could possibly handle. Lately Joey has been a handful. It's your turn to take over. Maybe you'll know what to do with him. Besides, I can't afford to raise him on the pittance you send.

Pittance!
Campbell forgot Harold was even there as he stormed down the hall to his waiting room to have it out with Carol.
''Campbell, I'm not done with you—''
Campbell barely heard Harold. He was consumed with irritation toward Carol. The boy wasn't his. She knew it, and he knew it. Not that he'd breathed a word during the divorce and custody proceedings about his doubts. At the time the press had been gutting him on a daily basis and he'd been struggling to keep his license. The last thing he'd needed to air was more of the dirty laundry of his marriage.
Pittance!
He should have ordered blood tests the day the kid was born.
How dare Carol turn up here with Joey!

Ten

As Campbell strode down the hall to his reception area and to Carol, he heard oohs and aahs and hushed laughter.

Strange. His waiting room was never a happy place. Clients who sought his services were anxious or angry—afraid to be there, afraid not to be.

All day long clients told him sad stories. They said they wanted justice when what they really wanted was money—someone else's. And they didn't care what he had to do to get it.

Campbell banged the door open. He was expecting manipulative, mean-spirited Carol. Instead he got Hannah in a soft white dress buttoned primly to her throat and a black-haired puny kid with big dark eyes and a cowlick as stubborn as his own.

A cowlick? Campbell's throat went dry, and he stared at the kid's unruly black mop and that signature swirl of hair. Then he looked at Hannah, and his throat went dry. She looked too good in the clingy white dress. *His kid?* She'd brought his kid to him. What the hell was going on here?

His mind did an instant replay of the drunken jabbering sentimental drivel he'd left on her answering machine last night. Embarrassed, he looked at Joey and that damned curl, and the skin under his collar got hot. Surely he'd seen his son's cowlick before. Why had Carol told him that the kid wasn't his?

Okay, you weren't ever home even when you thought your marriage was good. After the kid and the rumors about Carol…

Campbell jerked at his hot-pink tie and drew in a ragged breath. Fortunately, nobody had noticed him or how ill at ease he was. They were focused on Hannah and the runt she had in tow—*his* kid.

Hannah and the boy were kneeling in front of Maria Gastar, a young lady who'd lost her right leg working in a meat packing plant. Maria, who'd done nothing but weep in his office every time he'd seen her, was smiling at the skinny boy and something in the box he shyly held up to her.

Through the grill, Maria was petting the nose of the ugliest cat Campbell had ever seen. Half of this feline monster's face was black, the other half white. The kid sneezed, and Campbell remembered the boy was allergic to everything.

His kid? No way! But once again, he stared at the cowlick.

There was no such thing as a coincidence.

And Maria smiling? Campbell had never seen her smile in the six months he'd been representing her. If ever anybody had gotten a raw deal from a self-serving corporation, it was Maria. She was the one client who made him feel like something he was doing here was valid.

"Mrs. Smith, I believe?"

Hannah started.

"What are you doing here?" Campbell asked.

Hannah jumped, and he remembered grilling her yesterday.

"I wouldn't have come…except…" She stared at Joey, who was watching Campbell as warily as she was. With a little shiver, the boy set his miserable cat carrier on the chair beside Maria.

"You can hold him for me if you want to," the kid whispered before slipping behind Hannah.

"Cats aren't allowed in the reception area," Campbell said.

"Patches belongs to your son," Hannah explained. "I couldn't just leave him at your house."

"And what were you doing at my house?"

"I—I was trying to reach you," she said. "You called me last night, remember?"

His face got hot again.

"You weren't home. And… Well, Joey was there. I—I didn't know what to do…so I brought him here along with the note from your wife."

His clients were staring at him. At her. At Joey, who was still cowering as he clutched Hannah's skirt. Maria was frowning at him.

Campbell nodded at his gaping audience and said briskly, "Sorry for the extra delay, folks, but as you can see something has come up. I'm already running late. I don't know how long this will take.… Some of you may need to reschedule."

To Hannah, he said, "We'll discuss this in my office."

"But I have to go—"

He grabbed her firmly by the elbow and steered her

down the hall to his door. She protested, but he ignored her. Once inside his office, the kid persisted in his annoying habit of hiding behind Hannah. Campbell remembered being afraid of his father and despising his own cowardly behavior.

"I'm not going to gobble you alive," Campbell growled.

The boy's eyes widened.

"I wouldn't use the word *gobble*…in that tone," Hannah suggested.

Campbell ignored her gentle remark, too.

"What has your mother told you about me?"

"I wouldn't go there, either," Hannah warned. "And not in *that* tone."

"Hell, what do you know about any of this?"

"I'm a mother."

Campbell didn't know what to say, so he bought extra time by sending Muriel to get them something to drink. "And see if you can find cookies…for the kid."

"Do you have chocolate chip?" the boy asked, peeping at him from behind Hannah's skirt, his black eyes still huge.

"Your son has a name," Hannah murmured.

"Joey," Campbell said bleakly. For the first time he approved of the kid's name. He'd thought Carol had insisted on it to rub salt into the wound. Why had she told him she'd had that affair? Now the damn cowlick had him rethinking things.

Soon Joey had a Coke and a plateful of chocolate chip cookies, and Hannah and he had coffee.

"Cream? Sugar?" Campbell asked after Muriel set two coffees on a low table and left the room.

"Black," Hannah said, eyeing him over the edge of her cup with those incredible blue eyes that made his blood buzz even though Joey watched his every move as if he were a rattler about to strike.

"If you're going to be a full-time dad, you're going to have to read up on healthy snacks for children. Colas…"

"A full-time what?"

"Carol did drive off in a white Lincoln with another man. Destination—the Caribbean."

"I asked you what you were trying to pull," he repeated when Joey carried Patches and his plate of cookies to a wide table near the window that looked out over the harbor. Cat and boy stared at a tugboat pushing a barge under the high bridge.

"I—I…went by your house.…"

"Why?"

"Because…because you called…all those times and you sounded… I thought maybe we could…"

His skin heated and he looked away.

"I—I tried to call you back," she said. "I called your house and then here. I went over there on the chance I'd catch you. I want to end this situation as fast as possible. Your secretary said the O'Connors would take less, and I wondered how much less."

It wasn't smart to give her the lowest figure at first. "They'll settle for the limits of your policy."

She nearly spilled her coffee in her lap. "I don't think so."

"Do you really want this to go to trial? To get your name in the paper?"

"I—I don't know why I ever thought I could talk…"

The quiver in her low voice got to him just like it had yesterday.

"I—I—"

Damn. "You said you wanted to end this—" He scribbled a lowball figure on a legal pad and shoved it across the table.

She ripped the piece of paper off the pad. Biting her lip, she studied it. Then she looked up at him. "If I agree, you'll leave me alone, and leave my daughter alone."

"Of course."

"No more threats to expose—" She broke off. "You'll fire that detective…"

He wasn't able to meet her eye, but he nodded.

"And no more…strange phone calls in the middle of the night?"

Nodding even harder, he fought to make his face an expressionless mask.

"And I'll never have to see you again?"

He tried to smile casually. "Who says I even want to see you—" He paused. "Okay. Deal."

"Well, it's definitely something to think about. I—I'll just leave Joey with you and go."

Joey's eyes grew huge with fear, and he scampered out of the office to Muriel's desk. Campbell swallowed. The kid was scared sick of him, and, cowlick or not, Campbell didn't have the slightest idea what to do with the boy. "Not so fast. We haven't discussed Carol."

"She said she's getting married and…and, at least for right now, the boy, Joey…he can't stay with her and her husband's girls. Then, well, she just gave me the note and drove off."

"Without Joey? She trusted you—"

"She thought I was your girlfriend. Look, he's your son."

His son? Maybe. Probably. Carol had deliberately misled him. True or false, the idea was going to take some getting used to. He had a son… Maybe if he repeated it a hundred times, he'd believe it.

"He's scared to death of me." *I'm scared to death of him.* He thought of his own father. "I don't know the first thing about being a parent."

"You're going to have to deal with that on your own, Mr. Campbell."

When she blushed, he said, "I called you last night. I said…"

"I know what you said," she whispered.

"I wasn't…myself."

"It doesn't matter."

Her dress was so damp, it clung. Was that a leopard-print uplift bra she was wearing underneath it?

"But you went looking for me…. You drove all the way to my house in an old car with a bad tire in nasty weather."

"I—I… Not because… Look, you're smart, ruthless. I prefer sweeter types." She blushed again.

"I'd like to take you to lunch." His voice sounded way more controlled than he felt.

"I've known men like you before. I—I know what they can do."

"Is *Mr.* Smith the man you're so scared of?"

She jerked back in her chair and went very pale. "My life is none of your business."

"Right." His voice went cold. "Call me or drop by anytime…when you decide on that offer."

"No, thanks," she whispered. "I'll call my lawyer, and tell him to call you. I'd rather not see you or Joey again—once this…this highway robbery is over."

She got up. She was going, and he didn't want her to.

"It wasn't my idea to sue you," he said. "They would have hired somebody else. Africa forced the case on me. Hell, it's not even your money. It's insurance money."

"Is that really what you think?"

"Most people…"

"Maybe I'm not most people. There's a principle involved. Several principles. Right and wrong for one thing. Who do you think pays insurance premiums?"

He frowned.

"And what about justice? Is that such a strange concept? Oh, what's the use? You and I are so far apart. Telling the truth—there's another strange concept."

"The truth? There are always at least two sides to the truth when two parties are involved."

"More lawyer talk."

"I meant what I said last night. I do wish we'd met under different circumstances. Because I like…"

When she stopped at his door, Joey raced back in, grabbed Patches and sprinted after her. Hell, the kid hardly knew her, but he preferred her to his own father.

That hurt, which was idiotic. He'd only known Joey was his kid for sure for thirty damn minutes. Campbell knew he was about to make a fool of himself all over again, but he couldn't seem to stop himself. ''Joey wants you to stay,'' Campbell whispered, his voice softening when the boy saw a ship in the channel and ran across to the corner window.

''He's *your* son.''

''But you found him. You brought him here. You're involved. And, I want you to stay, too. You could help us through this adjustment phase. After all, you brought him here to me to be nice to him.''

Her eyes clung to his, so he pressed his advantage. ''Please,'' he whispered. ''Come to lunch. Why don't you agree to that low-ball figure and we'll settle the O'Connor thing, bury the hatchet, so to speak?''

''Why would I want to do that?''

''I don't know. But I called you last night and you dropped by my house first thing this morning.''

Shaking her head, she gulped in a big breath. ''Lunch? You and me? Today? When yesterday you said you'd expose—''

''I won't.'' He made a mental note to call off the Charger. ''Yesterday, I also said if we'd met under different—''

She cut him off. ''I wish you'd stop repeating…''

''I said I liked you.'' He couldn't believe he was actually restating his drunken drivel.

''But I don't like you.'' Still, she licked her lips, and her blue eyes weren't nearly so glacial.

He knew women, at least he knew how to get them in bed, so he pressed his luck. "We met. We click."

"Lunch with you?" She looked puzzled. "What in the world would we talk about?"

"What do strangers talk about at cocktail parties?"

"We're not strangers at a party. You sued me."

"Like I said…" His voice softened. "I didn't know you then."

"Would it have mattered?"

"Yes. I wouldn't have taken the case. Or maybe I would have—just to meet you."

"I'm no good at parties," she murmured, but he sensed a definite thawing in her.

"Neither am I. See, that's something we have in common. We can practice small talk over lunch—improve our party skills." His eyes were on her mouth.

"You're being ridiculous." But she licked her lips and laughed.

"I can't get you out of my mind," he admitted in a raw, hoarse tone that sounded so needy he hated himself.

"What about billable hours? What about all those people waiting to see you— You're a lawyer—"

"I'll have to work late, reschedule. Reshuffle. But Joey's here. And you're here. What are we going to do about that? About us?"

"Us?" She stared at him. "This is crazy."

"It damn sure feels good."

"This isn't happening."

He took her hand, and she didn't flinch or pull away. He gazed past her to the corner window where

Joey stood. And the kid… He had a son. Cowlick or not, the idea was going to take some getting used to. But maybe she could help him there, too.

Mr. Smith? Was she married or not? He had a thing about married women. He never messed with them.

Then he looked at Hannah again, and she was so pretty and sweet with those big, vulnerable blue eyes he forgot all about his damn rule.

Hell. Maybe he'd get lucky. Maybe there really wasn't a Mr. Smith.

Eleven

"Hot Ladies Murder Club?" Veronica's croaky voice blared from the television set in the cantina's kitchen. "Never heard of it!"

Hot Ladies. Hannah skidded to a standstill.

She'd been headed to the ladies' room, which was next to the kitchen in the colorful, hole-in-the-wall Mexican cantina Campbell had selected for their lunch date. The cantina was just around the corner from his building.

Windowless, the cantina would have been a nondescript box, except the owner had cleverly hired someone with considerable talent to paint lifelike murals of views of Taxco, Mexico, on the various walls. The colorful paintings opened the rooms up and gave the place an airy, exotic atmosphere that charmed Hannah.

Hannah edged closer to the television set just to make sure it was really Veronica.

Just her luck—*it was.* Veronica's platinum hair streamed down her shoulders like an uncombed mane. The writer wasn't wearing much makeup, but she looked as wild as a tigress in that same hot-pink suit she'd chosen to wear.

"Rumor has it," the young television hostess persisted, "that you started your little murder club right here in Corpus last night at a hotel bar, where you and your friends made up a hit list of local lawyers. You had the bar in such a riot, somebody called the cops. What in the world inspired you?"

"I can't imagine who would make up such a lie about me. Whoever she is, she'd better start writing novels. I'm already her biggest fan." Veronica's smile was thin. She stared at the camera instead of at the sexy hostess, her face showing nothing.

"Rumor has it that the four ladies in your club are being sued."

Veronica picked up the book in her lap. "Again—my compliments on a fascinating plot! But my book is called *Four Wishes*. You see, my heroine makes four wishes. They come true and throw her life into complete turmoil. My book deals with how she gets out of this jam she creates and—"

"Are four local lawyers on your hit list? Is Joe Campbell one of them? Were you throwing darts at his—"

Hannah groaned and prayed there wasn't a television set in the dining room. And Dom? What of Dom—

"What are the names of the hot ladies you went out with last night?"

"*Four Wishes* has nothing to do with lawyers or hot ladies," Veronica snapped. "It's about what happens when our wildest fantasies come true." Veronica mentioned the title of her book again. Then she quickly launched into a provocative sketch of her

characters and plot. She wouldn't quit talking until
her hostess said she was out of time.

When the commercials came on, Hannah rushed
into the ladies' room. She splashed water on her face.
If Campbell found out she'd put his name on that
ridiculous list—

Not *if. When.* Any guy who had his name on billboards was a publicity hound. Somebody would call
him. She crossed herself. She had to settle—fast. If
the story got more play, she would have to leave town
fast before Dom—

Two waitresses, a redhead and a brunette, were
laughing at something Campbell said when Hannah
returned. He cut them off with one of his charming
smiles, and got up and pulled out Hannah's chair.
"What took you so long?"

"Where's Joey?" she whispered, noting with relief
that the television screen behind Campbell was black.

Campbell pointed at a brightly lit machine against
the wall. "I gave him a handful of quarters and he's
playing games."

"I've decided to settle—for the figure you
named."

"Great. Not just to get rid of me, I hope?" He
looked at her so seriously, she lowered her eyes. "In
the future when we disagree, I'll have to send you to
the ladies' room."

"So you can flirt with the waitresses?"

He laughed. Then his expression grew more ear-
nest. "So, do you think that maybe we can put the
O'Connors in our past and go on from there…. Maybe
even become friends?"

"Friends? Us?"

"Why not—*us?*"

"Why?" She couldn't possibly tell him the truth— *hey, for starters, I drank too much and let this crazy writer put you on an imaginary hit list. And now you're on local TV. Hey, because you're handsome and sexy, and I've fallen for handsome before.*

Campbell was trying very hard to be nice, and probably because she had terrible instincts when it came to men, she was warming up to him fast.

Too bad. They were doomed. With a sinking heart she put her napkin in her lap. No doubt about it— this was going to be the most terrible lunch of her life.

"There's just something so special about you," he said.

With his dark skin and inky hair, he was too moodily sensual to believe. Guilt swamped her. "Now that we've agreed to settle, I should walk away while we're getting along so well."

Campbell reached for her hand and threaded her fingers through his.

The stillness of that big hand wrapped around hers was pleasantly comforting. His serious gaze locked on her face, blowing all her defenses. It had been too long since a man had looked at her that way and she hadn't wanted to run.

"I'm too easy," she said a little breathlessly. "The only reason you're interested is because I'm not your usual—"

"Don't—"

When he clenched her fingers possessively, she

searched his strong, incredibly handsome face for deceit or triumph or arrogance or for anything remotely dark and dangerous that she should fear. To her surprise, his gentle smile reassured her.

"I wish you could tell me what is going on in your life that has you so edgy all the time," he murmured. "Don't be afraid of me. I would never..." He stopped, but his grave gaze spoke volumes.

"I can be amazingly gullible," she whispered. "I've learned to be cautious."

"You won't regret taking a chance on me."

"You might regret taking a chance on me, though."

He shook his head and grinned. "Do you have a maniac after you or something?"

Even as she felt the color drain from her face, she slid her hand out of his and threw back her head, forcing laughter as she used to do for the camera.

"So, tell me about your beautiful secretary or receptionist—Muriel," she said, recovering herself. "She seems...quite devoted."

"That was a quick change of topic," he said. "Why?"

"You're hedging."

"What about you?" But he let it go and said lightly, "This is good. You and I haven't even had our first lunch together, and you're jealous of my secretary."

His quick grin made her feel ridiculously hot and confused.

"She's much more than a secretary," he admitted.

"Muriel and I go way back. Friends from the old days." A shadow crossed his face.

"You're leaving a lot out about Muriel and the old days."

"She doesn't want me talking about them," he murmured.

Hannah didn't press. "I suppose people always leave out a lot…in the beginning of a relationship."

"Is that what this is—a relationship?"

"I—I meant people shouldn't do that, hide things, fake emotions."

"So the mystery lady who can't talk about herself thinks we should show each other all our warts? Is this to scare each other off?"

"Maybe it's better to learn the truth before one gets in too deep."

"Ah, the truth. That most illusive of virtues—again. Everybody has his own version."

"That's lawyer think."

He laughed.

When the pretty redheaded waitress brought menus, Joey ran back to their table out of quarters. "I'm hungry," he said as he climbed into a chair. "Do they have pizza?"

"They have Mexican food," Campbell replied.

"It's good," the redhead waitress told him, smiling at Campbell.

"Better than pizza?" Joey asked.

"Nothing is better than pizza," Hannah said. "At least that's what my little girl, Georgia, thinks."

"Why don't we try some and see?" Campbell suggested.

Since Campbell knew the menu and what was good, he ordered for everybody. Hannah came up with more quarters. When Joey raced back to his machine, Campbell looked over at her as if he hoped to resume their conversation.

But Hannah turned away, realizing anew that she shouldn't be here with him. They lapsed into a silence that made her so tense she ran a hand up the back of her neck and then through the thick black hair at her nape. He watched her stroking herself, and that made her more nervous.

"Stop it," she whispered.

"What?" he replied.

"Looking at me like that."

He laughed.

"I told you we wouldn't have anything to say to each other," she said. "That this would be awkward."

"It's not awkward. It's something else—and you know it." He grinned. "Are those fingertips on your skin hot or cold?"

She jerked her hand from her nape to her lap.

His dark eyes teased. "All right. I'll be good. We can talk about why we're no fun at parties," he said. "Is it because you're shy or you think parties are stupid?"

"I'd just rather stay home and do my own thing," she said. "When I get there I'm forced to just stand around when I'd rather be doing something else."

"So, you're a girl of action, then?"

"This is ridiculous. We can't do this…be friends. Just yesterday I hated you."

"Not when I was fixing your flat. How's the tire, by the way?"

"Fine."

"I'm glad you got home safely."

"This is crazy. We…we can't be friends."

"We already are," he said.

"No."

He nodded.

"*Just* friends, then," she said, stressing the first word.

"For now," he agreed lazily, but his deep, dark, burning eyes took her too far more dangerous places.

Again they fell silent. When mountains of tacos and tamales and guacamole arrived, she hardly touched them. And when she did crunch into a chip dipped in hot sauce, she had no notion as to what it was. Joey loosened up and began to chatter, but she didn't hear a thing he said, either.

Campbell smiled at her all through lunch, smiled that dazzling white smile that soon had the two young waitresses hovering around him like bees around a honey pot. He had only to drink a few sips from his tea or water glass, and they danced up to him to refill them.

Finally Hannah got so annoyed, she took the pitchers from them and said she'd refill his glass. He laughed, and she knew she was a fool. He was a sexual magnet, the wrong kind of man for her.

And he was too well aware of his power over women.

"Why don't we go to my place?" Campbell said when he finished. "Get Joey settled?"

Hannah glanced at her watch. She'd missed an appointment to show a house. "What about all your clients who were waiting?" she asked, her voice tense.

"What?" Campbell asked. "Muriel—"

"I couldn't possibly go home with you and Joey—"

"Please," Joey said. Both his eyes and his voice implored her not to leave him alone with his father.

Campbell took her hand, and a fiery shock went through her whole body.

"You're too much," she whispered, frantic.

As if in a dream, she watched him pay the bill. She offered to pay her share, but he wouldn't let her. Then she was in his black Porsche convertible, and he put the top down. Joey looked as thrilled as she by his car as he buckled himself snugly into the back seat, and promptly fell asleep.

"I'll have to pick Georgia up at school...."

"But that's later. Three-thirty, and you're always late."

It was worrisome that he knew such private details of her life. She nodded.

"I'm as scared as you are," he said.

He took her hand in his and brought it to his lips. His mouth was warm, and when his tongue licked between her fingers, the heat was like an explosion throughout the rest of her body. She shuddered. How had this happened so fast?

"Wow," he whispered at her too avid response. "Wow!"

She swallowed.

"Cancel everything you have to do this afternoon." He leaned closer and whispered. "Everything but me."

Twelve

Lush bougainvillea dripped from the high white walls around Campbell's swimming pool in cascades of pink and orange and fuchsia as Hannah sank into one of the many chaise longues around his lavish swimming pool.

"Cancel everything," Campbell had said.

Glancing up at him from beneath her lashes, she said, "Nice pool." Then she slipped her cell phone out of her purse.

His pool hung like a magnificent turquoise jewel above the wind-whipped bay. How wonderful it would be to loll in this paradise with him the whole afternoon.

Not that she could really imagine a high-energy type like him innocently lolling around. He would have *ideas,* she was sure. Then once he'd had her, he would be done with her. Which was probably for the best.

"Nice house," she said on a little shiver. Then she looked up and saw a figure on one of the balconies of the high-rise condo building beside his property. No sooner did she glance at the person, a woman, she thought, than the person vanished.

"It's just a house," he replied lazily.

Did people who chose to live so lavishly ever view houses so casually? Not the people she sold such houses to. Not Dominic. Houses like this said, I'm somebody—look at me.

Campbell's house and grounds were gorgeous, but they didn't look lived in. That would change with Joey around. Obviously, Campbell paid a lot of people to keep the place up. Estates like this needed an oil well or the right title or a guy who was a money machine and could hire a staff, or they were a burden.

"Your next-door neighbors could spy on you if they wanted to," she said, glancing toward the high-rise. "Does that make you nervous?"

"Not usually. But not so long ago I sued a Dr. Crocker and his wife Kay, who lived there. Eighth floor. He was a real nutcase."

"Didn't they win?"

A shadow passed across Campbell's face. "There's just no making some people happy. He took the lawsuit way too personally."

"Most people do."

"Said I was accusing him of murder."

"Weren't you?"

"He gave an old man medication, and he died. The family brought the lawsuit. The firm asked me to represent them. Plaintiffs have a right to their day in court."

"Even if their grievance is frivolous and—"

"I lost. Crocker stayed mad, anyway. Partially, I think, because his wife came on to me. He was older than she. Kay still calls me. Somebody started sending me death threats."

"Did you sleep with her?"

"She was married."

"And you don't sleep with married women?"

He grinned. "Quit stalling. Just call your office."

Quickly, before Hannah lost her nerve, she dialed Alice, her bossy, know-it-all secretary.

"Yes...sorry, Alice, to put you to so much trouble," she said, feeling contrite when Alice began to whine. "I'm afraid—the *whole* afternoon. Something vital has come up." She spoke softly but firmly while Campbell dialed Muriel and told her the same thing. Muriel didn't argue the way Alice always did.

"Did you ever reach that lawyer?" Alice asked.

Hannah sighed. "Um, yes, he made me an offer...I couldn't refuse."

"Don't you dare let him bamboozle you into doing something stupid."

"Oh, and Zoë's coming by to make an offer this afternoon. Alice, cover for me, just this once—"

"It's highly irregular. Mrs. Rosner won't stop calling. I'm only a secretary, you know."

"You're much more, and you know it."

"I want to hear all about that awful Mr. Campbell—"

"I still don't know why we're doing this," Hannah mused aloud after she finished with Alice and Campbell hung up. She stared at him with a gripping sense of dread and anticipation. "I have an offer on a house—"

He placed his phone on the table beside hers. "You're doing this because I'm a clueless male and have no idea how to settle a cat and a little boy in my house. And because I'm hopeless when it comes to shopping." But his hot, dark eyes said more.

Uneasily she stared up at his mansion. Joey waved from the upstairs balcony, so she waved back. "Wave," she whispered, and Campbell, smiling at her and not really looking at Joey, lifted a brown hand.

"Well, at least you have plenty of room for him," she murmured when Joey ducked back inside. Campbell concentrated on her with an intensity that made her feel they had the pool and the bay to themselves, and that they were the only two people in the world. For a long moment she couldn't stop looking at him, either. His dusky features compelled her—the hard chin, the high, carved cheekbones, the black eyes and slashing dark brows. He was broad-shouldered and long-legged—all of him lean and hard. He was too gorgeous and dangerously male for words.

"You're a saint to stay and help me," he said.

Maybe he was no longer suing her, but did that mean she had to fall into his hands like a ripe mango off one of his fruit trees? Technically she was still married to Dom.

"Why don't I believe it's my saintly qualities that interest you?" she said.

He laughed. "Because you've been unlucky in love."

You put him on that hit list. And it made TV. Sooner or later he's going to find out.

Quickly, very quickly, she had to tell him about that. She would explain about Veronica and Taz and the bikers and the Hot Ladies Murder Club and how the night had spun so crazily out of control. But not yet.

His gaze grew hotter, and soon there was no mistaking the nature of his interest. He was making love to her with his eyes, stripping her, touching her, and although she flushed and turned so he wouldn't have quite as good a view of her breasts, she didn't mind nearly as much as she should have.

He laughed and moved closer. "Don't chicken out on me."

She erupted out of her chaise longue so fast she knocked her purse to the ground. "We have to make a shopping list."

"Do we really?" Sounding amused, he stepped back as she gathered up her purse and the things that had spilled out of it.

"You'll need a litter box," she said.

"Oh, God. What an awful-sounding contraption. Can't that damned beast stay outside?"

She shook her head. "You live on Ocean Drive, which is way too busy."

"What if it shreds—"

"We'll get something to spray on your furniture. And we need to go inside and see what room Joey has picked."

"I hope he hasn't let the beast out...."

"Patches."

"Patches." Campbell repeated the name slowly.

"And say it sweetly, not in that grumbly tone."

"Impossible," he growled, causing her to laugh.

"Did you ever visit Joey in Houston?"

"No."

"Did he come here?"

Campbell shook his head. His eyes narrowed. "Like I said, I'm not good with kids."

"That's sad. You both missed a lot."

"Joey doesn't think so."

"If you spend time with him, you'll get better with him," Hannah replied.

Campbell sighed.

"Lesson number one. We'd better go inside and check on him." She marched toward the glass doors. "You have to think about kids all the time. Otherwise, they get into mischief.... I mean...if you leave them alone."

His deep voice came from behind her. "And we adults don't...."

They had climbed to the gallery when he caught up to her and touched her face with the back of his hand. At the light graze of his fingers, she went still. Gently, ever so gently his thumb skimmed over the little scar at her hairline as she turned and waited for more.

She wanted him—shocking thought.

"What's this from?" he murmured.

Remembering Dom and that day by the Thames when he'd taught her what kind of man she'd married, she shivered. She remembered another glass door, a flying fist, and zillions of shards shattering all around her as her world had flown apart. One of them had hit her face.

With a frown, she put her fingers to Campbell's lips to stop his questions and her memories. His brows knitted thoughtfully as he kissed a finger, licked it, then ran his thumb over her mouth.

"So soft," he whispered, his eyes burning her skin. "You're not as afraid of me as you think you should be."

So, he was aware of her feelings. She closed her eyes because it was dangerous to look at him when she was so tense and confused, but when she opened them his wide shoulders loomed nearer. His dark gaze drifted down her face over her body, and Hannah felt her nerves heat.

She lowered her lashes, wanting him to kiss her, but he just stood there, smiling in that way that made her so breathless.

Time seemed to stop. When she could no longer sustain his gaze, she closed her eyes, expecting his lips. Maybe she even puckered her mouth a little, but all that caressed her was the humid breeze and the quick, raspy sound of his laughter.

"What's so funny?" she whispered, tilting her face to his and then blushing when his eyes glinted with mischief.

"Well, what are you waiting for?" she snapped.

"For you, precious."

"For me to what?"

"You know."

Her gaze climbed to his mouth, and that was a mistake. Wide and sensitive and very male, his beautiful lips parted in invitation.

"Hannah," he whispered hoarsely. "You know."

"I—I certainly do not know!" she stammered.

But the urgency in his black gaze melted her resistance, and her heart beat. *Kiss me. Kiss me. Kiss me.*

"You're dangerous," she whispered, edging closer, so that now all he had to do was lean down. As if to dare him, she wet her mouth with the flick of her tongue.

When he just stood there, she began to pout. Was he going to kiss her or not? Finally, when he did nothing, she gave into the fierce tide of longing and simply sprang onto her tiptoes and looped both hands around his neck. He laughed when she pulled his black head down to hers.

"Kiss me—darn it!" she pleaded.

Only then did his arms wrap around her waist and mold her slender curves to his harder contours.

"I thought you'd never ask," he said.

He felt so right, so perfect; it was difficult to maintain her pout. Her blood sang to a feverish beat as she gave herself up to him completely. In the next instant his mouth was on hers, and his kiss was perfect, even better than she'd imagined.

"You're delicious," he murmured.

"So are you."

"Then why are we still talking?" he said. "We should be devouring each other."

"Good idea." Good. Delicious, even. But not smart.

His next kiss was harder, and she lost herself in a flood tide of warm, escalating sensations. Everything, other loves, the heavy weight of her past mistakes, even her present terror, was erased in the searing flame of his mouth on hers. Her heart pounded errat-ically. Her senses were electrified. He was *that* good.

"My God." His words were low and thick as he picked her up and carried her to the gallery so that they were out of view of the windows of the house and Joey couldn't see them. Then Campbell pushed her against the wall. For an endless time, she felt the hot press of his muscular body against her softer limbs while their mouths clung. He was fully aroused, and he let her know it. When he finally let her go, he cupped her face in his rough palms and burned her with his eyes until she was thoroughly shaken.

She ran a trembling hand through her hair, fluffing it. "I can't believe I just kissed Mr. Billboard," she whispered in a light tone so he wouldn't suspect she was ravenous for more.

"Don't tease," he growled. "There's no telling what you might goad me to do."

"Behave."

"That's the last thing I'm in the mood to do," he said. "By the way, do your panties match your leop-ard-print bra?"

"What?" She blushed, realizing her white dress was too sheer.

What was happening to her? How he could he, of all men, with a kiss and his laughing eyes touch something deep and precious inside herself that she'd never known existed until she'd met him?

"We need to keep this light," she said.

"Good grief, why?"

"I don't think we should be here like this," she said, a little embarrassed.

"Neither do I. Not when kids have a habit of popping in on you when you least want them to."

"You said you didn't know anything about kids," she ventured shyly.

Running footsteps on the other side of the glass door signaled Joey's imminent approach.

"I have good ears." As Campbell pushed the door aside for her, he put his hand on the back of her waist to guide her inside. How could the mere graze of his fingers feel as searingly intimate as his mouth?

Oh, she knew it was wrong to want him, and wrong to yield even to a kiss. But it was the first honest thing she'd done for herself, maybe in years. She'd kissed a man she'd wanted to, not because she was afraid or because she had to, but because she simply wanted to.

He's bad. As bad as all the others. They were nice in the beginning, too.

"We only have a couple of hours before Georgia gets out of school," she said casually, attempting a light tone to cover the awkwardness she felt around him after their first kiss and her new insecurities.

"Then we'll pick her up...and bring her here, and we'll have all the time in the world."

"We can't do that.... You and I...we're strangers. I can't involve her."

Campbell put a finger to her lips and smiled. Then he called his housekeeper, Rebecca, on the telephone. Ignoring Hannah's protests, he asked her if she could come over and work late. No sooner had he hung up, than Hannah pounced, listing half a dozen reasons why she never left Georgia with strangers.

"Georgia is used to me," she began, "and to no-body else."

"Then you're overprotective."

"And Joey needs to get used to you."

"Rebecca loves kids. He'll need to get used to her, too. I have a job, remember?"

"I'm not likely to forget."

"You'll trust her as soon as you meet her. She's always telling me I should marry and have kids. When she heard about Joey, she said, *"Pobrecito, por supuesto."*

"Which means?"

"I suppose that she's coming right over."

"You don't know any more Spanish than I do."

"Okay. For now, let's go through Joey's things and figure out what he has and what I think he needs."

She nodded. Then Campbell brought all the suit-cases upstairs to the big airy bedroom Joey had se-lected. She looked through his clothes and toiletries and jotted notes on a pad. Then they left the open suitcases on the bed for Rebecca to unpack.

"Can we buy some toys?" Joey wanted to know. "Like maybe a GameCube for the television and some games?"

"If you're good," Hannah promised.

The afternoon was as bright and sunny and warm as the morning had been stormy. The sky was blue and the white clouds puffy, so it was wonderful to zip along in his sports car with the humid wind blowing through her hair as the three of them rode along the bay.

They went to a discount shopping center on South

Padre Island Drive, the main thoroughfare where the city's malls and retail stores were located. There, they bought everything Patches and Joey needed as well as groceries for Campbell. The hour and a half they spent pushing a basket through the colorful aisles, grabbing items off shelves and doing perfectly ordinary things together any couple might do seemed somehow magical and passed all too swiftly. They would each reach for the same item on a shelf at the same time. Their hands would touch. She'd feel a zing and giggle. He'd laugh.

"It's fun just being with you," he said at one point. "Even if you did buy carrots."

They were on their way to the cash register when they realized Joey must've disappeared while they were buying him a toothbrush.

"Where could he be?" Like a real father, Campbell was instantly alarmed.

"Let's go to the toy department. If he's not there—then worry."

Sure enough, they found Joey there holding a box with a GameCube and games in it. He was reading the back of another red box with spiders all over it. Campbell gave him a lecture as to what he'd do if he ran off again.

Joey crossed his arms and his lower lip protruded as he clutched the red box that contained the hideous-looking electronic spider to his heart.

"Mom kept all my toys. She wouldn't let me bring a single one. Not even my GameCube."

Anxious to leave, Campbell scowled, which caused

Joey's puffy lower lip to balloon ominously. Then a single tear streaked his cheek.

"Oh, all right. A GameCube and the spider thing."

"Thank you! Thank you!"

But when Joey couldn't or wouldn't make up his mind about the spiders without poring over the black print on every single box in the store, Campbell was at first impatient and then intrigued. Joey forgot his fear of his dad when he started reading the backs of boxes aloud to him and explaining in rapid, excited bursts that lots of the electronic toys and games needed components or other toys or they weren't any fun to play with. Watching them, Hannah smiled.

Finally, when Joey still couldn't decide, Campbell set his stopwatch and gave Joey five minutes to make up his mind. Joey ran wildly from shelf to shelf, reading the boxes until the very last second. When his time was up, he looked pouty, but he grabbed the spiders. No sooner had they checked out at the cash register than Joey was sure he'd didn't want the spiders and wanted to go back and exchange it for a gadget that would scream if anybody touched his doorknob.

"You made your decision," Campbell said firmly.

"But Mom always lets—"

"Mom is not here."

When Joey looked tearful, Campbell quickly said, "I'm sorry I said that."

On the way to the parking lot, Joey glumly ripped the box open and pulled out his new GameCube.

"You'll have to decide on whether you want Joey in private school or public," Hannah said when Joey was in the back seat and they were putting all their packages in Campbell's trunk. "As you know, I have Georgia in a private—"

"From what I hear, it's the best. Why don't we pick up Georgia early, so Joey can look at the school and I can talk to Hal Brayfield?"

By the time they'd collected Georgia and obtained the necessary enrollment papers and returned to Campbell's house, Rebecca had Joey's room in order. Georgia and Joey were the same age, and although they were a bit shy at first, they were instantly fascinated with each other.

Georgia was jealous because she didn't have a cat and Joey did, because she hadn't ever gotten to skip school, *never in my whole life,* she'd blurted, and because she didn't have any new toys or games.

"You never buy me anything," Georgia accused. "Not even new toe shoes. And mine are all tight."

Because money was tight.

"You can play with my new GameCube," Joey offered shyly. "And I'll let you pet Patches."

Happy to have someone to play with for a change, Georgia raced upstairs with Joey to plug Joey's new GameCube into the television when Rebecca, who'd been in the kitchen, spotted them and came out and introduced herself.

"I have grandsons and many cats...." Hannah, who was unpacking the groceries, listened as Rebecca recited the name of each and every cat she owned.

Joey told her about his new bouncy spiders and video games. Then he introduced her to Georgia. The three of them were chattering like magpies when

Campbell asked Rebecca if she could stay the rest of
the evening and keep both children.

"Why you never tell me you have a son who look
just like you?" Rebecca said to Campbell a little later.

"Well, now you know."

"Why you don't have no pictures of him anywhere?"

"Soon I will."

"What other secrets have you been keeping, Mr.
Campbell?" Rebecca asked, chuckling.

Hannah couldn't make out his answer. Then the
kitchen door swung open, and Campbell came up behind her at the sink where she was washing and peeling carrots and whispered against her ear. "Let's pack
a picnic supper and go sailing. And no carrots."

She had made a huge mess of vegetable peelings
and was cramming some down his disposal.

"Let me do that," he said.

Out of the corner of her eye she watched him dig
out all the peelings and carry them over to the trash
can. Next he got a sponge and scrubbed the counter.
He was too neat to be believed. Not like her.

"I really should take Georgia and go home," she
said.

"I've got a better idea," he murmured, tossing the
sponge in the sink. "You ever watched the sun go
down behind the city from the middle of the bay?
The buildings turn gold—"

"I should help Georgia...."

They said goodbye to Rebecca. She winked and
told them to have a good time and not to worry about
the kids. She'd spend the night.

Half an hour later they were on his yacht. He had the sails up, the engine on, and he was ordering Hannah, who felt lost and incredibly ignorant on his sailboat, to cast off lines as he backed out of the slip.

"Lines?" She glanced at him in confusion.

"Those ropes on those cleats!"

"Why didn't you say so, then?"

"If you're going to be a sailor, you must learn the proper terminology."

"I would if you'd quit acting like Captain Bligh."

"Are you planning to mutiny?"

"Not yet—since I don't know how to sail."

They headed across the bay in the humid evening air. The sky was gold, the buildings dark, and they quickly left them in their wake. She'd never been on a big sailboat before, but once they were away from the dock and he quit acting so bossy, she loved the way the sleek hull glided across the waves like a big, silent fish.

"We should stop this now," she said when she realized how much she was enjoying being with him.

"Why?"

"For one thing, you're obsessively neat. And I'm a slob."

"I'm not neat. I'm just never home."

"Even your boat is neat."

"Aah…boats… A man has to take care of his boat. After all, she's his mistress."

Halfway across the bay a school of dolphins played chase with them. Laughing, Hannah ran back and forth along the deck as one after the other, the dolphins surfaced and snorted geysers of water at her. Finally, she sat down in the cockpit beside Campbell.

He told her to pull in on a sheet.

"What's a sheet?"

"That rope on the starboard cleat. I mean that rope to your right on the big, shiny chrome thing."

"Then why didn't you say so?"

He laughed. "You'll catch on."

In between tacks, Campbell talked about himself, and she listened, fascinated as the waves rolled underneath them.

"I grew up in a bad part of Houston, near the ship channel and refineries. Maybe not the worst neighborhood, but bad. I wanted one thing—to get out and to have money."

"And you did…get out."

"Yes. But it's never like you imagine it will be, is it? Back then I thought having enough money would fix everything. When you're young, you think the answers are easy."

He was so right. Not that she could tell him her version of the same story. "So—how did you meet Carol?"

"At a firm party. In Houston. She seemed beautiful and glamorous. She married me for my money, for my law degree. I was working such long hours, eighteen-hour days to establish myself. I didn't notice anything was wrong—until it was all over. What about you?"

She wanted to talk about herself—about her parents, even about Dom and their marriage. But she'd been closed up so long, maybe she'd forgotten how.

Or maybe she was simply still too afraid. Or maybe it was too soon.

"It's too boring." He was clearly dissatisfied with her answer, so she continued. "Do you ever wish you could just start over...start with this moment...forget all that went before? Start over...and be different?"

"Like amnesia?"

She hesitated. "Do you think people can change?"

"You seem so familiar. Why?"

She didn't look at him. All she said was "A lot of people say that. I must have a sort of universal look or something."

"Some day soon, either I'll remember or you'll trust me enough to tell me," he said simply.

His dark face was so calm and kind, her heart skittered. "I'm on your side," he said. "As soon as I saw you, I wanted you even though I'm no good at—"

"At what?" she whispered.

"Relationships." His voice had gone a little hoarse.

"We can't have a relationship."

"Then what can we have?"

All lightness had dropped from him, and he sailed in a tense, abstracted mood, scanning the horizon, ignoring her for a while. She sat beside him, watching the gulls fly low across the darkening waves, watching the dolphins when they surfaced. The sun was going down, setting the city and sea aflame. Occasionally, a salty red wave rose higher than the rest and washed over the decks. She'd have to jump back to avoid being drenched. Several times, she landed in his arms. The last time she did that, he didn't let her go.

"Duck," he said, "we're going to jibe."

Before she could ask what he meant, the main sail, which was attached to a heavy boom, swung across the cockpit above their heads.

"Wow," she whispered from the safety of his hard, warm arms as the sun sank behind the skyline.

"Wow," he agreed, tucking her closer against his body. "We're running downwind all the way home."

"It's so smooth and fast," she whispered. "I've never sailed before. It's wonderful," she said.

"It's a dangerous tack. Anything can happen."

She smiled up at him, her eyes wide.

It was a wonderful evening. The night swam with stars and a big moon peeped over the horizon behind them not long after the red sun sank behind his house. By the time they reached his private marina, her perpetual homesickness and loneliness were gone. Her spirits were up for the first time since she'd moved to Corpus, and she almost felt at home…at peace.

Why had she thought him so hateful? She felt he was someone she'd known always. She longed to tell him about London and her real life and even her marriage, to speak of them as if they were things past, and he might be the future. Which was ridiculous. But some things like faith and sexual attraction or a blossoming friendship, didn't make sense, and yet, they made more sense than anything else.

They had a wonderful picnic in the cockpit— smoked salmon on crackers with capers and soft cream cheese was their first course. He opened a bottle of chilled champagne that he'd bought because she'd confessed champagne was a weakness of hers. Then they had fresh strawberries and a salad and sandwiches and store-bought chocolate mint cookies.

Sitting on the towel he'd spread out for her, she felt like a child on a camp-out, but not like a child at all. Eating on his yacht in the moonlight with him, with the champagne making her blood buzz, was wildly romantic and too wonderful to believe. The water lapped gently against the hull. The wind sang in the shrouds that clanged against the mast.

"A toast, *Mrs.* Smith," he said, holding his glass up.

She clinked her glass against his.

"To us," he whispered.

"Thank you for supper and for a lovely afternoon and lovely evening." Then she eyed the glittering windows of his mansion—every light in his house was aglow—and mentioned Georgia, saying, "I really should check on her—"

"No." He tensed when she stood up, and when he got to his feet and towered over her, she sensed some new danger in the taut lines of his tall body. "She's fine. Rebecca is an expert on kids."

Hannah was still protesting when he took her in his arms and kissed her hard. In an instant, she was soft, pliant, eager.

"Yesterday we were enemies," she whispered against that sexy mouth that tasted of champagne and capers and strawberries, but most of all, of him.

"Just goes to show you how quickly things can

change,'' he murmured as he took her hand and invited her below. "Truce?"

"Let me go! I must go to Georgia. Now. Please. I want this to be a light—''

"She's fine. Rebecca has my cell phone number.''

He pressed his mouth to hers and stifled whatever else she would have said. Her lips parted. His arms locked her against him until she grew limp. His lips were hard and hot, his tongue thrusting between her teeth. He kissed her over and over again until she began to tremble with some new, unnameable emotion, until her arms looped around his neck and her fingertips stroked his black hair. And even as she wanted to protest, she could feel herself yielding as something deep inside her welcomed him. The kisses went on forever.

After that his hands were everywhere, skimming over her soft cotton bodice, down her arms, across the crests of her breasts; his every touch causing tremors to go through her.

"I want to see you in that leopard-print bra and nothing else.''

"No,'' she gasped as he drew her down below. In disbelief she heard him snap the hatch, locking them inside. *She was locked in.* And yet she didn't panic.

A single light lit his tiny cabin. By its soft glow, she made out the blackness of his hair, the breadth of his powerful shoulders, the duskiness of his skin.

He smiled, and she smiled back at him. He had to stoop a little because he was so tall and didn't have full headroom.

"Snug,'' he said, lowering his head to hers. Then

she felt the heat of his lips nibbling their way from her throat up to her mouth again, and the warmth of his callused hands undoing a few buttons and sliding her bodice apart to cup her breasts and caress her nipples. Their tongues touched.

The yacht gently rocked beneath her, causing her to fall against him in a breathless heap and clutch his shoulders for support. She felt his hard arousal and gasped.

"We should stop," she said, a little shocked this was happening so fast.

"Is that really what you want?"

She shook her head, and he grinned. When had she ever been the kind of girl who did what she should? And he knew that about her. He'd always known—the longing was too powerful. Too true.

"I feel like a swimmer caught in an undertow," she whispered as she melted against him.

"So do I," he murmured, stroking her nape. "From the first moment you walked into my office, you had me."

"I don't believe you."

"You underestimate your power, then." He took her hand and placed it on his body, made her feel him there so she would know how much he wanted her.

"You are very lovely, very desirable, Hannah."

His words thrilled her as much as his kisses and touch. "You would say anything. You're a man, a lawyer...and a notorious womanizer—"

"So you get three villains for the price of one." But he flinched. And suddenly he pushed her away gently. Reaching up, he unsnapped the hatch. "All right. I'll stop being so unbearably arrogant. I want you, but I like you and respect you, too.''

She stared up at him.

''Go. Or stay. Your choice. But make it fast. Nobility is not my strongest trait.''

''You are the devil,'' she whispered.

''I'm trying to be a gentleman. It's not so easy for me, you know.''

He held himself very erect, his black eyes blazing. His fists were clenched, but he moved aside to let her go.

''Hurry,'' he urged. ''I'm not very patient, either.'' The line of his mouth was thin and set.

She lifted her chin in the air and put a slim, determined foot on the first narrow step. Then she heard him sigh in fierce disappointment. When she climbed the second step, a fist seemed to tighten around her heart.

When she hesitated, she heard him catch a breath. She could still taste him. He was so close, she could feel his body heat. Oh, God, whatever, whoever he was, no man had ever made her feel as he did.

Suddenly, before she even knew what she was doing, instead of rushing up the stairs, unlocking the hatch, and escaping him, she turned, and with a little cry, flung herself into his waiting arms.

''I know I'm being totally stupid.''

''Then, don't be. Go.''

''I want you too much.''

''So, finally, you admit it.'' His dark eyes jerked to hers, and she felt her cheeks flame and her throat go dry.

He swallowed, too. "Do you have any idea how beautiful you are?"

"Oh, God, please help me," she prayed as his arms tightened around her and his mouth gently grazed hers, carrying with it the precious, hopeful, honeyed sweetness of a new beginning.

One kiss ignited a firestorm of desire and doubt and hope.

"Make up your mind," he whispered against her lips.

She felt so shy, she was afraid to open her eyes. "I already have."

Thirteen

From the sagging navy sofa that dominated a wood paneled den littered with art books, stacks of video-tapes and DVD disks, the watcher pointed the slim black remote at the TV and seethed.

Suddenly there it was again on another local channel—the Hot Ladies lawyer hit list. The local shows were having a field day with it.

The watcher squinted at the billboard shot of Joe Campbell with his crotch blown away that dominated the television screen. Next the pictures of the four founders of the Hot Ladies Murder Club flashed beside those of the lawyers who were suing them and who had therefore made their hit list.

Frustration gnawed as the television host yapped unceasingly about the right of aggrieved citizens to the country's court system. Everything the idiot said, especially his comments about how lawsuit abuse was wrecking the medical community by causing mal-practice rates to soar made anger burn like a slow fuse inside the watcher. The stupid bastard thought this was some kind of joke. What would it take to make them see the light?

The checks and balances that normally restrained an organized interest group had failed, creating an opportunity for attorneys to hold the rest of the economy for ransom. The bastards could pick off industries one at a time. Reform, they called it. All you had to do was read their Web pages to see what they were up to. Hell, it was high time somebody got fed up enough to stop them.

When the program cut to a shot of Hannah Smith, the watcher leaned forward. Hannah Smith was certainly a pretty little thing. Again, he thought she looked familiar. Next there was a clip about Veronica.

"Witch! The blond witch stole my idea!"

Then the watcher flicked the remote, and the screen blackened.

This might be good. Yes, this could work.

Glancing from the television set, he noted his rifle case in front of the instant-open gun safe. The rifle lay where he'd thrown it after his drive out to the island. Thinking he should put it in the safe, he got up. But instead of opening the safe, he unzipped the case. Lifting the rifle to his shoulder, he sighted in on his blond cocker spaniel, Tracy, who was curled up at the patio door.

Lazy, no-good, tick-laden mutt if there ever was one—always wanting in or out. Dogs were trouble, more trouble than they were worth. Same as most people.

Moving toward Tracy, he began dry-firing.

Tracy lifted his golden head, gave a little shudder and began to whimper. Then the dog rolled belly up and stuck his paws in the air. Big brown eyes pleaded for mercy.

Bang. Bang.

The dog whined.

"Am I that scary, fella?" He dry-fired two more times.

"Yes, you are," said a voice behind him.

He whirled, the gun still raised in his hand.

And he thought about it.

The scary thing was, she read his mind.

In the dark cabin Campbell licked between Hannah's lips, exploring her mouth, until they both were so feverish they sank to their knees trembling.

"I've always been too easy," Hannah confessed on a heated sigh. Guilty desire for all that was forbidden flared in this safe sealed enclosure of his yacht when his mouth skimmed her bare neck. "Oh, God..."

"Not a problem," he muttered on a ragged breath, cupping her bottom.

"You're a man. You say that tonight. Tomorrow..."

"You don't know me—"

"Which should be a reason not to sleep with you."

"Sex has nothing to do with reason and you know it. Maybe this is the beginning."

In a furor they stripped each other. She unbuckled his belt while he undid the buttons on her bodice as fast as his hands could fly. Laughing, they fell against the bunk.

"To hell with tomorrow," he said, peeling her leopard bra off and studying her in her matching thong panties before kneading her breasts with his rough palms.

"You're right," she whispered. "I don't want commitments of any kind any more than you do."

"That's not what I meant." He caressed her nipples until she shivered and he laughed.

"We have tonight. Just tonight," she persisted.

"So your panties do match your bra."

"Did you have a bet on or something?"

"Only with myself."

Outside the water sloshed against the hull, rocking them gently. Palm fronds roared. A gull cried.

"What if...I want more than a one-night stand?" he whispered huskily, pressing his mouth to the nape of her neck again and sending another hot spasm licking through her.

"What if...I'm not available?"

"You seem kinda available," he murmured.

"Not for anything long term."

"Okay. Neither the hell am I." But his voice was so rough that for a frozen moment she felt near tears.

"So, tomorrow we can say goodbye? I mean, if one of us wants to?" she persisted.

"And what if I don't?"

She grew rigid and fought to ignore the pleasure of his mouth on her shoulders. Sex had led her through dark passages to chambers of horrors she never wanted to visit again.

Her voice tightened with pain. "All it will take for you to leave me alone is for me to say I want out...and...you'll leave? Okay?"

"But what if it's not okay?" His low voice grated harshly.

"All right. I've changed my mind." She was in a

panic suddenly. The cabin walls seemed to press toward her. "Let me go, Campbell. Now! I mean it!"

In another lifetime she saw a fist smashing glass. She felt glass raining against her face. She heard a man's deep, husky voice say, "You're mine—forever." She'd been young and naive then and so foolishly, oh, so foolishly wild with desire, she hadn't understood.

Trembling at the memory, Hannah tried to push Campbell away.

"Easy. Easy."

"Just let me go. You have to let me—"

"Hey…this is really important to you, isn't it?" With the utmost deliberation and gravity, he lifted his lips from her throat and drew her into his arms and pressed her close. Only now his motive was to soothe her, and the fact that she found reassurance in his embrace scared her even more.

Her heart raced while he held her.

"Honey, honey, what are you so scared of?"

She couldn't meet his gaze. *Of men who can't say goodbye. Of men who can possess and hurt too easily. Of men…of love…because I don't know where the lines are, where to stop, how to stop….*

Then she remembered the Hot Ladies Murder Club hit list and was afraid of what Campbell would do if she didn't tell him before he found out on his own. Oh, why did she always screw everything up? She couldn't have sex with him without getting that out of the way first. But she couldn't tell him now.

"I'm afraid of repeating my mistakes over and over," she confessed.

"Me, too."

"I want to break the cycle."

"You will." He stroked her hair. "We will."

"Sometimes I watch happy couples and wonder what their secret is. I want to know if somehow, some way, I could have what they have."

"You, too?" His deep voice was soft with understanding against her ear.

"I grew up in a crazy, free-spirited world. You wouldn't believe—"

"Ah, a hint…of who you really are, at last. U.K. Free spirit. Any more confessions?"

The word *confessions* zinged. Remembering he was at the top of that hit list, she gasped. "Bottom line—will you let me go…if I ask you to?"

His hands were in her hair, stroking her neck and shoulders, pulling her even closer. "Of course I'll let you go. Of course. Just don't be scared. Not of me."

"Okay, then… Those are the rules. This is just sex."

"You think so, huh? You hope so. But what if we can't make the rules. What if…heaven forbid, this thing between us turns out to be love?"

Then her already complicated life would spin totally out of control.

"There's something else," she began. "Last night I did something—"

"Another man?"

"No."

"Then I don't give a damn about it." His mouth covered hers before she could go on. "Wrap your legs around me."

She laughed shakily. ''There really is something I have to tell you.''

''Later.''

When he clasped her to him, she felt his heavy, muscular body strain against hers. Involuntarily, she circled him with her legs.

He kissed her mouth, her nose, her throat, and her body shifted to shape and accommodate his. He was hard and naked, and he certainly knew what to do, but what he did was layered and textured, complex, not like anything she'd ever experienced before. Not with Thomas, whom she'd adored as a young schoolgirl, Thomas, who had stolen her virginity and left her when she'd told him she was pregnant. Not with Dom, who'd rescued her and married her and taught her a new kind of pain.

She felt safe and adored as Campbell's mouth closed over the rosy tip of her nipple, and when his tongue lapped at the rough peak, she got wet instantly. It was as if he were her first man, as if Thomas and Dom had never been. When Campbell's lips moved to her other breast, he gave a gentle tug and she felt wild sensations of hot pleasure shoot from her womb all through her.

It was wonderful until her mind started talking back, the way perverse feminine minds do sometimes no matter how great the sex.

How can I feel like this? So involved on such a profound level? With Joe Campbell of all people—a man I've known for what—a whole day? Am I as naive as ever? Am I repeating...

His mouth and tongue moved lower and turned her body to molten sizzle and her perverse mind to mush.

Then thankfully her body took over as bodies do—maybe because Campbell aroused some deep, vital core of passion inside her that had never been awakened before. Whatever, because his hands and his lips sparked volcanic need. All she knew was that she went wild, climbing and twisting all over him, craving things she'd only endured before. She welcomed him into her mouth, welcomed the most intimate caresses of his tongue anywhere and everywhere. And in every smoldering kiss, in every surrendering touch they shared, her lonely, tortured soul rushed to his. Somehow his hungry lips and eager body washed away past sins and made her feel whole and new.

He lifted his mouth to hers again and again with an eagerness that shook her. Then bliss took over, and she forgot to worry about the past or the future. Blood roared in her ears, and she urged him on top of her. Straddling her, he touched her cheek and then neither spoke nor moved for a long, tense second while he stopped to put on a condom. When he finally lunged, the tissues of her velvet warmth had to stretch tightly to accommodate him. But soon he fitted her perfectly, this inner Hannah, who had never surrendered so fully before to any man.

Again, he hesitated for a few more precious seconds, as if to pay homage to her, the person, before letting the wild rhythm of their mating dance begin. A stab of wonder went through her as her entire being warmed at his every stroke until she was so hot she was burning up.

Soon her hands, which had been gentle on his back and shoulders, became claws, her fingernails raking the sweat-dampened sheets of his bunk. She didn't dare to touch him now because if she had, she would have drawn blood. He rocked wildly on top of her body, and she wanted him to go on and on, but the burning force that consumed them both swept them to explosive, shattering release. He stiffened, his buttocks bunching on top of her. He gripped her to him, his final lunge, causing intolerable waves of pleasure as she met him all the way, exploding when he did.

When it was over, his muscular body lay sprawled across her, but he continued to fill her for a long time and let her cling to him, weeping, laughing, sobbing, unable to let him go.

She stroked his hair and his wide shoulders. "I've never felt like this before…like I'm part of everything that is beautiful and timeless in the universe."

His face was dark above hers when he raised his head and kissed her tears away. "Why are you crying?"

"Because I'm so happy…and confused."

"Because you're afraid?"

"The good part can't last."

"How do you know? Maybe it will get better."

Or worse, she thought. Her fears seemed to mushroom in the dark, and she clutched her hands into fists. She still hadn't confessed the hit list.

"Hey, I'm not those other men."

"What if there's something wrong with me that will make me do stuff and make you react like them?"

"Hush." He kissed her hard.

One kiss led to more. Almost immediately, they were making love again. And again their coupling was both sexual and spiritual. He swept her into a world of dark eroticism that terrified her because she'd been there before and known such terrible pain. Only he touched her whole soul and gave her release and joy that was sheer poetry.

Later, lying beside his long, lean form, she stroked his warm shoulders with the back of her hand, marveling that he was so perfectly made. Marveling that for the first time in her life she felt whole, and not so totally alone. Still, sex always made her feel like a dark, uninhibited angel, who went to dream worlds she didn't trust, who opened secret doors inside herself that made her feel excruciatingly vulnerable and afraid of this wild creature she'd unleashed that was a vital part of herself.

She'd halfway hoped that if they did it fast and got it over with, she could forget him and he would forget her. Maybe she wouldn't have to confess about the list, after all. But sex with him hadn't just been sex. It was more, and she didn't know why. How could she hate him one night and joke about his death and tonight feel so unbearably close to him?

Why did women like her always want to know the whys?

Whatever, lying beside him, just listening to him breathe, made her loneliness fall away. Even in the beginning of her romances with Thomas and Dom, she'd felt alone. When Campbell pulled her against his taut, bronzed chest, she fell asleep in his arms, her mind churning, overanalyzing what had happened and finding no easy answers.

Despite all that was hanging over her head, including his name on that stupid list, she slept as peacefully as a child cuddled against him. The shrouds clinked against the mast, singing like a lullaby in the soft breeze while the waves rocked them like a cradle.

He, too, lay awake as he gripped her close. Why had he confessed that he'd been born poor and told her things about himself he'd never told anyone since he'd left the neighborhood? Not that he'd told her the worst—about his mother or his father.

Hannah's eager hands had undressed him, caressing him, shyly at first and then not shyly at all. And yet underneath her every tenderness, he'd felt a thread of tension and fear.

The first time she'd come, she'd screamed and had clawed the sheets like a wildcat. Afterward, she'd shaken and wept and clung to him.

Usually if he slept with a woman, he got up and drove home immediately. Or if she was at his house, he made sure she got up, and he followed her home.

Not tonight. Not Hannah. She was incalculably, dangerously special. He didn't want to let her go. His hold on her was too fragile. Sensing some unknown terror in her heart, he wanted to protect her and make her feel safe.

He wanted to wake up beside her, to lean across the bunk and kiss her good morning. Would her eyes sparkle? Or would she blush as they ate breakfast and drank coffee? Would they drive the kids to school?

Their kids. He could almost see them as a normal happy couple. The kind he watched sometimes.

Finally, the soft crush of her small, warm body curled into him and lulled him to sleep. For the first time since forever, he wanted the night to last forever.

Fourteen

Hannah awoke to the smell of salt and the sound of waves and gulls. To warmth, incredible warmth, wrapping her. To Campbell. She stretched beside him and smiled shyly. Then she remembered the stupid hit list, and that theirs had to be a superficial, brief relationship.

Alarm warred with the drowsy pleasure of feeling so safe and adored in Campbell's arms. Her head rested on his shoulder, her inky-black hair spilling in waves of silk all over his dark biceps. Their naked legs were intimately entangled. She could tell by his breathing that he was still asleep, so she watched him as she sometimes did Georgia.

He was beautiful, so beautiful, but in his own virile, masculine way. His broad chest rose and fell, and she resisted the urge to comb her fingers through the black mat of curls growing at the center of his chest. She wanted to kiss his lips and invite a session of morning lovemaking. First, she would press her lips to his eyelashes. They were dense and curly and as black as a crow's feathers. Then maybe she'd smooth that unruly cowlick with her tongue.

But as the little red rectangles of light pouring inside the cabin began to brighten her shyness intensified, and she knew she'd better go before he woke up. Thus, with a sinking heart, she disentangled her body from his, stopping all movement when he stirred. When she was at last free of him, she bent and gently covered him with a sheet.

Then she picked up her clothes, which had been flung all over the cabin. Remembering her wild abandon with a hot blush, she slanted her eyes toward his dark, sleeping form, and she dressed even more quickly. How could she have let him do all those things? Cautiously, oh, so cautiously, she slid the hatch open. When it squeaked, she gasped. He rolled over, reaching for her.

When he groaned and grabbed her pillow, she scampered up the stairs and ran across the deck that was covered with dew. A single flying leap, and she was on the dock. The bay was still, glassy satin. Another leap and she was running through the thick-bladed, wet St. Augustine grass up his bluff. Fortunately, the patio doors of his house were unlocked, and his alarm wasn't set. A brief search led her to Georgia in the upstairs bedroom next to Joey's.

Georgia and Joey must have played until all hours because Georgia, who'd fallen asleep by the GameCube, didn't bat an eyelash, not even when Hannah scooped her into her arms and fled down the staircase. Latching her sleeping darling into the back seat of her Mercedes, Hannah rattled out of Campbell's estate onto Ocean Drive just as Campbell, clad only in his jeans, streaked barefoot across the lawn, shouting her name loud enough for the whole city to hear.

She rolled down her window and whistled at him and yelled, "You're beautiful."

Oh, dear, what would the neighbors think? What if someone recognized her car?

Blushing shyly when Georgia stirred, she jammed a bare, wet toe on the accelerator. Spewing clouds of diesel, she headed to the island. Campbell raced out onto the boulevard waving his hands. With a fingertip, she tilted her rearview mirror and waved, watching him until he was no more than a speck.

When she got to the beach house, she woke Georgia up. Again, her mailbox was empty. Strange. A little ominous, even, since Dom used to steal her mail and read all her letters. She'd have to ask Mrs. T. if she'd seen anyone else snooping around.

Upstairs Hannah made Georgia cereal and bananas for breakfast. Georgia said she wanted Pop-Tarts or a *taquito* and not stale cereal with a mushy banana that had black spots on it.

"All we have is cereal, darling."

"You should've gone to the grocery store—"

How could I? I was too busy having wild sex.

"When I suggested it, you didn't want to." Trying to look prim and properly maternal, Hannah grabbed the banana and a knife. "See, I'm shaving the black spot off. When you're done, young lady, be sure and brush your teeth and comb your hair and change into—"

Georgia eyed the offending banana suspiciously. Then she began shoveling teaspoonfuls of sugar into her cereal until Hannah commandeered the sugar bowl and put it on top of the fridge.

Then Hannah left her, scooping up dirty clothes off the floor on her way to her bedroom. Funny, how everything, even laundry seemed to be painted in a rosy afterglow.

Hannah wanted to call Campbell. But what if he'd seen the hit list? Besides, they'd had sex.

Big deal. Sex *was* a big deal to her. It always had been...despite what the tabloids had written. She wasn't one of those women who could be casual about whom she gave her body to. In the end she felt too shy to call.

She took a shower. Not to wash Campbell away but to savor the warmth of the water on her naked body. Not in years had her body felt so alive, so feminine so...so eager. She was aware of her breasts, of the soap suds drizzling down her skin and pooling in a mound around her toes.

For so long she had not thought of her body as anything at all, and her new awareness of it surprised her. She'd been oddly responsive and newly hopeful to everything since she'd left Campbell's bed. To the vivid color of the red sky as the sun had climbed above the bay and gulf, to the ever-changing brightness of the waves of the Laguna Madre as they'd driven home in the early morning on the causeway, to the feel of the salty air blowing through her hair when they'd finally gotten out of the Mercedes at her beach house.

She felt as if she'd been born to make love to this particular man.

What about the hit list? She pushed the question to the back of her mind. Campbell made her feel so

cherished and special. And shy. How could she ever
face him again?

*You're still married. You had a great time, but you
have to end this—now.*

Still, every time she thought about Campbell's
tongue between her thighs or his hand inside her she
tingled from head to toe.

The phone rang as she stepped out of the shower
and wrapped herself in a thick towel. Her windows
were slightly open, and a salty mist from the gulf
crept into her bedroom. Before she picked the receiver
up, she read Campbell's name on the caller ID.

She got hot all over. Even as she told herself to
ignore the phone, female hunger made her heart beat
like a drum. She grabbed it on the first ring.

"Don't ever run off like that again," he ordered
huskily.

His voice filled her with guilt and pleasure and
made her body thrum with desire. "Work."

"Liar. You were afraid to face me…to face us."

No argument there. She swallowed.

"No goodbye kiss?" he persisted.

"One kiss would have led…" Her stomach quivered with utter longing. "How do you know I didn't
kiss you? You were sound asleep. Snoring."

"I don't snore. And I didn't sleep long—once you
quit snuggling with me."

*God, he was being so sweet. But he was so out of
reach. A relationship right now was simply out of the
question. Besides, sweet never lasted.*

"You don't seem like the snuggling type," she de-
murred as doubt mingled with desire.

"I'm not. But, there you go. One night of bliss and you've caused a profound change in my habits."

Oh, how she craved the comfort of his deep voice. She knew she should hang up even as she pressed the receiver closer to her ear. "Look, I've got to go. Work—"

"Right, work," he agreed, sounding weary and pressured at the thought. "Muriel called a while ago from home. Sounds like I've got a rough couple of days ahead of me. Says my desk is piled to the ceiling. I hate that. Can I see you tonight? Maybe around eight?"

Hannah gulped in a breath. More than anything she wanted to say yes. Instead she watched her curtains bell as a sea breeze caught them. "I...I think we should slow this down."

"Why?"

"Why? I hate that question." She fingered her hair. "I don't know. My life is complicated."

"So, I'll go back to my original question. Can I see you tonight? That's a yes-no question, so all you have to do is say yes."

She felt a flash of heat flare in the naked center of her being as she stroked herself dry between her legs with the towel. "No."

"Then when?"

She gulped in more air and ran a shaky hand through her damp hair. "Maybe in a week or so."

"A week! That sounds like a damn lifetime. Somebody could shoot me by then."

She sighed uneasily, remembering the hit list. "Yesterday you promised...you wouldn't push."

"That was before you were so incredible last night."

"You were incredible, too," she admitted shyly, twisting a strand of her hair.

"Tuesday. Dinner? Five o'clock? Right after work?"

"Since when do we stop work at five? And Tuesday's only four days away."

"It's called negotiation. Compromise. Mediation."

"Always the lawyer."

"At least I'm not suing you anymore. We're on the same side."

But will you be when you find out I put you on a hit list? Worse was the thought of telling him about Dom.

"So—Tuesday?" he persisted.

"Okay," she breathed, caught up in his eagerness and her own, feeling almost cherished, and yet wary of him and her own feelings. "Tuesday."

"What are you wearing right now?" His low voice sparked something hot and wild and made her breathing stall.

"I—I just got out of the shower."

"So, you're naked—and wet all over."

His deep, dark voice branded her body and her soul.

"I—I'm drying myself with a towel."

"You *are* naked, aren't you?"

She gasped.

"Admit it," he growled.

"I'm naked."

"I wish I was there. You know what I'd do, don't you? We'd do it against the wall."

The moist air in her bedroom seemed to thicken. She imagined his rapier cheekbones, his black, black hair and that adorable cowlick. Then she thought about his bristly chest hairs rasping against her breasts. When she swallowed, she could still taste him.

Suddenly she was so hot, she could barely breathe. "Okay, so—I'm naked."

"I'm going to put the phone in my lap," he whispered on a raw, edgy note. "Between my legs."

She felt so warm she was sure she was the color of ripe raspberries.

"Blow me a kiss over the phone," he whispered harshly. "And make it hot. Like last night when you blew me."

She giggled, remembering the salty flavor of him filling her mouth. "You are terrible."

"Do it," he commanded softly. "And talk in that low, dirty, incredible voice of yours."

"What? I don't have a dirty voice."

"Yeah, you do. Now, touch yourself down there."

"This is…"

"Just do it."

She pursed her lips as her hand slid lower, and maybe she was about to indulge in a bit of phone sex when Georgia burst into the room, looking like a street urchin.

Hannah yanked her towel around herself and snapped out a single, final, terse word to Campbell. "Goodbye!" Then she hurriedly slammed the phone down and whirled innocently to deal with her little girl.

"Your hair's still tangled. And you're not dressed—"

Indeed, Georgia was still in the same wrinkled T-shirt she'd slept in, and she was wearing only her panties.

"Why are you all red, Mummy?"

"Mommy!" Hannah corrected primly.

"Can we go to Joey's tonight, Mommy?"

"Not tonight, sweetie." Hannah flushed anew at the sexual charge the thought of seeing Campbell again gave her. He'd said he felt like slamming into her against her wall.

Oh, dear. A sigh welled in her chest as she eyed her Sheetrock with utter longing. Then she remembered her failure to confess about the hit list.

"You need a clean shirt, darling. And…let's go find your jeans."

"I want to wear this shirt!"

"And…and where's your lunch pail?" she said in her strict, mommy voice.

"I want to go to Joey's." Georgia's voice was pipingly eager.

"Tuesday," Hannah whispered, stepping into a pair of bikini, zebra-print panties.

"That's a whole week."

"Four days."

"It feels like a week."

Hannah's eyes flitted to her white wall again. *Tell me about it, darling.*

Five minutes later they were both dressed, and in

equally grumpy moods as Georgia swung her lunch pail off the counter and was galloping out the door.

Pretending not to notice Georgia hadn't changed her wrinkled shirt, Hannah followed her, locking the front door behind them.

"Woof. Woof." A small red sausage hurtled across the dunes toward them.

Georgia was skipping down the stairs when she suddenly knelt in excitement, her eyebrows flying together. "Matilda! Here, Matilda. Here, girl!"

Now the woofs were right under their gray wooden staircase and getting louder.

"Matilda!" Georgia shrieked as the dachshund, nails scratching, scrambled up the stairs to her. Wagging her tail, tags jingling, she was dragging her leash through the sand and over the rough boards. A red-faced Mrs. T. waved wildly and tooted her whistle in vain from the beach.

At every whistle Matilda whined and panted guiltily but wagged her back end even harder as she nosed Georgia's lunch pail, begging with her big brown eyes.

"Methinks she wants a cookie."

Delighted, Georgia knelt and Matilda began sniffing her lunch pail and licking at the latch and then moaning most pitifully. "She seems awfully hungry." Georgia looked up at Hannah. "I think she wants my tuna fish sandwich."

"Have you fed her your lunch before?"

"Sometimes a little."

Matilda's imploring gaze and whine confirmed this

fact. To win Hannah over, Matilda licked her leg and whined even more mournfully.

"Just pet her and then let's go. Mrs. T. will feed her."

"Why can't we have a dog, Mummy?"

"Mommy! Yesterday you wanted a cat."

"I want a pet. Why can't I have a pet? A mouse even...?"

"Absolutely not a mouse!" Hannah opened the door of her Mercedes.

"Why can't we ever have anything good here?"

Hannah felt a rush of guilt as Georgia kissed Matilda's wet nose, and Matilda's butt wagged even more wildly.

"I've told you and told you not to kiss her! Dogs put their noses in awful things."

"Like other dogs' bottoms?" Georgia giggled.

"Excellent example, love."

"Yuck."

"Exactly. And don't ever feed her again."

"Can I give her one tiny, little bite of my sandwich?"

"No."

"But, Mummy—"

"Mommy!"

"I hate calling you that. It sounds daft. I hate it here. I like grass and trees and my old school and my friends. I miss Charlotte. It's too bright here. The sun makes my eyes hurt."

"I know. I know."

Mother and daughter got into the car, bickering as usual. Matilda flung herself at Georgia's door, raking her toenails into the paint and whining most pathetically.

"Can't I just give her one tiny bite of tuna?"

Hannah shook her head, but secretly she was glad of the distraction. The dog made her forget Campbell. Which was good.

Fifteen

His door was locked when Campbell got to his office that morning. For once, he was earlier than Muriel. Guy James wasn't there yet, either.

Switching the lights on, Campbell tensed at the towering stacks of file folders on his desk waiting for his attention. He hated stacks. Obviously, Muriel and Guy had been their usual, efficient selves yesterday. But there was only so much they could do.

He rolled up his sleeves. On each foot-high pile they'd attached neon-bright Post-it notes with urgent messages from his clients along with appropriate phone numbers. James had copied two pages from Muriel's calendar with the next two days' appointments and had highlighted the most important ones. Every time slot was jammed with double entries. Muriel had allotted a mere thirty minutes to Maria Gastar.

In bold red ink Muriel had scribbled on three separate pads that Chuck had called about Hannah Smith. She'd written Chuck's number down twice and underlined the word *urgent*. Guy James had added another note about Chuck, this one with exclamation marks around the word *urgent*. What the hell had he found out?

Stuffed to the right corner of his desk was a new death threat in the same loopy handwriting as all the others. He started to read it, getting as far as the words *you disgust,* before he wadded it up and pitched it toward the trash.

A rush of dread swamped Campbell as he sank down into his soft leather swivel chair and tried to wrap his mind around his work, even as images of Hannah from last night rose up to distract him. Sifting through his stacks of mail, he thought about lifting Hannah's dress over her head. God, she'd looked great in that leopard-print bra and matching thong panties. She'd felt even better—quivery and warm when he'd clasped her against his body. And, oh, how sweet and soft her mouth had been under his even when she'd quivered with fear.

He tossed his mail aside. Thumbing through the O'Connor folder, he pitched it aside, too. Then he dialed Chuck, intending to fire him. The Charger's machine picked up on the first ring, which meant the lazy, no-good giant was asleep, stoned, out partying, dropping acid, or worse, out snooping on Hannah. He dialed his cell phone and got no answer.

Campbell swore. Then he logged onto the Internet. He let out a groan when he saw the number of e-mails in his inbox. The first e-mail contained an attachment titled Naked Georgina. Thinking it was porn, he almost deleted it. Then his gaze fixed on the name, Georgina.

Her kid was named Georgia. Coincidence? Campbell didn't believe in coincidences.

Next he noticed that half a dozen more e-mails below the top one all read Georgina Phillips.

Georgina Phillips—the name, at least that first name, rang a bell, the way names like Cher or Madonna or Twiggy did. Why?

He scratched his forehead. Wasn't Georgina the name of that cute British model who'd had those huge, incandescent blue eyes? She'd been skinny as a stick, and yet sexy, too. So sexy, she'd made Campbell feel like a pervert.

Yeah, Georgina had been one of those celebrities who went by only her first name. She'd made a big splash a few years back and then had dropped out of sight.

Campbell's heart plummeted. His mind flashed to the photograph of the blond angel on the beach in the bikini.

Naked Georgina.

This he *had* to see. Hesitating, his fingers as tense as claws as he gripped his mouse now, Campbell leaned slightly forward in his chair. He'd been warned by Africa never to open attachments from unknown senders. Not only was the firm very paranoid about viruses crashing the firm's complex computer system, the firm was very specific about policy regarding what would happen to anyone who disregarded orders and introduced a virus—especially a nonpartner.

Campbell tapped his mouse and opened the attachment.

Georgina. Hannah! One and the same!

In all her childlike, womanly glory—breasts, thighs—Hannah filled his computer screen in vivid

color. His gaze locked on her brilliant, blue irises
ringed with black for a long, electric instant. He was
a pervert all over again with a racing heartbeat and a
stiff groin.

Hannah!

Hating himself, hating her, he kicked his chair back
from his deck and sprang to his feet. For several
minutes he paced back and forth along his windows
to get over his physical reaction.

Hannah Smith, or rather Georgina, looked even
better without her clothes than she had in the thong
bikini.

He should know. He'd had her last night.

He walked briskly with the frenzied energy of a
caged-in tiger. Not that he saw the bay or the bridge
gleaming in the pinkish gold sunlight. All he saw was
the image burned into his retina. Georgina had huge
blue eyes that lit him up like a fire, a waiflike face
and virginal body, and a lioness's mane of coppery-
gold hair. Her arms and legs stretched taut; she was
tied to two posts with gauzy red ribbons. To cover
her modesty, red ribbons streamed between her
thighs. Her navel stared at him like a third dark eye.
The expression on her childlike face was that of wom
anly ecstasy.

He felt a rush of anger for being such an idiot. He
remembered that shot all too well. It had been a panty
hose ad plastered to every bus stop in Paris. He had
been in France on business for Rod that spring.
Campbell remembered a long view of Versailles, its
grounds burning with color, banks of tulips, peonies
and daffodils along walkways and a deep blue sky

above. His limo had stopped near a bus stop, and then all he'd registered was the girl. The sign had been enormous. There'd been no way to miss those eyes, her navel, the ribbons streaming between her incredible thighs.

When he'd returned to the States, the shot had made all the back covers of the fashion magazines here, too. Yes, Hannah—Georgina—had struck a chord in him even back then.

Fool. He sat down at his desk again and opened the second attachment. In this one an older, more mature Georgina was tied by her wrists and ankles to a massive bed with red ribbons. Her wide blue eyes had caught the flash and were red with terror. Someone had looped a ribbon tightly around her neck and tied it in a gruesome bow. There was a birthday cake with a butcher knife stuck in the middle on a table by the bed. The photograph was amateurish, grainy, private, and so personal, it sickened him.

Who had taken it? When? Why? And why the hell had the sicko sent it to him?

Campbell punched the next e-mail with the title Georgina Phillips. The file was thirty pages long and included biographical articles about her life, none of which were flattering. Sitting rigidly before his computer, he skimmed them swiftly.

There was a shot of Georgina in a dress that looked like liquid gold poured over her nipples and curves. The scandalmongers fixed their gaze upon every facet of Georgina's flawed character, writing stories that dealt with her trawling through London's pubs and posh parties with her groupies, younger models usually, looking for men. She'd married Sir Dominic Phillips for his money, and then she'd cheated on him. These stories contrasted with those about Dom visiting land-mine victims in hospitals.

Well, now, at least, Campbell knew who the hell she was.

She was married. But that was the least of it. She'd cheated on her saintly, well-bred husband and tried to kill him. Then she'd run. The courtroom lawyer in him couldn't help overdramatizing.

To Texas. To ensnare me.

Campbell got up and turned out the lights. Then he sat in the shadows alone and stared unseeingly out at the brightening ship channel and bay. Somehow it was always easier for him to think in the dark.

Leave it to me to pick a woman like her. If there were a hundred virgins and one married witch in a room, I'd be drawn to the cheating witch like an iron filing to a magnet—every time.

Fifteen minutes, maybe half an hour later, the Charger called him on his cell phone.

"Did you get the packet I left about Georgina Phillips on your desk?" Chuck's voice was edgy with excitement.

Campbell wanted to punch him in the jaw.

"Upper right hand side of your desk?" Chuck finished, breathing hard.

"Hidden under my latest death threat? I don't know how I missed it." Dazed, Campbell ripped Chuck's fat parcel open. Clippings of the sexy waif with golden hair spilled onto his desk along with several more articles about her and her rich playboy husband, Sir Dominic Phillips, who, according to his adoring press, was a modern-day Prince Charming.

"Aren't you supposed to be stoned or something— at this hour?" Campbell grumbled. "Why the hell did you call?"

"If you got the hots for this broad, you've got exciting tastes, old friend. You should have seen her night before last at this bar I followed her to."

"Was she with another man?"

"She was out on the town with her girlfriends, partying in a bar with bikers."

"Bikers?"

"They were throwing darts at your crotch. They had this newspaper clipping of you pinned to the dartboard. Then I caught a talk show last night. I think these four wild gals might have started some weird ladies club that somehow made the local—"

"Are you the bastard who sent me pictures of Georgina over the Internet?"

"No—all I got on her is in the packet. She's married. She tried to kill her husband."

"Tell me something I don't know already."

"The poor, heartsick bastard she's married to loves her too much to press charges. There's something funny, though. I'm out on the island where she… Oh, did you or did you not catch yourself on the local news last—"

"Look, I'd love to chat about the local gossip and news, but—"

Campbell slammed the phone down and then pitched the photographs and articles into his shredder. Not that he could forget Hannah's real story, even though, he, of all people, who'd had reams of lies written about him, should know better than to believe a single word. But he was too emotionally involved not to devour the gossip about Georgina.

Georgina Phillips had been born Georgina Hayes. She was the daughter of Claudia Hayes, a world-famous American artist with a somewhat confused sexual orientation. Claudia had done huge, boldly colorful figurative paintings that had caught on big time in London in the eighties. Her paintings hung in every important museum. The artist had been high-strung and difficult.

Georgina's father was Gabriel Johnson, the moody British photographer. Her parents had had a turbulent, modern relationship, marrying and divorcing each other three times, living and loving, at times in houses side by side, at times on opposite sides of the world. Free spirits, the press had called them. Georgina had had a room in each house and had been shuffled between them. Apparently, they'd fought over her like they'd fought over everything else and then would ignore her completely at other times.

Claudia and Gabriel had each had many lovers and many houses. Claudia had once bragged she slept with all of Gabriel's lovers. They'd dragged their little girl all over the world. Besides being an artist, Claudia had been a fiercely competitive stage-mother type, believing her beautiful child had to be as famous as she was.

When Georgina had shown no talent in art or the theater or photography, Claudia had used her as a model and then had turned her into a child fashion

model. Georgina had worked until her late teens.
Then, like many models, her career had abruptly
ended. Apparently, Georgina had gotten pregnant and
run off to the States to have her baby. She'd gained
too much weight, at least for the camera. At nineteen
she'd become a has-been. While in the States she'd
worked for her grandmother in San Antonio and had
obtained her Realtor's license.

Bingo.

When her mother had had a car accident and then
a mental breakdown, Georgina had rushed back to
London to nurse her. There was a story about her
mother meeting Georgina's plane naked. Then, out of
the blue, Georgina had married Dominic Phillips, the
most eligible bachelor in England. Voilà! Georgina
Hayes Phillips was no longer a has-been. Once again,
she was a sought-after beauty in London society.
They'd had the wedding of the decade.

Their marriage had been a wild, fast, much-written
affair—red meat for the scandal sheets. The couple
had hung out with rock stars and royalty and flitted
from party to party on grand yachts with the rich and
famous. In England they'd lived in a castle by the sea
in Cornwall, a town house in Belgravia and a flat on
the Thames. In short, Georgina had copied the wild,
free-spirited life of her famous parents as closely as
possible.

Not just a playboy prince, Dominic was also a phi-
lanthropist, and as a result, he was popular with the
press, while his wife had soon lost favor and been
deemed a shallow clotheshorse and later, worse.
While Dominic had been knighted by the queen for

his good works in poor neighborhoods, there had been rumors that Georgina had been involved in affairs. Still, the fabled Phillipses had seemed a charmed couple, at least for a while.

Then one night, Georgina had attacked her paragon of a husband, left the poor besotted bastard on the floor of their posh flat on the Thames and had vanished with their only daughter. Only, technically, the daughter wasn't Dominic's.

Campbell could relate. Just reading about Dominic's and Georgina's lives brought up all of Campbell's insecurities and demons.

So—here Georgina was in south Texas, temptress extraordinaire, pretty and soft-spoken, well bred, at least compared to him, just the filly to tie the noose around Campbell's *dumb-ass* neck and lead him to the slaughterhouse.

Even as Campbell cursed himself for his stupidity, he couldn't forget how frightened she'd looked when she'd walked in for the deposition, nor how wild with fear she'd looked staked to that bed in the picture some sicko had sent him. He remembered his mother and how his father had screamed at her. Most of all, he remembered the fear in his mother's eyes.

Georgina's married. She tried to kill her husband.

Campbell flushed with anger and jealousy and ignored his cold lawyer's mind that told him there were always two sides to any story.

If she's so bad, why is she so scared?

He was too jealous, and he felt too betrayed and too big a fool to think logically or intelligently.

When Guy James arrived sporting a new haircut

and wearing a dark suit and tie, Campbell merely
scowled at him. Brusquely he set his eager clerk to
work on a stack of files he could handle, while Campbell saw clients. Once or twice, in between appointments, he tried to call Hannah but got her secretary,
Alice, a nosy, hostile old biddy. "Aren't you that lawyer who plasters…?"

"Is she there or not?"

Her voice grew more precise. "I already took your
number—sir."

"Three times already," he growled. "So—take it
again. She has yet to return my call."

Before he could hang up, Alice got in another
aside. "Listen to you. Would you call you back?"

"Where the hell is she, you old biddy?"

"Listen to you." Alice hung up on him.

When Hannah—no, *Georgina* did not call him
back, Campbell's mood worsened. When anybody,
even Africa, or one of the other partners, came to his
door, Campbell was brusque—almost rude. Everybody except Africa took the hint and left quickly.

"You made the news last night," Africa said when
he came by to check on the O'Connor case again. "I
got a laugh out of it until—"

"Good." Campbell was used to bad press. Having
a bad reputation was sometimes useful in his line of
work. "So what if I'm not the most beloved attorney
in the city? So what if some people think I'm an
ambulance chaser? If we don't show up at a disaster
site first thing, the insurance adjusters and defense
lawyers damn sure do."

"You're preaching to the choir, buddy."

"Those defense bastards make their big hourly salaries regardless."

"Gotcha, buddy. So—who do you think blew out the crotch in your billboard?"

"What?" He scowled. *Probably the same minx and her biker buddies who threw darts at my picture in a bar.* "Don't you have something better to do than pester me?"

With that, he immersed himself in work to get his mind off her. Halfway through the day when Georgina still hadn't called, Campbell was edgier than ever and totally exhausted from working so hard.

He drove Guy James like a workhorse, too, but as always the kid good-naturedly applied himself with such unrelenting enthusiasm Campbell wasn't so far gone that he didn't feel a qualm of guilt. Not that he let up on the kid or himself. If he had, he never would have gotten through the day.

But he owed the kid, and he knew it.

Later.

One minute Hannah was thinking about all the people she still needed to call that afternoon, including Campbell, as she climbed her steps to her beach house, and the next, disaster.

Her cell phone rang. When she answered it, nobody was there. "Hello? Hello? Hello—"

Dom used to call and not say anything.

"Mummy! The door's wide open—"

Hannah didn't bother to correct her as she ran past her up the stairs. "Stay back, Georgia...."

Georgia dashed heedlessly inside the beach house.

Slashed envelopes, scraps of newspaper and magazines, what was left of Hannah's mail littered the balcony and the sandy drive below. Hannah's rusty black
mailbox hung at a cockeyed angle on a single broken
nail against weathered gray siding.

A caustic bite of fear made Hannah's mouth go dry
as she heard Georgia racing nimbly through the rooms
inside. What if whoever did this was still— What if
Dom knew she'd slept—

"Georgia…" Hannah's voice broke when she
stepped through her gaping doorway. Kitchen bar-
stools had been overturned and her darling set of
white dishes with the little blue seagulls were
smashed on the floor.

Scream, she told herself as she stumbled through
her front door, her feet crackling as she stepped on
dish chips. But her tongue stuck to the roof of her
mouth when she saw the slashed phone book and the
rest of the chaos of her living room and kitchen.

On automatic response she locked the door. Her
purse and keys fell through her fingers onto the li-
noleum floor. Somebody had cut her phone line and
thrown the phone against the wall. A framed mirror
that had come with the house had fallen to the floor,
shattering the beveled glass all over the sofa.

Again she tried to scream for Georgia but could
only gulp in a strangled breath. To her wild relief,
Georgia came running back down the hall with her
dolls.

"Look, Mommy! Pretty red ribbons around their
necks. Aren't they pretty? Daddy used to do that."

A high-pitched scream rang in Hannah's ears as she

sank to her knees to take a doll and embrace her daughter.

"Mommy—" Georgia's blue eyes filled with tears. "You're squeezing me too tight!"

"I—I…"

"You're scaring me, Mommy."

"I—it's okay," she gasped as she undid the bow around the ballerina's neck.

"Don't! Me like the bow!"

"Well, I don't!" Savagely Hannah tore it off the little ballerina.

"Mummy, who broke the tewephone?"

Usually baby talk drove Hannah crazy.

"Maybe it just fell off the table."

"Maybe a big wind—"

"Yes, a great big wind, darling—"

"I'm glad we weren't here," Georgia said, her blue eyes huge and worried as she puckered her brows.

While Hannah checked the rest of the house and deadlocked the doors, Georgia went to her bedroom and turned on her computer.

The worst of the wreckage was in Hannah's bedroom. Even her mattress had been slashed and all the mirrors broken. All her underthings and nightgowns had been ripped to shreds.

This felt personal, way too personal.

The mirrors made her think of Dom. Had he somehow found out about Campbell?

"Look, Mommy," Georgia yelled excitedly. "Somebody sent you an e-mail. It says Georgina—"

"Don't open it, darling."

Hannah gulped in air as she ran to Georgia's room.

"Darling, would you bring me a glass of water? Not from the kitchen…er…from my bathroom. And be careful of the broken glass."

When Georgia raced down the hall, Hannah opened the e-mail.

It was the picture Dom had taken of her staked to the bed right before he'd threatened Georgia. Memories of how his eyes had gleamed with hellfire as he held up that knife flooded Hannah as she tearfully punched Delete. She'd been terrified of her life that night and for Georgia's, as well. That's when she'd finally realized their relationship would only get worse and that she had to find a way out.

She began to shake. Dom was here. He'd been here, in her home. He knew where she lived. He knew about Campbell. He'd done this. She felt as violated as if he'd touched her again, as if he'd raped her again. Only he hadn't raped her, he'd explained when he'd loosened the ribbon around her throat afterward, in that soft, sweet voice, the voice she'd once loved.

"Darling, sweet darling, husbands don't rape their wives because wives belong to their husbands," he'd whispered.

What if the sick monster still wanted Georgia like that headmaster had wanted him?

All Hannah knew was she had to get out of here, just as she'd had to flee London. She pulled the plug of the computer out of the wall just as Georgia screamed.

"Mummy, Daddy's at the front door! Give me the key so I can let him in!"

* * *

Campbell left Guy James at his desk, doing research, and then stalked blindly out of his office, punching Hannah's number into his cell phone as he left.

"Can I help you?" Alice said.

Doesn't she ever answer her own damn phone? "Is she—"

"Oh, it's *you* again. She *still* hasn't called you? Well, I wouldn't hold my breath if I were you."

"Thank you. I'll try again later."

Instead of waiting for the elevators, Campbell took the stairs, since he'd parked only one floor down. Just as he opened the door to the stairwell, a short man carrying a cardboard box got out of the elevator.

Campbell was too engrossed by the message on Hannah's voice mail at her office to pay the man hurrying down the hall much attention.

Downstairs he was starting his Porsche, which was parked a little too close to Africa's fancy, new red Beemer, when he heard what sounded like a muffled gunshot. Probably a car backfiring on one of the higher levels, he thought. But when he got to the lowest level of the parking garage, he heard the sirens. Then his cell phone rang, and Muriel was sobbing.

"I—it's Guy James. He's been shot. I called 9-1-1. I—I think whoever did it…was after you."

The death threats…

Campbell slammed on the brakes and got out of the Porsche. Leaving the keys in the ignition, not even bothering to slam his door, he raced for the stairwell and took the stairs two at a time.

Africa was doing CPR when Campbell stumbled

into his office, breathing as heavily as a hard-run horse, and collapsed beside James.

Bob looked up, his hands bloody, his face ashen. "I think he's gone."

"He can't be gone, damn it." Campbell threw himself onto the kid and began to breathe him, counting, praying, swearing, going insane until the paramedics finally stormed through the door with their gurney and other medical equipment and took over.

"Is he going to make it?" Campbell whispered in a voice that sounded thin and disembodied even to himself. Suddenly he was remembering the morning he'd found his mother and how helpless he'd felt.

The men's grim silence and white faces made Campbell sick to his stomach.

"Maybe it's that damn hit list." Africa's voice swam in a sea of voices in the background. "I—I thought it was a joke. So did the newscaster. But I think whoever it was… Hell, maybe one of those hot ladies… Maybe one of those crazy women was after you, buddy."

"What hit list? What the hell are you talking about?"

"What planet do you live on? *The hit list.* It's on every TV channel. *You* made the first slot on the list. I made it, too. Guy was hunched over *your* desk. It's either those death threats…or…that damn hit list that, like I said, was all over TV last night. An anonymous caller tipped off the television station with the names of the four women who wrote the list. That Realtor you sued for mold put you on a hit list."

"Hannah?"

When Campbell stared at him, Africa completed his thought. "Yeah. She got together with three other women in a bar. One of them is Veronica Holiday, the writer. She's famous. Because of her the list has had a lot of play. But this damn rancher is after me, too. I'm going to call her and tell her I'm off the case."

"What the hell are you talking about?"

"The O'Connor case! Hannah Smith put you on a hit list. Her method to kill you was to have you fall down an elevator or something. The whole town is laughing about it. Then somebody blew the crotch out of all your billboards, too. I thought it was a joke. Then this short guy with wild white hair, black glasses and a big gun came in here and blew James away."

Campbell was too shocked to think or speak. Blood pooled around the kid's chest. So much blood. Could you lose that much blood and live? Guy's face was as white as his mother's had been.

A terrible silence filled the room as the paramedics worked to save the boy.

"Move. We've got to get him to the hospital," a paramedic finally shouted.

Guy was strapped to the gurney. His face was covered by a mask. They were racing him to the elevator, which meant he must still be alive.

Campbell loped after them. He hadn't felt this helpless in years. Not since that awful morning when he'd found his lifeless mother in her bed. What could he do? All he knew was that he had to follow the am-

bulance to whatever hospital they took the kid. Then
he'd notify the family.

Live, he prayed. *Live.*

He'd deal with Georgina or her husband or whoever else did this later.

BOOK FOUR

In a dark time, the eye begins to see.

THEODORE ROETHKE

Sixteen

Mummy, Daddy's at the front door! Give me the key so I can let him in!

Her purse? Where was it? Her car keys?

Broken glass glittered on the floor and bed.

In this mess, Hannah would never find them. Had she dropped them at the front door? Seconds ticked by with agonizing slowness.

Hannah risked a glance down the hall and saw a still-shadowy, broad-shouldered figure silhouetted against the kitchen shade. Dom? No matter how hard she squinted, it was impossible to see through the shade. It could be anybody.

Whoever it was, she wasn't about to risk going back for her purse and keys. When the arm lifted against the shade, and a hammer crashed through the glass, Hannah grabbed Georgia and pulled her down the hall and out the back door. Racing down the wooden stairs, she tugged Georgia along. They were scrambling along the shell path, which twisted through the dunes and yellow tangles of wildflowers that grew in thick clumps all the way to Taz's beach house.

They were halfway up the stairs before Hannah realized Taz's motorcycle wasn't parked on its concrete slab under the house, and her windows were dark. Not that that stopped her from beating on the wooden door and ringing her doorbell. In a panic when Taz didn't come running as she usually did, Hannah crossed herself and pounded one more time.

She should run. She shouldn't be wasting time, not with some man stomping through her house with a hammer. But she was in panic mode and couldn't think rationally. So she just stood there gasping, holding onto Georgia's hand.

Taz. Please. Somebody help us.

"You okay, lady?" growled a deep, furry voice from underneath the pilings of Taz's beach house.

Hannah jumped back, flattening herself against the door. When she saw it was only the same gap-toothed, redheaded biker from the bar, looming out of the shadows, Hannah flew down the stairs, pulling Georgia behind her.

"You know that bastard with the hammer?" he demanded, his earring flashing.

"Maybe." Under normal circumstances she would have been scared witless of the behemoth in black leather. "Who...who are you? What are you doing here? Why did you follow me here?"

"Campbell hired me to check you out. Is this where your cute black friend lives?"

"You're...why *you're* the detective!"

He beamed. "Campbell and I go way back."

She stared at the blank space where his front tooth used to live. "I knew all along you weren't a dentist."

He pointed to a big, black motorcycle. "If you've got the guts…I'm your ride out of here."

"I'm sorry. I've told Georgia to never ever get on a motorcycle. Not even Taz's, not under any circumstances—"

A gunshot crackled in the humid, salt-scented evening air.

"That sounded like it came from your beach house," Goliath said. "You sure you don't want to rethink your priorities? Me—I'm getting my fat ass outta here."

"Mommy! I'm scared!"

The giant hopped onto his bike and revved it.

Georgia climbed on behind him. Hannah scrambled onto the seat behind them, too.

"Put your arms around both of us and hang on tight—"

Hannah didn't have to be told twice.

"Where to?" he said.

She wanted Campbell, she thought, as she wrapped her arms around the man's thick waist. But the last place she could go was to another man if Dom was really after her.

"The airport!" she yelled, feeling sad she'd never get to tell Campbell goodbye.

The giant was revving his bike when a second shot came from her beach house. Georgia shuddered and hung on tighter. Then they were flying out of the drive just as Mrs. T. and a yapping Matilda rushed onto their porch to see what was the matter. Mrs. T. was red-faced and big-eyed and gripping her cordless phone.

"Call 9-1-1 and get the hell back inside!" Goliath yelled just as Taz rolled up on her bike.

Taz had on a tight, chartreuse tube top and low-cut purple jeans and those same sandals with little bells that showed off her green toe polish. Her dark chocolate eyes lit up when she recognized Goliath and Hannah and Georgia crammed behind him on his big hog.

"How come you won't even ride with me and you'll ride—"

Another shot was fired. Hannah gulped in air. "Taz...get out of here."

"Oh, I get it," she said. One quick smile at Goliath and she was turning her bike around in whorls of shell dust.

Then she was beside them, and the two bikes roared out of the drive onto the narrow street and raced side by side through the dunes, taking the back roads to the causeway.

The bikes screamed down cracked asphalt.

"Mummy, me scared."

"Me, too, darling. But we're going home."

"Back to London?"

"As fast as a big old airplane can take us."

"Will Daddy come, too? Will he shoot us?"

"Daddy would never hurt you, darling."

If only she believed that.

Red lights danced viciously before Campbell's closed eyes as he sat in his darkened den, clenching the neck of the Glenlivet bottle as he stared at the black bay. He got up and paced restlessly. Thank God

Rebecca was upstairs with Joey. Joey kept asking about Hannah and Georgia, wanting to know when they could see them again. Campbell didn't know what to tell him.

When he opened the patio door and was about to go outside a blast of music hit him. Somebody in the high-rise was giving a party. Guests spilled out onto one of the balconies. A woman, her dress swirling around her, stood up there staring down at his house.

Valet parking had parked so many cars in front of his house, it looked like *he* was the one having the party. To add to the confusion, the press had trucks double-parked at the entrance of his drive. He'd had to hire a private-duty cop to keep them off his grounds.

Campbell raised his bottle to the woman on the balcony in a mock salute and then went back inside, slamming the door and locking it.

The bullet the James kid had taken had been meant for him.

Because of Georgina? Because she had put him on a hit list?

Campbell had the headache from hell. Hospital smells always got to him. They reminded him of his mother and the hours he'd waited to learn whether she'd live. Reporters camped outside his front door got to him, too. They made him remember Rod's company going down and him being blamed. Georgina's betrayal had hit him hard. He cared about her more than he'd believed possible.

When he'd stormed through the front door, the first

thing Rebecca had showed him was Joey's bad report cards from the Houston schools.

He'd been concerned, but he hadn't been able to face another problem. "Watch cartoons with him or something," he'd said. "Just keep him quiet—upstairs."

Joey was addicted to cartoons. The boy needed to read. Campbell would tackle that one later.

Campbell slumped back down into his favorite leather chair and began drinking Glenlivet straight from the bottle and staring moodily at his yacht as it bobbed against its lines. He'd made an ink mark on the label after his last drinking session and dated it.

You'll end up like your father or worse—if you don't get a handle on the problem....

Tonight he didn't give a damn about his mother's repeated warnings. He didn't care if he became violent or died penniless in some gutter or fried his brain and ended up in a nursing home prematurely, staring at everybody with vacant eyes and hating his own son, the only person in the whole world who gave enough of a damn to ever visit him. What the hell did it matter what his mother had said? She'd been dead and buried for years. She'd lied, hadn't she? She'd said she'd be there for him. Then she'd gone and taken pills without even bothering to say goodbye.

"I didn't want my boy to work for a man like you, Mr. Campbell," Guy's blond mother had told him tonight at the hospital in the ICU waiting room.

Her words had cut deep.

Campbell had forced a bitter smile.

"He said that you were a lawyer because you

wanted to help the little man, and that if you didn't advertise, uneducated people in trouble wouldn't know you were there for them.''

"Your son's a great young man. Someday he'll make a great lawyer."

"But a bullet in his spine, the doctor said."

"I know." Campbell had forgotten the rest of the medical mumbo jumbo that had followed that terrible pronouncement. He'd represented people who couldn't move from the neck down.

"Did you know Guy got up an hour early every morning before work and stopped off at the Episcopalian school where his little brother Sammy goes and watered all the new trees he and Sammy planted?. He...he did that this morning before..." She'd stopped, choking on a harsh sob, unable to go on.

"He's a helluva kid. He took a bullet meant for me because I was an arrogant jerk."

A talkative nurse, who'd reeked of cigarettes, had interrupted them. "If he lives, he'll never walk or move his hands again."

Campbell had grabbed the pasty-faced nurse and shoved him against the wall and told him to keep his mouth shut in public. Campbell had been booted out of the hospital as a result.

When Campbell's phone rang, he grabbed it, hoping it was Dr. Crocker, but the caller hung up. That was the second time tonight.

Remembering his exchange with Crocker who, as bad luck would have it, happened to be the one doctor he'd sued. Every time Campbell thought about how

Crocker had treated him blood washed across his pupils in a red wave.

"I did what I could," Dr. Crocker had said in an offhand tone when he'd come out of the ER in his blood-splashed green scrub suit.

Crocker was short and old. He believed in right and wrong, and held on to a grudge.

Still, Campbell wished to hell he hadn't beaten the guy up in court so badly.

"He's stable," Crocker had said. "But he needs a neurosurgeon. The operation he requires is extremely delicate and highly risky. Unfortunately, we don't have a neurosurgeon available."

"Then get one, Doctor. I don't care what it costs, if it gives him a chance, I'm good for it. I want the best possible doctor—"

"There's nobody left in town—"

"Then make arrangements to fly Guy out of town—to Houston...."

"If he were my son, I wouldn't risk moving him anywhere."

"Then get some doctor from Houston here. I don't care what it costs—"

"You lawyers think nothing counts but money. You don't value human life. Apparently, a lot of people agree with you."

Campbell had clenched his fists. "That's a bald-faced lie, Doctor."

"Is it? I've been sued frivolously half a dozen times. Every case but yours was thrown out, and I beat the hell out of you, didn't I?"

"This isn't the time or the place—"

"Those lawsuits cost my insurance company a bundle, counselor. I've been dropped by my carrier twice."

"So is this some kind of personal crusade to get me?"

"You lawyers stomp around the courtroom telling us how to practice medicine—call a lawyer. Give him a scalpel."

"Doctor, Guy James is just a kid. Medicine is supposed to be a higher calling."

"You called me a murderer in a court of law. I didn't like it. I don't like you."

"Lawsuits aren't personal. Besides, you won."

"You cost me months of my life...my marriage..."

"Doctor, I'm sorry."

"Not good enough."

"All right. There's nothing I can do to make up for what you think I did to you, but I'm begging you to forget your hatred for me and find Guy James a surgeon. I'll pay—"

"You still don't get it. It's not a question of money."

"Okay. For whatever it's worth, I'm sorry—"

"I don't give a damn."

Campbell felt guilt-ridden and numb. He was burning up inside at the same time. His TV was on, but he had the sound off, and the stillness and silence in his big lonely room engulfed him as the booze haze thickened in his brain like a dark fog.

Nobody had really gotten a good look at the shooter carrying the cardboard box. How could you fire a big gun and then get out of the building without anybody seeing you?

Georgina and her hot ladies? What the hell was that all about? Did that have anything to do with James?

Campbell had plastered his name on billboards and phone books. He hadn't given a damn who hated him or who sent him death threats.

Until now.

The phone rang and Muriel said, "You're a star. Channel 3. National news."

Campbell punched three and turned up the sound. Sure enough, there he was outside the hospital with a microphone shoved against his face.

"Do you think the shooter was after you, Mr. Campbell?"

Campbell's television self ducked his head.

"Come on, Joe, do you think the shooter's the same person who's been using your billboards for target practice?"

His dark face betrayed nothing as he rushed through the throng toward his Porsche. A flash went off in his eyes.

"What do you think about the Hot Ladies Kill-a-lawyer Club?" the reporter shouted. "Do you think it catches what a lot of people around here feel toward the legal community?"

He'd reached his Porsche and was opening the door when the reporter started in on him again.

"Why do you think Hannah Smith put you at the top of that hit list? Is it true she agreed to settle the case the next day?"

Campbell's face was a cold mask. "Go to hell."
He got in his car and slammed the door.

The reporter beamed at the camera. "Folks, the law
clerk of prominent Corpus Christi attorney, Joe
Campbell, whom you just saw getting into his car
after hospital security evicted him, was shot late this
afternoon while working at Mr. Campbell's desk and
is in critical condition. As we reported earlier, Joe
Campbell's name made the top of the Hot Ladies
Murder Club hit list, and now today—"

Campbell switched channels. A local talking head
was saying, "It seems that four ladies who don't like
being sued decided to get even and got together at a
local bar with a bunch of bikers during a biker convention—"

A list, composed of four lawyers' names and their
pictures, and the names of the women who wanted
them dead along with the ladies' pictures, flashed
onto the screen.

Georgina's fine-boned, pale face was paired with
his. Next there was a shot of the lipstick-smeared hit
list itself.

"Police would very much like to speak to Mrs.
Hannah Smith, the local Realtor who allegedly tar-
geted Joe Campbell. Mrs. Smith couldn't be reached
for comment. Neither could Veronica Holiday, who
has disappeared...."

Campbell couldn't believe what he was seeing and
hearing. Next, a sun-burned biker named Chico, who
had a shock of greasy dark hair falling over his
moody dark eyes, filled the screen. He wore a black
T-shirt with a winged skull and thick chain necklace.

"I don't know nothin' about no hit list. But them's the Hot Ladies that was at the bar. And yeah, one of 'em got the Charger to pin a picture of Joe Campbell on the dartboard, and we threw darts at it. The Charger won the contest and danced with one of the hot ladies on a table...."

The Charger?

"Ain't no law against throwing no darts. None that I ever heard of, anyways. Them hot gals didn't seem like no criminals to me. They wuz just havin' fun. That hit list could be bullshit for all I know. Probably is."

There was a shot of one of Campbell's billboards with a gaping hole where his crotch had been. A seagull was perched inside the hole.

Campbell flicked his remote to another channel. A newscaster was filling in his viewers with the story of Campbell's precipitous rise and fall in Houston. Campbell punched a button and the screen went dead.

Compared to Houston, this whole hit-list thing could have been a joke. But it was no joke. Not with Guy James fighting for his life. Had the kid been hurt because Campbell had threatened to expose Georgina Phillips? Had she wanted Joe Campbell dead so much that she'd scribbled his name in lipstick on a hit list?

His doorbell rang as Campbell lifted the bottle of Glenlivet. His throat tightened convulsively. Who the hell could it be—some reporter or the short shooter here to blow him away?

Campbell got up and swayed unsteadily for a long moment. Then he went to the nearest closet and yanked out a golf club. Padding silently to the door, he threw it open.

When he saw Georgina's white, terrified face, Campbell lowered the club and flung it violently aside, sending it clattering across his Saltillo tiles and smashing into a wall. It made a long black mark.

Georgia was in one of his dark blue wicker chairs at the end of his porch hunched into a ball. Her arms were wrapped around her legs and she seemed to be trying to squeeze herself into a tight little ball.

"You've got nerve." His voice was low, as he focused on Georgina, and yet his pain felt as raw and cutting as a knife's edge.

She colored. "I—I didn't want to come here. But your friend the Charger won't take me to the airport until I talk to you. Then I remembered I left my house so fast I forgot my purse and my passport...credit cards, everything—"

"So, you were running out—"

"Something's happened— Somebody might be after..."

"You're damn right something's happened. You started a firestorm."

"I—I don't know what you're—"

He took a quick rasping breath. "Two days ago, you wanted me dead. Right or wrong, honey?"

"But I—I don't feel like that now."

"You put me on a hit list. Everybody in town knew about it but me."

The Charger and a biker pal lingered at the end of his drive near the cops and the reporters, revving their bikes. Obviously the Charger wasn't leaving until Campbell told him to.

"Oh, Campbell, I wanted to explain about that list. I did try even on the boat, but you…we…Joey… It all happened so fast. My feelings about you changed so quickly. One night I hated you, and the next night I made love to you."

"Did you want me dead?"

"That stupid list wasn't my idea…. Campbell, you've got to believe me. It was a joke. We were drinking, just fooling around."

"In a bar full of bikers?"

"It was a joke. I'm sorry. And if I could undo it, I would."

"Not good enough."

"You know how upset we both were after the deposition. I was still half-crazy when I went out with Taz, my next-door neighbor, that night. We met Zoë, a client of mine, and her star writer, Veronica, at their beach hotel. There were a bunch of crazy guys at the bar."

"Yeah—bikers."

"All I want to do is to go home…to London.…"

"Sure."

"Oh, Campbell, something horrible has happened. Everything is catching up to me."

"Tell me about it."

"What's the matter?" she murmured, suddenly more aware of his dark emotion than her own.

"You mean you really don't know?"

Her frantic eyes clung to his. "Know what?"

"Don't look at me like you give a damn!"

"I do. I never wanted to hurt you." Tears brightened her deep blue eyes, making them appear larger and as painfully innocent as a hurt child's. She was *that* good. Model's tricks, he told himself.

"I'm sorry. I really shouldn't have come," she began in a wounded, low tone. "The Charger made a mistake. I'll go."

When she spun around, he grabbed her by the arm, his fingers closing in a viselike grip. She held her breath, and he could see her pulse knocking wildly in her throat.

Last night he'd made love to Hannah Smith. Tonight he held Georgina Phillips, and she was scared to death of him again.

The sea breezes stirred the palms and brought the sweetness of oleander and her perfume, Chanel, wafting to his nostrils, and those fragrances were a cloying, nauseating combination on the humid sea air.

Georgina. London. Modeling. Who was she really? What had her glitzy life really been like with Dominic Phillips? Sir Dominic Phillips? What had she suffered at her husband's hands that had made her strike him and run? Was the man really such a paragon and she such a monster? Or had the press gotten it all wrong?

Georgina was watching him with big, scared eyes. She loved her daughter and was a good mother. So, why hadn't she had children with Dom if he was so perfect?

The tabloid stories and the woman didn't add up, and Campbell didn't like mysteries. Still, he was in a black mood, and he wanted to hurt her for starting a vicious chain of events that had led to Guy having

been shot. He wanted things to be simple for once.
You were bad, you got hit. Lessons his father had
taught him with the back of his hand, with a belt, a
whip, or with whatever was handy.

But her vivid beauty and her gentleness struck him
like a blow. Even with coal-black hair that did nothing for her pale complexion, she looked so gorgeous
and sweet his heart dropped to his stomach. He remembered the aching glory of lying with her last
night, the rightness of it on so many levels. Her parted
thighs, her velvet warmth, her strangled moans of
pleasure before she'd turned into a wildcat, her gentleness afterward—had all those things been lies? He
wanted this woman, both her passion and comfort,
more than he'd ever wanted another. A knife turned,
cutting deep into his heart.

Pale as a ghost, she glued her sapphire eyes on his
dark face; that pulled at him on a profound level. He
was enraged that he was such a sap. All she had to
do was turn up on his doorstep, and he was falling
for her all over again.

"Let me go," she whispered.

With grim resolve, he jerked her across his threshold. "You're not going anywhere until you give me
what I want."

"Which is?"

"The truth for a change."

"Campbell, I never wanted you dead. But if I stay
here—"

"Before this night is over you're going to tell me
who you really are." He clenched a fist and fought
for control.

His hands were shaking when he let her go. He was scared of her. Of himself. Of what he might do if he kept touching her.

"Tell Georgia to come inside. Tell Chuck he can go. Then get in the house."

"No. You don't understand—"

"Then I'll tell them myself." He stepped onto the porch again. "Georgia!"

He had only to snap out her name, and her kid came running. He touched Georgia's shoulder gently before he waved goodbye to the Charger and slammed the door. For an instant the little girl grabbed him and clung trustingly before her mother pulled her away.

Campbell slammed the door.

The bay was lit by silver moonlight. The night was one of those warm, smooth evenings made for lovers.

Ignoring the other party guests, the watcher leaned forward against the balcony, fighting the little sting of an adrenaline rush.

What was going on down there, anyway? Motorcycles? *Her?* Running across *his* drive?

Her? At his house?

Hannah Smith, yes, it had to be her again. She and her little girl disappeared from view, but the two big bikes drove round and round in Campbell's drive in great sweeping circles.

Hannah must be talking to Campbell on his porch.

And what was that? That dark figure racing fast, from behind the garage? How had he gotten past the cops and the two motorcycles?

Was that the same weirdo who'd been in the parking garage the other day, who'd flattened the tire of Hannah's Mercedes?

The same weirdo from the bar?

If so, he was becoming a problem.

Seventeen

Inside his house, Hannah sucked in a nervous breath. She didn't know what to say to him or what to do. Then the phone rang and Campbell answered it.

"Nobody there," he said, hanging up abruptly. "Third time tonight." His tone accused her.

Dom? No. Everything bad isn't necessarily your fault.

Her eyes widened, and to distract herself, she stared out the window and watched the pair of big motorcycles going round and round and making lots of noise in his drive now.

"Who the hell is Chuck with?" Campbell demanded.

"Taz."

"Taz?" Campbell's black brows slashed together. His mouth thinned.

"I told you, she's my next-door neighbor. She's a high school principal. When she bikes, she goes by the handle of the White Ninja. Oh, and she's my spiritual adviser."

"Right. One of the Hot Ladies. Hell," he said, looking away when the two motorcycles roared away into the night together.

"I think your Chuck's taken a fancy to my Taz."

"He's not a spiritual guy."

"She could change that. She's powerful. Not that I think she could change him into somebody she could take home to meet her grandmother."

"Her grandmother? I can't believe I'm having this ridiculous conversation," he muttered.

"So, why did Chuck bring me here?"

"He works for me. That's why."

"As if that explains anything."

Campbell wore jeans and a long-sleeved, hot-pink shirt that made his tawny skin seem darker and the glitter in his hard, black eyes seem hotter. Tonight his carved face was implacable and cruel.

Why was he looking at her like that? Like he hated her all over again? Like he lusted for her, too? With all the tenderness for her gone? Why were all the television trucks camped at his house? He smelled of whiskey and that scared her.

"Campbell?" She blinked and tried to bring him into focus.

Joey came running down the stairs to see what was going on. Campbell waved him away, but she knelt to be on eye level when the little boy approached her shyly.

"How's it going, Joey?"

"Good." He looked up at his father shyly, too, but with affection, she noticed. "I was watching cartoons."

"He needs to read more," Campbell said.

"Hi, Joey," Georgia said. "A bad man shot bullets inside our house. I thought he was Daddy, but he wasn't."

"Bullets?" For the first time Campbell's face grew concerned as he regarded Hannah. "Upstairs, kids."

He waited as they rushed up the stairs like two little whirlwinds on flying feet before speaking to her again. During the awkward silence of being alone with this man she'd slept with, a man so changed that he seemed more a stranger than ever, she scanned the furnishings and the high-beamed den with a sense of unreality. Already the house looked a little more lived in. There were sneakers and socks littering the polished floor. A baseball bat and a soccer ball lay at one end of the couch, comic books with dog-eared pages at the other.

"Yes, somebody broke into my house with a hammer," Hannah whispered.

"Who?" A muscle in his jawline ticked. "*Mr.* Smith maybe?"

"Maybe. I—I don't know."

"So, were you ever going to tell me about him?"

She swallowed. "I didn't want to involve you, to involve anybody."

"I'm involved, okay?"

"And furious about it."

"Yes. Furious. And mixed up as hell."

"Me, too. But if I stay here, you could be in danger."

"Tell me about it," he said darkly.

"No, I mean it."

"So do I. Some maniac shot my law clerk this afternoon. He was after me." Campbell's voice was thick, odd.

"Oh, my God—"

"Now you tell me some maniac broke into your place and shot it up. Same guy? Might be your husband? You think he's mad because I went to bed with you? Is that what you think? How'd he find out? You tell him? Were you using me…to make him blow his stack?"

"No! But if it was Dom, I really might be endangering you by being here. Call me a cab and lend me some money, and I'll get out of your life.…"

"Just like that…" He laughed. "No way in hell are you leaving—not till I find whoever shot Guy. If you're the bait he needs…"

She shuddered. "I—I wish I hadn't come here.…"

"You wish?" He laughed. His black eyes burned her. "I wish I'd never laid eyes on you." Then his big, dark hand reached for her.

"Let me go.…"

He caught her to his hard body. Even as his rough, bruising fingers set her on fire, she gulped in a panicky breath, knowing too well from past experiences where such an embrace might lead.

He pressed her into the wall. "What the hell was last night all about?"

"I don't know anymore. Maybe it was a mistake."

"You're the one who's married, honey. What'd you do it for—kicks? I've known women like that—"

"I bet you have." Dom would have hit her if he were in a mood this black and she talked back.

"You're scaring me," she whispered.

"Maybe you'll tell me the truth."

He reeked of whiskey, and she could feel the heat

of his body against hers. Still, she forced herself to meet his gaze.

"And I was already scared when I came here tonight." She gulped in another bite of air. "I—I've been so scared for so long.... I ran away because I was scared. I guess I got crazy and thought you were different from all the other men I've known."

"Don't play me."

"Okay. I was married to this man...."

"Was?" He groaned. "That's a lie."

"I told him I wanted a divorce. He went crazy. He said he'd kill me if I left. He threatened Georgia. There was no way I could stay after he made those threats."

"You'd better be telling the truth." His eyes were dark as his hand came toward her throat. Terrified, not knowing what he intended, she felt his broad fingers bury themselves in her hair. Gathering up a fistful of the thick, silky mass, he brought it to his lips and inhaled her scent. The gesture was tender, and strangely at odds with the violence and anger she sensed in him.

As abruptly as he'd grabbed her, he let her go.

"Th-thank you," she whispered, "for releasing me."

"Go upstairs." His raspy tone was low and unsteady. "Third bedroom to the right. There's a bathroom, too. A tub. Towels. You'll find the thing things you need. Women's things."

Whatever she had expected, it wasn't this sudden about-face. He looked wounded and moody, and she felt a strange animal need to comfort him. Instead of running to tend to her own needs, she lingered beside him in the shadows. "I—I want…"

"Goddammit, don't tell me what you want!"

He leaned toward her, his eyes glinting as they moved from her face to her breasts. "Move. Go upstairs. Leave me the hell alone. Last night you asked me not to push. Well, don't the hell push me. Not right now. Later… Later I want to hear all about your husband."

Quietly, quickly, she stepped out of his range. Then she ran, not daring to turn around even though she felt his eyes burning into her back until she disappeared upstairs.

In the kitchen, while Campbell heated a cup of water in the microwave to make instant coffee, he poured out the rest of his Glenlivet. Then he pitched the bottle so violently it smashed to pieces in his metal trashcan. Lowering his black head into the sink, he splashed cold water over his hair and his face and his neck, not caring that he soaked his collar or got water all over the floor. By the time the bell on his microwave rang, he was a sloppy, wet mess and so was the kitchen.

The tile counters spun crazily; every nerve in his body buzzed. He was still furious. On fire. Hurt. Crazed with fear and guilt and remorse over James. Scared for her, too. Some bastard had shot up her house. What the hell was going on?

Campbell had to sober up fast if he was going to figure all this out. And he had to stay the hell away from her until he got a grip. Or he'd do something really crazy. *Like his father.*

He drank two cups of black coffee. Then he went outside, changed into swimming trunks and dove into his lighted pool and swam laps, never guessing that a killer had him in his sights.

On the balcony outside Hannah's beach house, Taz looked up at the black sky and then at Chuck's broad face and said, "I'm not sure we should be doing this."

"Neither the hell am I." With a grin, Chuck ignored the police tape and stiff-armed the front door of Hannah's dark beach house.

He flipped on the light, and Taz nearly screamed when she saw Hannah's broken white dishes with the little blue seagulls, only Chuck's beefy hand closed over her mouth.

"Hush," he said.

His voice and his hand were incredibly gentle. Taz felt her stomach flutter. She went for big and gentle.

"We don't want to get caught here," he said.

"You're right. I'm a high school principal."

"You're kiddin', girl," he said as he let her go.

"No, I'm really not."

"I never would've guessed. I like that. My mother was a schoolteacher."

"I won't be a principal long, though. I took some heat today for being one of the Hot Ladies. Lucky thing I'm opening my own business."

"What kind of business?"

She produced a hot-pink card.

"Wow! Sister Tasmania. Fortune-teller."

"Spiritual adviser."

"Cool."

"You wanna come over to my place…after you get through here?" she invited.

"For a little spiritual advice?" His earring gleamed. His grin was cute even with the gap.

"For coffee?"

"Sure. This won't take me long. It better not take long. Somebody might see the light."

"Don't get any ideas, Goliath."

"Goliath. I like that. It would make a good handle."

"I said coffee. That's all."

"I don't think so," he murmured, grinning at her.

"You're mighty sure of yourself, white boy."

"Shouldn't I be?"

"This won't go far. See, I don't think my grandmother would approve of you."

"If it matters, she will."

"You're arrogant."

"No, I just like you." He stared at her before turning his attention to the wreckage. "I'd better get to work here."

Taz knelt and picked up a broken saucer. "Man, she loved these dishes."

"Whoever did this really has it in for her. This is vicious. This is personal, primal. It was a lucky thing I was here when he bashed in her door."

"Yes, it was. I like that…your being lucky. It's a sign." She paused. "You got something against dentists?"

"Recent injury. I've got an appointment."

They smiled shyly at each other.

A few minutes later Chuck called Campbell on his cell phone.

"The bastard came here to kill her. You don't even want to think about what he would have done to her if I hadn't gotten to her first. I think he must've gone a little crazy when she rode off with me. He cut her clothes, cut her mattresses, masturbated and defecated on all her underwear. The guy's a real loony-toon, and Joe, he's still out there. Watch your step. You'd better call the cops, first thing. When you can, get your own ass out here and take a look at this mess."

Taz heard Campbell say in a loud voice, "I owe you…for saving her."

"I'd still be some cheap thug in Houston if it weren't—"

"Cut the mush."

Chuck laughed.

Knowing Campbell was downstairs, Georgina felt almost safe. His charming guest bedroom was papered in gold and silver. She opened a closet and found that it contained women's clothes in various sizes—jeans, shorts, skirts, blouses.

So, he had women here on a regular basis. Why shouldn't he? He was a rich bachelor.

There was bubble bath on the side of the tub, too. When she ran the water and sprinkled some pink powder, the bathroom smelled of steamy roses. Not that she took a long bath. She was too tense. When she got out, she pulled on a white floor-length bath-

robe. Then she went to the window and saw Campbell
in the pool swimming like a madman.

Instinctively she sensed he was working off his anger and maybe sobering up, too, and she relaxed a
little. He wasn't like Dom. He wasn't. He hadn't hit
her or forced her to do anything she didn't want to
do, and he'd been furious. But not crazy furious. Still
thinking about him, she wrapped her wet hair and lay
down on the bed, intending to rest only a minute or
two and gather her courage before going downstairs
to find him.

What had possessed the Charger to bring her here?
To him? What if Dom— She couldn't let her mind
dwell on Dom. She needed to tell Campbell more
about the break-in and really explain about the hit list.
There were other calls she needed to return. Katherine
Rosner had called a dozen times with growing impatience, according to Alice. Then there was Zoë. But
first of all, she should call Mrs. T. and see what the
police had found out, but her eyelids felt so heavy
suddenly. It was all too much. She'd lived in the
shadow of violence so long, she was worn out by it.

Later, she would call Mrs. T. Later, she thought as
she lay down. Sometime during the night, she heard
the phone ring and the deep timbre of Campbell's
voice. He spoke for a long time. She thought she
should get up, but she was so tired. So very tired.

Campbell was in the den when the Charger called.
He was on his mobile. Chuck's voice was low and
hard to hear over the static on the line, but it sobered

Campbell up fast. He had a blinding hangover after Chuck hung up.

His heart pounded. He was scared. He hated being this scared. It made him feel like a weak, wimpy kid again, at his father's mercy. It made him remember why he'd strutted around, acting like he was some sort of Hun with a law degree.

Georgina could have died. What if he'd found her in that beach house, all white and crumpled and blood-streaked, the way he'd found his mother. Georgina would've been gone forever, like his mother, without a goodbye, without anything. Death was a familiar enemy. It cut a huge black hole in your heart forever. And just the thought of Georgina's death brought him up sharp. Every nerve in his body stung him into a fever pitch state of alertness. He'd been too tough on her. Who was he to judge anybody—ever?

His rage toward her hadn't just been mere rage. Even when he'd been more furious at her than he'd ever been in his life, love and fear and disappointment had been there, too. He'd thought she was special. He'd thought she was cutting out on him.

Hell, she was special.

Now all he could think about was how close he'd come to losing her. Suddenly he knew how much he loved her. He didn't want this. Damn it, he loved her.

How had that happened? Love didn't happen in a few days. But it had. How was he going to protect himself? Lady Phillips? She'd go back to London. He was from a low-class neighborhood. A lot of people thought he was just an educated thug with a law degree.

He and Georgina didn't have a chance of making it.

Sometime during the middle of the night Georgina opened her eyes again and realized she wasn't alone. Bright moonlight streamed from the window across the bed, revealing the broad-shouldered form of a man sitting on the bed beside her, smoothing the blankets, smoothing her hair, his touch infinitely gentle.

Campbell. Dark and tall, he looked as lethal and fierce as some ancient Viking warrior, and yet he was tender now. He must've been watching her while she slept, watching over her, maybe. Funny, just his being there made her feel safe, and it had been so long since she'd felt safe. Maybe she'd never felt safe before, not even when she'd been a little girl. Only rarely had her famous mother come to her bedroom and kissed her good-night.

She snuggled deeper into her pillow, studying his profile through her dense lashes. "Campbell?"

"Go back to sleep," he said gently.

"You sound different…better…."

"I shouldn't have come in here," he said. "But you screamed in your sleep."

"I have bad dreams sometimes. I'm glad you came in. There's so much I have to tell you. About Dom. About me."

"In the morning—*Georgina.*"

"So you know?"

"Some of it."

Sheets rustled as she sat up and reached for his hand in the dark. "In the morning you might be all mean and hateful again. Not like you are now—nice."

"Nice. I hate that word."

Their hands touched. As always, the connection of palm to palm lit a fire inside of her and made her want more.

"Damn you," he muttered. "Don't use sex—"

"I'm sorry. I wasn't. Just listen," she pleaded. "I've got to say this fast before I lose my nerve." She gulped in a breath. "Yes, I'm married. And my husband's trying to kill me. Or at least he will, if I don't go back to him. We live in a beautiful old house in London that's filled with antiques and heirlooms. Belgravia. But I can't go back there. I can't. And nobody understands, so I don't expect you will, either—"

"You're tired. So am I."

"Just listen. Quit putting up walls."

"All right." He was silent.

She closed her eyes. "I don't want you to hate me because I didn't tell you before last night. You and I—we happened so fast."

He nodded.

"One minute I hated you, and then..." She breathed deeply. "And I haven't ever told anybody else about him, either. Except my mother. And she didn't believe me. Nobody would, you see. He's very clever. And Mother wants me to be famous, and since I failed at acting and modeling, the only way I can be famous is to be married to somebody famous."

"You really expect me to believe—"

"There's more. It gets worse. I—I…"

"I know it all by heart." His deep voice sounded dead and lost, so she gripped his warm fingers more tightly, to hold on to some part of him because she was so sure she was losing him with this confession.

"No, you don't."

The air in the room felt thick with her fear.

"You're Georgina Phillips, aren't you?"

She nodded, instinctively brushing his forearm with her fingertips.

He jerked away even from that slight touch. "I read all about you today."

"I can imagine what you read. How you must feel. And…I'm so ashamed," she said. "I feel so undeserving. So dirty and awful. Dom did terrible things to me. And I let him because I thought things might get better. Only they got worse. And then… I—I didn't tell you. I let you make love to me. I should have told you. I know I should. But you wouldn't have wanted me. And I wanted you…so desperately. Before you…I never had a clue what love was."

She felt a hot tear slide down her cheek. His hand reached toward her as if to brush it away. Then he caught himself, and she ached because he didn't want to touch her.

"What about that damn hit list?"

"Oh, dear. You brought that up earlier, and I'm sorry about it making TV and embarrassing you. I saw it when we were at lunch in the cantina downtown. I was going to tell you, but I barely knew you then. Like I told you, it was a joke. A stupid joke. I really didn't even want to participate. It was Veronica Holiday's idea.''

"The writer?"

"She met somebody in the bar at her hotel earlier that day, a doctor, I think she said. He gave her the idea. He'd been sued, and he wanted to start a lawyer-killing club. It was the night of the deposition. I didn't even want to go out that night. I was still pretty upset.''

"But you did—go out."

"Because of Taz and Zoë."

"Zoë?"

"A client of mine. Veronica's editor."

"You put me on a hit list, got bikers to shoot darts at my crotch, and then you slept with me. You change tack fast."

"The dart game…" She moaned. "Taz thought of that."

"Your Taz who rode off with Chuck?"

"Yes."

"So—is it true what the papers say about you? That you tried to kill Dom Phillips, your husband…for his money?"

"You want me to say yes, don't you? You want to believe the worst, so you can hate me and go back to your blondes. So, all right, yes, I married him for his money. And I tried to kill him for it, too. You obviously know all about Georgina Phillips, her famous parents, her failed modeling career, her affair with Thomas, the American designer. When he got her pregnant, she went to the States to have her baby…. You think you know all about Georgina's jet-set life and the extravagant wild parties. About her lovers. Don't forget them. Marriage was too dull for famous, spoiled Georgina...."

"Stop it." His voice was low and savage.

"No. Isn't that what you read today? It's exactly like they say. Money. Because of the money, I left Dom for dead. Only he isn't dead, is he? Because he loves me, he didn't press charges. Because he loves me so much. And he's such a great person."

She stopped, suddenly at a loss for words. Another tear streamed down her cheek.

"That's enough," he whispered. "You're torturing yourself."

"No. I'm the luckiest woman in the world. I was married to the most brilliant man. He was knighted by the queen. I am Lady Phillips. I live in a castle. He took care of my mother when she was hurt and ill and I was too plump to model and had an illegitimate daughter to support. He did all that because he is so good. He married me, and I tried to kill him for his money."

She was repeating herself, her voice shrill and hysterical, but she couldn't stop. "Then I slept with you casually. You're just one of many lovers. You're nothing to me...nothing...." Her voice broke.

She was sobbing wildly when he grabbed her and kissed her. He tasted like Glenlivet and Campbell, and he sparked an all-too-familiar need that seemed to intensify with every hurried kiss.

"Don't leave me," she pleaded, grabbing hold of him, rumpling his bright pink shirt. "Don't ever ever leave me."

"Who said anything about leaving? You're a drug and I'm an addict."

He was pulling her robe aside, and she was unbuttoning his shirt as fast as she could. He was tough, made of nothing but sleek, dark muscle. How was that possible when he worked at the computer all day? Her perverse mind was doing it again—thinking, asking stupid questions, when all her body wanted to do was surrender.

He lifted her in his arms and carried her to the wall. Once there he propped her up, knelt and began to lick between her legs until she could almost feel the heat pouring out of her, so great was her desire.

"Oh, Campbell…" Her hands were in his hair, her nails digging into his scalp.

When she was hot and ready and weak at the knees, he stood up, unzipped his jeans and drove into her with an urgency that made her buck and writhe and cover her mouth with her palm, which she bit until she tasted coppery blood, so she wouldn't scream.

His shuddering release detonated the same explosion in her. They held each other for a long moment.

"That was good," he whispered when his shudders subsided. "Too good. Better than last night."

"You don't sound happy about it."

"Go back to sleep."

"Stay with me."

He led her to the bed, but the phone rang downstairs and he used it as an excuse to leave her.

She pulled the sheets around herself and stared at the bars of moonlight that splashed dazzling silver against the far wall.

The impossible had happened. She was still married to Dom and in love with Campbell. Which meant she had to leave him before Dom found them together and killed him.

Eighteen

When the phone rang, the last person Campbell wanted to talk to when he was still warm and damp with sweat after making love to Georgina was Bob Africa.

"It's two o'clock in the morning, Bob. Go to bed."

"Can't. Working late." Africa hesitated, and Campbell imagined his wolverine smile. "Hey, Daniel isn't too happy."

Daniel Gannon was the managing partner

"Daniel can go to hell."

"Man, that attitude of yours."

"So fire me. Is that what this is about?"

"Not yet. A little leave of absence may be called for until this blows over."

"Fine."

"How's the kid?" Africa asked.

"James? If you're so damned concerned, call the hospital and ask about him yourself. Ask for Dr. Crocker. After all, it was your bright idea to take that case."

"Hey—I'm your only friend, buddy."

"Too bad for me. And for you, too. You fire me, and I'll sue you till hell freezes over for damaging my career."

Africa began to splutter. "You don't have a case."

"Save it for the jury."

At the soft sound of a woman's footsteps on his staircase, Campbell hung up.

He turned and saw her. Georgina was gorgeous in her white fluffy bathrobe. "Go back to bed," he said.

"I need some air."

"Me, too."

When she opened the patio door, he got a strange, paranoid kick in his gut. Anybody could be watching them. When she strolled out to the pool, he followed her, glancing around in all directions like he used to do in the old neighborhood after dark, not finding anybody, but not feeling any easier, either. The vegetation around the house was too dense and tall. He wrinkled his nose like a big cat smelling the air. Something felt wrong. He couldn't shake the feeling that some alien presence was near.

Campbell glanced up at the high-rise apartment building to the south. The Crockers lived up there. During the lawsuit, he'd never risked going out in his backyard or swimming in his pool. Good thing he hadn't known Crocker was a hunter. He remembered their run-in at the hospital.

"Who in the world called you at this hour?" she asked.

"Bob Africa."

"So, now you're in even more trouble—because of me?"

She moved toward him in the dark and he could no more resist her than a fly could resist honey.

"Georgina... Georgina..." Softly he touched his

mouth to her nose, but when she tried to snuggle into his arms, he pulled away.

"Why not?" she murmured shakily. "Is it because I'm married...or because you believe I'm this would-be murderess who wanted you dead...."

"Shut up." He put a gentle finger against her lips and watched Georgina's face in the moonlight for a long moment.

"Listen to me. I don't care who you are or what you did. Whatever you've done or haven't done, I've done worse. Do you understand?"

"Worse?"

"I'm no saint. I brought Rod's company down."

"Surely he had something to do with it, too."

"Not according to the newspapers and the investigators."

"Okay. I'm glad you're not perfect."

"His wife Sheryl committed suicide."

"Oh, Campbell, surely you can't blame yourself for that."

"Everybody else did. I slept with her only because we both felt so vulnerable since Rod was sleeping with Carol. I shouldn't have done it. Her husband had left her. I could have been a better friend."

"Oh, Campbell."

"I never told you about my mother, either. She killed herself, too. Suicides get to me. I always think there's something I could have done different. I was fifteen the morning I found my mother."

"Why did she do it?"

"I don't know. Sometimes my father hit her. She seemed so strong. She was always telling me she was okay with the way he was, that her father had had a bad temper, too. And then one morning she took a handful of pills. I didn't find her until it was too late. She's the last person you'd ever think would have done something like that. My father blamed me. Said they'd quarreled because I was wild.''

''Twisted logic.''

''I was raised on twisted logic.''

''Oh, so was I,'' she said.

''I guess if you're determined to talk...we might as well really talk.''

''So, let's go up to bed,'' she said, taking his hand.

Opening the patio door, he carefully locked it and set the alarm once they were inside.

When they reached her guest room and got into bed together, he pulled the covers over her and then leaned back against the headboard and wrapped his arms around her slim shoulders.

In his deep voice, he told her about growing up with his parents' constant quarrels. His father had been an attorney, but he hadn't worked because he'd hated being an attorney and hadn't been any good at it. So, he'd drunk too much, and his mother had earned money any way she could—baby-sitting, cooking, cleaning.

''My mother did everything. She told me I had to get an education and do something with it, make something of myself. She was smart. But there wasn't ever enough money.''

''Is that what they fought over?''

''They fought about everything. Once she started yapping at him, she didn't stop even when he told her to. Then he'd get sullen. Sometimes, he'd bash her. She'd squall.''

"I don't blame her.''

"But why'd she stand there arguing, pushing him, knowing how it always ended?''

"Why does anybody do anything?''

"Once he hit her, she'd usually run out into the street screaming for the neighbors. She liked an audience. There were always these big embarrassing scenes. Sometimes the cops got called. To this day, I hate the sound of sirens.'' He paused. "I remember her lying on her bed, barely breathing, while the sirens grew louder and louder.''

She touched his face. She knew too well what shame felt like. "My parents were just as wild and reckless.''

"When I got older, my father drank more. I was always the one who had to go down to the jail and get him out. She'd told me not to be a lawyer, that the work wasn't fulfilling.''

"And now she's dead and you feel guilty because you didn't save her,'' she said softly. "I'm not sure you can save people from themselves.''

"All I know is I don't want to be like him.''

"You're not.''

"I look like him.''

"You're you.''

"People thread themselves through the entire fabric of your being and you can't get rid of them. Parents. Spouses. Relationships always cost more than you bargain for. My dad pickled his brain on booze. He's in a nursing home here. I check on him every couple of weeks or so. Not that he wants me to. I wonder if that's me in thirty or forty years."

She grew silent. "Relationships are scary."

"That's why you've got to be careful who you pick to fall in love with."

"And did you pick?" she asked.

"I'm not sure. Maybe it's more a matter of going with your instincts."

"I can't trust mine," she said.

"Maybe it's our turn to roll a winner."

"I wish," she whispered, snuggling closer to him beneath the covers. He felt so warm and solid.

"Why me, then? Why do you want me?"

"You were the last man on earth I'd willingly choose...but with my instincts...maybe that's a good sign."

"More twisted logic."

"I'm a woman. I'm entitled."

He laughed.

"When I first came here, I just wanted to end it with Dom and find a way to go home. And be safe."

"So tell me about the first guy, the one who got you pregnant."

"Thomas? I was young and naive. He was a handsome clothes designer from New York. First I fell in love with his clothes, which were bright and wild. Then I fell in love with love and sex. I was modeling then, but beginning to have trouble getting assignments. I had my own money and not enough common sense to see how my career was heading. I wasn't careful with Thomas, either, so I got pregnant. He split because I wanted the baby. My parents agreed with Thomas. They said I was nineteen, and for God's sake, not to have the baby. So, I called my grandmother in Texas.''

"The one in San Antonio?"

"She *is* wonderful, a Realtor, too. I lived with her, got my Realtor's license, had the baby. Then Mother was in a wreck outside London and she suffered a mental breakdown. I went home to take care of her. I was young, not up to all the responsibility. She'd do crazy things—like run through the airport naked just because she wanted attention. That's how I met Dom, actually.''

"What happened?"

"She met my plane when I came home from San Antonio with the baby and stripped off all her clothes to get attention. Suddenly Dom was there. He wrapped her in his overcoat, used his title to talk the police out of doing anything, and whisked us away in his stretch limousine. Dom was so good with Mother. He was famous, and because he was, he reminded Mother of the old days with Daddy and made everything seem wonderful to her again, just like a fairy tale. Only it didn't last. Grandmother said it wouldn't, that he was too intense, not right somehow.''

"Funny, how life plays little tricks," Campbell said.

"Right from the first, he never wanted me to have anyone around except him. She was the only who suspected there was something seriously wrong with him.''

"Well, no wonder," Campbell said.

"What?"

"No wonder you were so spooked of men, of me."

"Once, right after we got married things got too wild, so during a party, I went upstairs to bed. Dom didn't follow me, and the next morning I found him on the floor of the ballroom naked with two of my friends who were only partially clothed."

"Did you confront them?"

"They were asleep, so I ran away, but I felt trapped and terrified Georgia might come down some morning and discover something like that. The house and grounds were always trashed mornings after Dom's parties. Then he made me do things in bed I didn't want to do. Even when I became frigid and couldn't stand sex, he forced me. But he was always so careful about his public image. If he'd been that man, we would have had no problems. I don't want to ever live like that again."

"You won't have to. I swear."

"Oh, Campbell, I'm so afraid that by being here, I'm putting you in danger."

"I'm not letting you out of my sight until this is over."

"But, if I just left tomorrow, maybe it would all stop. He wants me. Just me."

"Hush. You ran away because you can't stand to live like that."

"But look what happened. Guy James—" she said.

"If we keep this up, we'll talk all night. We'd better get some sleep. Tomorrow we're calling the cops. They're going to want to talk to you. You're telling them everything. We'll figure this out."

"Oh, dear. Police?" she said.

"I'll be here, and so will Chuck."

"But police?"

"Do you trust me, Georgina?"

She nodded. She moved closer, so close her head shared his pillow.

"Don't look at me like that. You're too adorable. Are you seducing me, you minx?"

"No, I'm too sleepy." She yawned, and then suddenly, she wasn't sure she was *that* sleepy. She wasn't sure at all.

"You can get inside me if you want to," she said in the low voice that turned him on.

She didn't have to ask twice. His mouth closed over hers, and he eased himself on top of her. "I can't believe I'm thinking about sex again after this hellish day."

Within seconds, they were both naked, he was deep inside her, and the magic took over. At first she was gentle and sweet. Then he was riding her, and a dark power built in them both. He felt big enough to burst and she was wild and abandoned, moaning his name, clawing the sheets.

He ground his teeth together when he exploded, and she cried out. For the rest of the night he held her close, their bodies fused together. He dreaded the morning when the cops would show up along with the media.

But morning came as it always does, and just like he'd thought, all hell broke loose.

Nineteen

"I felt so dirty afterward. I—I still hate myself. I—
I have nightmares...." Veronica's voice trailed away.

Veronica was sitting on a beige couch with huge
cushions. Not that she felt comfortable. No, she was
tense, afraid. She always felt like something might
burst apart inside of her when she was here, and Janice was staring at her with her wide brown eyes that
seemed to bore into her.

"I—I don't know why I told you about him."

"Think about it."

The walls of her therapist's office in south Austin
were pink. The color was probably supposed to be
soothing. Glass doors opened onto a green garden
where several cat bowls were lined up. The garden
was probably supposed to be soothing, too.

Janice, her therapist, had had four divorces and had
a kid on drugs, but she'd never met a cat she didn't
like.

"Cats never disappoint you," she'd explained one
day. "They are totally honest. Maybe that's why the
strays in the neighborhood land in my tiny walled
garden."

"I love your thick, soft ferns."

Janice smiled. "Every so often when the mood

strikes me, or another tenant complains about the cats, I get the janitor of the building to help me catch them. I load them into my station wagon and take them into my vet. I get them sterilized and vaccinated, then I bring them back. It's not an easy task. Most of them are half-wild.''

Janice had a soft, easy, lived-in face. Her fine, pale skin was lined, but the lines were soft, and her smile was kind. The smile was probably meant to soothe, too.

"I ran, Janice. I didn't know what else to do. Cops called. But I didn't answer my phone.''

She didn't tell Janice about the kid who'd been shot, maybe because of her.

"But you finished your book?''

"I used it to finish my book. I always finish my books.''

"When are you ever going to live your real life with the same dedication you put into your novels?''

"That's why I'm here, Janice. You're supposed to teach me how to do that.''

"I can't do it in a weekly hourly session.''

"I can come more often.''

"Why did you seduce that man in the hotel when you said his eyes look so dead, and he scared you nearly to death? When you made a vow to me and to yourself—no men until you did some serious work on yourself?''

Janice fell silent.

"I—I...''

Suddenly Veronica didn't trust herself to speak. She looked away into the wise jade-green eyes of a calico cat that was as round as a butterball. The creature was staring imperiously at her through the glass door, as if he owned the place. The cat expected something, probably to be let in. Not that she really saw the self-assured, bossy cat.

No, she saw a scared little girl hiding under her bed in the dark. Her heart began to pound when the door to the hall opened, spreading a triangle of golden light across the gray floor. She almost wept with fright when the man walked across the room, knelt and carefully lifted the bedspread. Even before he knelt and spoke to her, she knew who he was, and the knowledge made her heart knock louder.

"Come to Daddy, sweetheart…"

The little girl stuck her thumb in her mouth and inched as far back against the wall as she could get.

"Damn it." His big hand snaked under the bed and caught her ankle, dragging her out of her hiding place.

Tears were streaming down Veronica's cheeks when she realized where she was again. "Aren't we done yet, Janice?"

"We still have five minutes." Janice's voice went lower. "Why are you crying?"

"You're not my friend," Veronica said. "We can't run one minute over…ever."

"I'm not supposed to be your friend. I asked you why you're crying."

Veronica was brushing wildly at her eyes. "I'm not. And you don't care about me."

"We have a professional relationship."

"Not anymore. You can't tell me what to do. Nobody can.'' She got up recklessly. ''I'm Veronica Holiday.''

''Veronica, I can check my calendar and see if I can extend your session today.''

''You're fired, Janice. I don't need you to do me any special favors. Not if you're not my friend!''

''But—''

Driving home down Lamar, Veronica felt so defiant, she stopped at the first bar she saw.

She needed a man. She needed to forget. More tears fell. Nobody could tell her what to do. Not Janice. Not the cops. Nobody. She was Veronica Holiday. The prettiest little girl in the whole world. She knew that because her daddy used to tell her so.

Every night. Right before he stuck his tongue in her mouth and pulled her panties down.

She'd run from him when she could. But when he'd caught her, she'd never fought.

Dom felt highly agitated when he walked into the hotel bar. Every day his field of vision seemed to be narrowing. He needed some coke or a beer, but when he sank down on a plush stool and ordered one from the bartender, the rotund man, Mac, seemed to recede from him, growing smaller and smaller. His shiny bald head came in and out of focus.

Vaguely Dom saw Mac's fat hand slap a foamy mug in front of him. He hated foam—it meant the pig had just slopped his beer into the mug. His legs felt stiff, as if they weren't his own. He turned his glass round and round, sloshing beer onto his napkin as he positioned it where he wanted it on the bar.

What was wrong with his brain? Something had snapped when he'd stood on the dock and watched Georgina go inside the lawyer's house. They'd been smiling at each other and holding hands. He'd watched a bedroom light go off upstairs and he had run away, imagining the worst.

Mac, the bartender, was saying something, something about sports, but Dom couldn't hear him. He was thinking about Georgina with that lawyer and wishing that hot writer, one of the hot ladies, was here. He was still thinking about her when a short redhead with brilliant eyes slid onto a stool beside him. Her black skirt was slit to the thigh and she had a red scarf around her throat, which she fingered nervously, while her eyes devoured him. He'd seen her before, drinking alone. She'd been here *that* night, he remembered.

She ordered a beer and then went over to the jukebox and pinged in a few quarters. When she came back to the bar, she moved her hips, showing him a bit of leg. Obviously, she worked out. She had the body of a gymnast.

"I played my favorite song so I'd have an excuse to ask you to dance, handsome."

American women were too fast. He preferred to take his time, to be in control. But she was the best-looking woman in the bar. And she was like a wild cat in heat. "What else do you need an excuse to do?" he asked, his soft voice suggestive.

"Have you got a room?"

"Do you?"

"No."

So, she was a local. "The penthouse suite. But I thought you wanted to dance."

She smiled. "I'm lonely."

"Same here."

"Then I'm all yours."

That didn't take long, he thought smugly as they headed for the elevator. Which was good. What he had in mind would take a while. Maybe all night.

"You married?" he asked.

"I was." Her smile was bitter. "You marry a professional, a man with money. You think you're something special. Or that at least he is."

"But—"

"Then you find out he's a wimp." Her eyes flashed. "And not sophisticated at all. He was tight, too, a real pain in the ass. Once he even cut up all my credit cards."

"Marriage," Dom muttered. "You think you know the person. You think you can trust them...."

She laughed. "My husband...he should have been a farmer, driving a tractor. He should have been a goddamn farmer."

When they were inside his room, she looped her red scarf around his throat and kissed him. "But I don't want to talk about that loser. I want to forget him."

The police swarmed about the kitchen. When Chuck slouched in the doorway, his face in the shadows, it occurred to Georgina the big, redheaded hulk was as scared of the police as she was. There were only two of them, but it felt like more, at least to Georgina.

They'd been out to her beach house yesterday. They were very curious about her. Suspicious of her, too.

While being interrogated, Georgina kept gulping in bites of air. She wore jeans and a short-sleeved navy top that had been in Campbell's closet, and her black hair was caught messily in a clip at her nape. She sat rigidly beside Campbell at the little round table and faced Lieutenant Dawson, who played bad cop while he drilled her relentlessly. Georgina fidgeted with her silver ring until Campbell folded her hand in his and brought it to his lips.

Dawson was a big man with a rawboned face and a thatch of sandy hair. Gregory Page, a slim, swarthy, boyish cop, leaned against the refrigerator, smiling affably at the group around the table while he munched powdery doughnuts. He was the good cop. But they were a team; they worked together, like wolves in a pack. She mustn't forget that.

Campbell had gone out early and bought freshly made doughnuts. Rebecca had made two huge pots of coffee and then vanished upstairs with several books Campbell had instructed her to read to the children, who weren't going to school today because of all the excitement.

"Aren't doughnuts and cops a cliché?" Georgina had asked Campbell when he'd returned with three boxes of doughnuts.

"I guess I wasn't thinking creatively."

"Well, don't let Georgia near them. I'm trying to

keep her away from junk food and all that processed stuff."

"In America?" He opened a box. "She'll starve."

She eyed the doughnuts. "I—I got so fat once."

Campbell gazed at her. "Well, you're not fat now. You're breathtaking."

As soon as Dawson had arrived, he'd attacked, sneering at Campbell when he saw the doughnuts. "You're too much, Counselor."

"Just trying to be friendly."

Dawson was all bluff when it came to doughnuts. Five minutes into the interview, he'd already gobbled down two.

"Did you try to kill your husband in London, Lady Phillips?"

"No." All she could manage was a breathy whisper.

"And you think he's here and he shot up your beach house?"

"I don't know. He used to follow me."

"Why'd you leave him, a rich fancy lord like that?"

"He hit me. He threatened me. The violence and the other abuse were escalating. Then he threatened Georgia after I asked him for a divorce. I called my grandmother in San Antonio. She wired me some money and found me a job here."

Dawson jotted down her grandmother's name and address. Then he asked all the same questions and made her go through it again as though he thought she was lying.

"Do you know where my husband is?" Georgina asked.

"We're asking the questions, ma'am. Did you try to kill him?"

"Don't be ridiculous, Dawson," Campbell interrupted. "She told you she didn't." He squeezed her hand. "Georgina, you don't have to answer that again without a lawyer."

"But I want to answer it," Georgina cried. "He had his hands around my throat. I'd just told him I wanted a divorce. I—I grabbed the paperweight because I couldn't breathe, and it was there on the table. I never tried to kill him. I don't want him dead now. I just want a divorce and to be able to live in peace with my daughter."

"*His* daughter, too?"

"No."

"Were you married before?"

She'd already answered that once. "Look, I know what you've read in the newspapers, but Dom has PR experts who plant the stories they want in the press…about me…about him. They make him seem like he's this perfect person.…"

"But you know better.…"

"Don't answer that one, either," Campbell ordered.

"He's not like the papers say he is," Georgina said. "And neither am I."

"He hurt you and you wanted to punish him." Dawson's face was inches from hers. "Does that about sum it up?"

"No, the hell it doesn't." Campbell slammed the

doughnut box shut. "No more questions. Chuck was there last night. Talk to Chuck."

Dawson eyed Chuck's broad shoulders and grizzled red ponytail. "A very reliable source, I'm sure."

"Why the hell aren't you out rounding up the guy who shot Guy James?" Campbell demanded.

"Because other than those death threats you gave us, a vague description of the shooter, and your pal here, Georgina, we've got zip. The only fingerprints on those letters were yours and your staff's." Dawson sipped coffee from his mug and frowned at her.

"So, you think your husband broke into your house and trashed it when you weren't home?" he repeated. "Then he came back when you were there with a hammer—"

"That's right," Chuck said. "He had a gun, too. She was downstairs with me when the bastard started shooting the place up." Chuck strode across the kitchen and stuck a beefy paw into the doughnut box. "These look good, but we're running low—"

"Did you see him?" Page demanded.

Chuck shook his head as he pulled out a doughnut. "Maybe the landlady did. Mrs. T...."

"No, we asked her."

"One more question for the lady," Dawson said. He was scribbling on a notepad. "Where were you at 5:00 p.m. yesterday afternoon when Guy James was shot?"

"Driving to the island with my daughter."

"Okay, guys." Campbell shut the boxes of doughnuts and threw them in the trash. "She told you that twice already."

"Hey," Chuck said. "There were two more—"

"Ever heard the word *moderation?*"

"No—and I damn sure don't want to." Chuck dug the last box of doughnuts out of the can.

Even after the police left, their presence lingered.

"They think I shot James," Georgina whispered to Campbell, twisting her ring.

Campbell gathered her close. "They're fishing. In the wrong fishing hole. But at least they're fishing. Maybe they'll catch something."

When the cowboy pulled out and came all over her naked belly, Veronica shot bolt upright in her bed. Placing her palms against his wide shoulders and pushing him away, she felt like she was flying to pieces again. She jammed a thick pillow under her head and tried to hold on to her sanity as she pushed him off her.

"Was I good?" the cowboy whispered, licking her throat with his talented tongue as eagerly as a puppy might.

"Great," she said in a raspy tone, yawning. "You can go now."

"You don't want to do it again?" he queried hopefully. "Maybe a quickie."

Not in a million. "I'm tired."

"Wore you out, did I?"

Why did men always seek praise? Why couldn't he just shut up and scram? "You sure did."

Thank goodness, he didn't argue about leaving. He had a pleasant, accessible, babyish face, which was why she'd hit on him instead of a rougher type. She hadn't forgotten the sicko in Corpus, and wasn't ready for a repeat of his brand of rough, sick sex. She felt guilty about not talking to the cops. Had that sicko gotten the list and shot the kid? Should she be doing more to help?

The cowboy was a pleasant, obedient sort, but not the sharpest knife on the cutting board. Not by a long shot. Not somebody you wanted to have a conversation with afterward or wake up and have a chat over breakfast with.

He got out of bed, snapped on his jeans and pulled on his shirt. He had a great tush, lean hips.

"Don't forget your hat," she whispered when he headed toward the door.

"It would've been my excuse to come back."

"I know. Goodbye."

He slammed the door behind him.

When she heard his truck start and his tires squeal, she turned off the light and tried to sleep. She only felt edgier in the dark, worse than ever after the beers and the sex. She hadn't come. She hadn't been able to reach orgasm since that night in Corpus. She kept thinking about the kid who'd been shot and that sicko. She should do something.

She lay in bed for a while, hating herself. Ever since Corpus, she'd been a mess, unable to sleep, unable to enjoy sex. He'd scared her badly, so badly she'd left town the minute her interview was done, so badly she hadn't even bothered to go to her book signing or to call Zoë and thank her.

Slowly Veronica dragged herself out of bed. First she went to her bathroom and showered, then she turned on her computer. When she began to write, her heroine in her new book was a mess, a sexual mess, just like she was.

Poor Judy went from man to man. And like herself, Judy, who was in her thirties, wasn't getting any younger. Each stranger she slept with made her feel a little more desperate. But she couldn't stop.

Why couldn't she stop?

Janice, her therapist, had told her not to date. She should call Janice.

You fired know-it-all Janice.

Veronica grabbed a notepad and a pen. When she was really inspired, she always wrote longhand.

After a few pages, the writing gave her some measure of control, and the pain in her head and the tightness in her chest diminished.

Her heroine still believed her life would eventually work out. Poor kid. Poor dopey kid.

Not like me—I learned a long time ago—life never works out.

Then why did she write happy, sappy books, or at least books with happy endings?

She was rich and famous. Hell, she was Veronica Holiday. She was a real somebody.

This is as good as it gets.

She had a mansion on Travis Lake. Her neighbors were dot com zillionaires, or at least millionaire wanna-bes. Life was good. Everybody wanted to be her. That's what she told herself, anyway, when she felt like blowing out her brains. Like tonight.

Who was Veronica Holiday? Writer extraordinaire? Or a pathetic little loser when it came to men?

All of a sudden she was remembering her parents' marriage, the long silences in the morning over breakfast. Veronica had never known what to say when they stared at her and then stared at each other as if she was to blame for whatever was wrong.

She'd kept her head lowered over her cereal bowl, but she'd felt her parents seething as they watched her until finally her father would say, "I've got to go."

Then he'd get up. He never used to kiss her mother goodbye. Only her.

He'd say, "Come to Daddy." Then he'd kiss her cheek, and his lips always smacked wet and sloppy in her ear and so loudly her ear rang for a long while after he was gone.

His morning kiss was never like the night ones when he came to her room and stuck his tongue into her mouth so deeply he sometimes gagged her. But it was the other things he'd done that had made Mommy hate him, that had made Veronica feel so guilty about her parents' thick silences, that had made her feel she was to blame for everything in their lives that had been sick and wrong.

Veronica stopped writing. Sucking on the tip of her pen until she tasted ink, she held her breath. She hadn't spoken to her mother in a while. She should call her.

Suddenly she wanted to call Janice. She had to call Janice.

But when she did, she got Janice's answering service. A lady took her number and promised her Janice would call back.

But Janice wouldn't. Veronica had called before.
Someone always called back and reminded her that
she wasn't Janice's patient anymore since she'd fired
her.

"Can't I tell her I'm sorry?"

"You fired her. You're not her patient anymore."

Feeling all alone and not knowing what to do with
herself, Veronica turned on the television. The news
was all about Guy Jones and Joe Campbell and Hannah Smith. Only, Hannah wasn't Hannah. She was
Lady Georgina Phillips.

I should call *her,* Veronica thought. I'll call *her*—
not the cops.

Twenty

Twenty-four hours after James had been shot and Georgina's beach house had been trashed, Campbell sat on the floor of his den holding the phone against his ear. Georgina, who was stretched out beside him, watched him.

He was deep in conversation with a police-woman—who fed him inside information from time to time whenever he needed it…for a price.

Campbell wore a red shirt and black slacks. Georgina had on white shorts and a white tank T-shirt. She looked good, so good he was distracted even as he spoke softly into the mouthpiece.

She was eating popcorn. He was drinking lime water, and she was drinking beer before dinner. Dinner, which was a pot roast he'd put in the oven, smelled great, too. He'd put in lots of spices, especially garlic. He'd even let Georgina talk him into a few carrots.

Rebecca's mother was sick, so he'd given Rebecca the day off. The kids were swimming in the pool with Taz and Chuck.

"Dawson is trying to tie Georgina Phillips to the shooter," the female cop said.

"That's absurd," Campbell said, his grip tightening on the receiver.

"So far he doesn't have anything. His men tore her place apart and came up with nothing that incriminates her."

"Thanks." Campbell hung up the phone and pulled Georgina into his arms.

"So?" she whispered.

"So—nothing." He took her hand in his, spread her fingers out so that he could lock them through his. His fingers were longer, browner, but he loved the way her hand fit so perfectly inside his.

"I want this to be over," she said.

"So you can go home? Back to England?"

She frowned. "So maybe my life can get back to normal. Yours, too."

"What's normal? I don't think I know anymore."

"You can go back to suing people, to making money.... Maybe you could move back to Houston and marry one of your pneumatic blondes."

None of those ideas excited him much. "What if I decided I wanted something different?"

"Then go for it," she said, her blue eyes burning him.

He smiled down at her, gazing at her lips. "Maybe I will." He drew her closer, so he could taste her mouth.

And as always, one taste wasn't nearly enough.

The patio door slammed open, and Georgia screamed, "Mummy, Joey won't share the kickboard...."

"Then stay inside with me."

"No! Come out and make him give me the—"

"I can do this," Campbell said.

He got up to follow Georgia back outside. "You all will either share, or nobody will play with the kickboard."

"I'll go check on dinner," Georgina offered, winking at him.

Campbell's quick grin stretched from ear to ear. She was so damned beautiful. He couldn't wait until the kids were in bed and they were alone.

Maybe they had a maniac after them, but it was funny how normal his life felt, normal and right. He had two fighting children on his hands, kids who made him impatient as hell at times, but he had a pretty woman who was great in bed, who said she'd check on dinner. The kids were great most of the time, and Georgina. God, how he loved just lying in bed holding her.

"Since everybody knows you're Georgina Phillips and you're here, when are you going to go back to being a blonde?"

"You going to suggest implants, too?"

"Never. You're perfect the way you are."

"Really."

"I like *you*."

Georgia ran toward the patio door.

"Don't run with wet feet," he said, in voice that didn't brook disobedience.

She slowed, but only just a bit, as if to test him. He felt his temper rise, but when he reached the pool and saw Joey's eyes widen, probably because of his grim expression, Campbell was careful to speak softly.

"Kids, you've got to take turns. Joey, let Georgia

have a turn. Five minutes. I'll set my timer. Then you can have your turn.'' Campbell fiddled with his watch.

Georgia hopped into the pool and grabbed the kick-board. Then she splashed back and forth in front of Joey, kicking water at him.

Five minutes later, Campbell told her it was Joey's turn. Then Joey splashed back and forth in the aqua pool. Occasionally Patches made a mad dash out onto the sunny lawn to chase a butterfly before slipping quietly back into the shade of a flower bed.

And so it went until Campbell went into the pool house and changed into black bathing trunks. When he came out and jumped into the water, he suggested that the kids race each other for a prize.

''I'll pay the winner a dollar—''

''A whole dollar!'' Joey cried.

After the kids raced each other, Campbell raced Joey and let him win. Joey beamed.

The Charger laughed when Campbell climbed out of the pool, grabbed a towel and took a sip of lime water.

''Man, has Georgina got you pussy-whipped.''

''What?''

''Hey, it's a compliment. I like the new you.''

''Just shut up—okay? I like you better stoned.''

''Well, I don't,'' Taz said.

''Look who's calling who pussy-whipped,'' Campbell said.

''Maybe, but you don't see me getting all grumpy about it.'' The Charger winked at Taz.

''What can I say? I'm just a grumpy guy.''

* * *

Georgina was in the kitchen with Taz. The guys were still out at the pool monitoring the kids.

"I'm taking Chuck to meet Sister next week," Taz said.

"Sister?"

"That's what we all call my grandmother."

"Have you slept with him?"

Taz's grin was bright. "Sister isn't going to like it much that he's white."

"If that's all…"

"So, how are you and Georgia doing with—"

"It's kind of scary."

"I mean, is Campbell good to you?" Taz asked.

"He's great. I mean it's scary when you feel a lot for someone, but you can't believe the good stuff can last."

"Just take it a day at a time."

"But is that any way to live?"

"Baby, that's the only way to live."

"Taz, it's just that I'm so scared. I want to break the cycle of violence in my life. I don't want to hurt Georgia any more than I have. I never told you about my life before, but I made mistakes—"

"Girl, you didn't have to. I could see it in your eyes."

"You, too?"

"My daddy. I ran away from home when I was sixteen. No other man has ever hit me or touched me. You can stop it," Taz told her.

"How can I be certain, I mean with Campbell? He's got that edge. He drinks sometimes."

"Tell him if he is ever violent with you, you'll leave him. If you mean it, he'll believe you," Taz said.

"It's not that simple."

"Yeah, it is," Taz insisted.

"You make it sound so easy." Georgina chewed her lip.

"Campbell—easy? Please. The easy part is deciding to draw that line in the sand. If he steps over it once—it's over."

"You know what he did?"

Taz didn't say anything, so Georgina continued. "He hired men to go to the home where my mother lives to watch over her just in case Dom goes really crazy."

"He loves you," Taz said. "He's trying to take care of you."

"I don't know.... I'm so confused."

"Then just play it by ear. Every day, you get a new chance to start over. Take it."

When the phone rang during dinner, Georgina answered it. "It's a Dr. Crocker," she said. "For you."

Campbell bolted up from the table.

"I've found a surgeon. He's in Houston, though."

"Thanks."

"I didn't do it for you. I did it for James and for myself. I got so far off the track because of that lawsuit, I almost forgot that I was a doctor first. Whether it was right or wrong, I have to let go of what you did to me. I have to realize I can't fix the system alone...and I can't take the law into my own hands."

"What about your marriage?"

"That's over—thanks to you."

"I never came on to her."

"I disagree. I saw the way you looked at her. She saw me as a wimp after the way you hammered me in court. My hands were tied. You could say any damn thing you wanted to...."

And he had, Campbell thought. He'd been so damn angry about Houston and Carol and Rod, he'd blasted everybody he'd had the least excuse to blast. And even the jury had thought he'd gone too far. "I'm sorry, Doctor. I really am."

"So the hell am I. Personally, you and your kind can go to hell. You can go straight to hell—but the kid...James... I'm a doctor, not some vigilante. I'm sorry about the kid. I—I blame myself. Maybe if I hadn't dreamed up the idea of a club that kills.... Maybe if I hadn't ranted about it for months to anybody who would listen... Maybe if that writer hadn't stolen my idea and used it to promote herself, some nutcase wouldn't have fired that gun at James. I'll have to live with that."

"I've got a lot to live with, too."

In a gruff voice, Dr. Crocker told him where and when in Houston the surgery would be before hanging up on him abruptly.

They were in the hospital waiting room, just the three of them: Campbell, Guy's mother and Georgina. Campbell was pacing inside the pale green walls, and the pacing was driving Georgina so crazy, she felt almost claustrophobic. Still, she couldn't take her eyes off him, even though she sat beside a rigid Mrs. James.

Campbell wore a bright orange shirt and navy slacks. Even in the loud color, he was handsome. She loved the way that lock of ebony hair fell over his dark brow, the way he pushed it back impatiently, only for it to fall again. She loved everything about him—his intensity, his energy, his fierce determination to protect her during this difficult period, his dedication and concern for Guy James and his mother and little brother. He'd even gone so far as to charter a plane and had flown them here. He'd been generous to a fault. Not that he would admit it, or accept any thanks.

"We had to fly. The firm plane was in Lubbock. I love my car, but I can't hack driving the Porsche more than a couple of hundred miles and that's with no luggage and no passengers. Your car is too old— I was being selfish to charter the plane, not generous."

"It was nice of you."

While he continued to pace, Georgina shut her eyes and prayed. She prayed for Guy James and for the surgeon, but most of all she prayed for Campbell. If James didn't get a good result, she wasn't sure how Campbell would handle it. He blamed himself, and it wasn't his fault. She'd had something to do with it, too. So had Veronica and the doctor.

Every night lately, he'd told her he had a lot to answer for. She would ask him what he was talking about, and he would say, "Just a whole lifetime of mistakes."

"You can start over," she told him, wishing she believed it herself.

But could he? Could anybody? Was every day a new start on life as Taz said?

It seemed like hours passed before the surgeon came into the colorless little room to talk to Mrs. James about the fate of her son.

"How's my boy?" Mrs. James whispered, her face draining of blood as she groped for Georgina's hand.

"I'm guardedly optimistic," the doctor said. "The operation went so well, we might get full recovery."

"You mean he might be all right? My boy might—"

"Will he ever walk again?" Campbell asked.

"He says he will."

"He's awake?" his mother demanded.

"Yes, and he's a very determined young man."

"Can I see him?"

"He's asking for you. And for you, too, Mr. Campbell."

They rushed past the doctor.

The pink walls seemed tighter than Veronica remembered. The lines in Janice's face seemed deeper, and her smile seemed a little more strained.

"I can't believe you took me back," Veronica whispered uneasily. *I can't believe I want to be back.* But she did desperately. "Thank you."

"As long as you remember my condition."

"I know—no men for a while."

"Men trigger an automatic self-destructive response."

"Why?"

"We're going to have to work very hard to answer that question."

Veronica felt the need to say something, but all she could do was open her mouth several times, take a deep breath, lick her lips and stare wildly around the room. She wanted out of here. More than anything in the world, she wanted to escape.

But the cat, that damned, obese calico cat was at the patio door staring at her with those intelligent green eyes. That know-it-all cat was blocking the door.

"That cat," she said, but was unable to go on because it seemed crazy to blame a cat.

Suddenly Veronica was a little girl again, crying when she woke up in the dark. Her father wasn't in her bed, so she got up. Then she was running down the hall to her mother's room.

Her mother and her father had separate bedrooms, of course. She'd beat on her mother's door, and her mother hadn't let her in. But her daddy had opened his.

Another scene flashed in her mind. She and her mother were at breakfast the next morning after Daddy had gone to work. There was gas leak and the kitchen reeked of gas and burned cheese. To this day Veronica hated the smell of gas and burned cheese.

"Are you in love with Daddy?"

Her mother had looked at her as if she was crazy. "Go to school, why don't you." Then her mother had gotten up, her knuckles white as she grabbed her plate. She'd turned her back on Veronica and had begun washing dishes so noisily, she broke one.

"Look—see what you made me do! Go to school! Don't stand here pestering me!"

Veronica had rushed to her mother and put her arms around her. Then they'd cried together. Afterward they'd packed suitcases and fled. But the memories hadn't been so easy to run from. Just like now. She couldn't forget the sicko or her part in getting that kid shot.

She had to call Georgina Phillips. She had to. Janice leaned forward. "What are you thinking about? Why are you crying?"

"No, I'm not. I'm not crying." But when Veronica dabbed at her cheeks, to her surprise they were wet.

"On my first date, I went all the way with a pimply-faced boy I didn't even like."

Where had that come from?

"I hardly knew him. I hated myself after it was over."

"Why did you do it?"

"I don't know. I just didn't know how to stop him when he started touching me. It just seemed like the thing to do."

"You did the right thing—coming here," Janice said softly. "People have hidden agendas in their subconscious that drive them to do things that seem incomprehensible, things they don't want to do."

"But I keep doing them. I run from my problems. I write to escape them. I never face them."

"You won't always run. I promise you. We're going to find out why, and we're going to break this cycle.''

For the first time, Veronica felt a thin ray of hope shining into the darkness of her locked heart.

When she got home, she *would* call Georgina.

Twenty-One

The River Road
New Braunfels, Texas

As if he were a man without a care in the world, Campbell lay asleep on a quilt underneath a huge, spreading pecan tree beside the Guadalupe River in the Texas Hill Country. It was a warm, drowsy, balmy kind of day, an afternoon made for napping lazily. The air smelled of cedar and the river.

Not that Georgina, who felt tense all the time, could nap. Not out in the open. Thus, she was busy catching up on her phone calls while she lay stretched out beside him. She was wearing a black bikini and using Campbell's hot-pink shirt as a cover-up. His shirt swallowed her, and the sleeves kept coming unrolled and falling over her hands. But she liked wearing it because it smelled of Campbell.

While she made her calls, she kept an eye on Taz and Chuck with the kids, who were swimming in a shallow part of the Guadalupe River. The water was green and cold, especially where it ran deeper beneath the towering cliffs on the opposite bank. She also watched every car on the road that wound on the opposite cliff on the far side of the park.

Guy James was doing better every day. Like any ordinary couple needing to celebrate, instead of a pair being stalked by a maniac, Campbell had suggested they drive to Canyon Lake and rent a condo with Chuck and Taz for the weekend at a hilltop resort above the lake. At first Georgina hadn't wanted to come, but the resort had a beautiful pool with stunning views of the lake. The children loved the pool so much, they hadn't wanted to come along to the River Road today.

"I hate driving," Georgia had said.

"Well, you'll have to handle it," Campbell had said firmly. "Today we're going to see some country."

Georgina liked the way Campbell was kind yet firm with the children. When they'd turned off the River Road at this private park with lush green grass and unpacked their quilts and towels and picnic hamper, the kids hadn't wanted to swim in the Guadalupe River, either.

Joey had stuck his toe in the dark green water and said, "Cold!"

"You get used to it," Campbell had countered.

"There might be snakes," Georgia had protested. "I like swimming pools."

"There might be," Campbell had agreed. "But you're a lot bigger than they are, and they'll swim away. Trust me. I've never seen a snake here."

"Do you come here a lot?" Georgia had wanted to know.

"Not much lately, but I love this river, and this place. I've loved it since I was a kid. I wanted to show it to your mother."

"Why?"

He'd turned to Georgina, his black gaze so rapt, it had thrilled her. "Because it's a special place to me."

So here they were, under a bright afternoon sun in central Texas, four hours north of Corpus, loafing on a quilt while their children swam with bikers, who went by the handles, Goliath and the White Ninja.

The kids had two kickboards now, thanks to Taz, who'd bought the second one because she couldn't stand all the bickering every time they swam in Campbell's pool at home. The river was crowded with people floating slowly down it on rubber rafts and in big black tubes.

For the most part the rafters weren't athletes. They were sunburned and overweight and wore T-shirts that read River Rats. Their thick legs sprawled untidily over the sides of their rafts, while they leaned back, smoking and drinking. Some had tattoos and looked tough. Behind their main raft they trailed more rafts that held ice chests or their dogs.

Georgina, who scanned every face, and scanned every arm for that distinctive blue dragon tattoo, couldn't really relax.

Dom had a bad habit of picking the worst possible moment to show up.

In an attempt to stop thinking about him, Georgina punched in Zoë's phone number. "I've got good news," she said when Zoë answered. "The seller has accepted your offer."

"Oh, that's great! Tony will be so thrilled. Not that he'll let me off the ranch until that maniac is caught."

"How are you feeling?"

"Perfect. I had a sonogram. We saw the baby. She's a little girl."

"Oh, that's wonderful."

"I must have watched the video seventeen times. More good news. Bob Africa called. He's dropped the case. Says there is no merit to it."

"He's smart," Georgina said.

"So, the Hot Ladies are turning out to be a pretty fearsome bunch."

"According to the media."

"Well, at least something good came out of all the furor over the Hot Ladies. But Veronica is really running scared. How's Guy James?" Zoë asked.

"Better." Georgina sighed. "He took his first step yesterday. It was shaky, but we're up in the Hill Country to celebrate. And Veronica? You said she's scared?"

Zoë hesitated a fraction too long.

"Is she okay or not?"

"As far as I know." Zoë said.

"But you haven't talked to her?"

Georgina wasn't through asking questions, but she got another call.

"I—I do hope she's okay. And you...you take care of yourself and the baby girl," Georgina said, trying to end the call even though she wanted to know more about Veronica. "I'll call you, or I'll have another agent call you when it's time to close."

"Another agent?"

"I may be moving back home."

"What about Campbell?"

"I've got another call—"

The other caller was Katherine Rosner. "Finally," Katherine said, sounding annoyed. "You never answer your phone these days."

"I—I thought another agent had been assigned—"

"Why don't you ever answer your home phone?"

"I moved in with a friend."

The silence felt heavy. "I know about the Hot Ladies." She paused again. "So, you're hiding out until the publicity blows over?"

"Something like that."

"I just can't make up my mind about that house on Ocean," Katherine said.

"You will. You have wonderful taste."

"I do things the way I want them. My parents finally learned that." Katherine's laughter was loud and too abrupt. "I just know if you came and we looked at the house together, I'd know for sure."

"Katherine, I would if I could."

"Please, I feel so abandoned."

"Feelings aren't always realities. Look, I've got to go."

Poor Katherine. Campbell had forbidden her to work because he was afraid Dom might get to her.

As she and Campbell dressed for dinner, she couldn't stop thinking about Katherine. Even during the drive into Gruene, she thought about her. Thus, while Campbell and the others toured the antique shops of the Gruene Historic District outside New Braunfels, she wondered how she could mention

Katherine to him. But Campbell was too busy telling
the children about Gruene, which was a quaint 1870s
cotton-gin town containing the oldest dance hall in
Texas.

Finally, when the children were shopping with Taz
and Chuck and she was standing in line beside Campbell as diners poured into his favorite restaurant, the
Gristmill, she found her chance.

"Katherine Rosner really thinks she needs me to
help her decide about this house on Ocean Drive."

Campbell, who looked like a hunky cowboy in a
peacock-blue cowboy shirt, jeans and black boots,
pushed his black Stetson back with a frown.

"Rosner?" he repeated, his frown deepening.
"She's the spoiled, rich doctor's wife?"

"Her husband left her."

"She still has that mentality. Rosner... That
name... Where have I heard it?" He paused. "No,
we're sticking to our plan. You and Georgia are to
keep out of sight...until Dom surfaces."

"What if he's running scared or on another conti-
nent? I can't imagine him finding Corpus amusing for
very long."

"And how about you, Lady Phillips? Are you
amused in Corpus Christi?"

"Very amused," she murmured, lifting his black
Stetson from his dark head and placing it on hers.
When the hat fell down over her forehead, he took it
off her and put it back on.

"We can't take the chance that your husband is
anywhere around," he said, readjusting his Stetson.
"So, stay away from Katherine Rosner."

"I never knew I had such a thing for cowboys."

He grinned. "So—that's a vote for the hat?"

She nodded.

"Even in bed?"

She laughed. "Maybe."

After dinner he took her to the historic dance hall next to the old mill where she drank beer and he drank a Diet Coke, and they listened to a country-western band. The place was authentic, nineteenth-century Texas. It had creaky wooden floors, fans and lots of open windows. The kids were fascinated with a little boy on stage, who was even younger than they were. The kid was pretending to play a guitar that the lead singer had strapped around the boy's shoulders.

Campbell smiled at Georgina. "That guitar is nearly as big as he is."

"He's cute."

"So are you. You want to dance?" Campbell's eyes gleamed; his voice lured her.

"Nobody else is dancing."

"Which means somebody needs to break the ice."

"All right. But the kids…"

"You two go ahead," Taz said. "We'll shoot some pool with them."

Campbell's hand came around Georgina's waist. When they reached the dance floor, she lifted her hands to his solid shoulders. Pulling her tight against his body, he began to sway with her to the whine of a country waltz. He knew all the right moves and was easy to follow, turning her, catching her, dipping her back and pulling her close against his body. At first she felt self-conscious, but soon other couples

streamed onto the dance floor. The next song was a
polka, and so fast she was soon breathless. She lost
herself in the music and Campbell, and she paid no
attention to the dancers swirling past them on the
crowded floor.

He was a great dancer, but that wasn't why she
was enjoying herself. She felt young and adored, as
if she were a carefree young girl having fun with the
man she loved.

With the man she loved. The thought registered,
slamming her into a new reality that caught her by
surprise.

The man she loved.

When the music ended, she clung to him. He
squeezed her waist, his eyes intense as he regarded
her. Then he tilted her chin and backed her into a
shadowy corner, where he kissed her mouth gently.
Not for long, though, because the children came running up, their eyes aglow, wanting to dance, too. So,
Campbell danced with Georgia, who wore his Stetson
even though the black brim fell over her nose, and
Georgina danced with Joey. Georgina was aware of
Campbell's eyes following her as she leaned over
Joey, who stepped all over her toes. Laughing, she
felt tingly and aglow and a little breathless, too, just
from the heat in Campbell's eyes.

That night when Campbell made love to her, Georgina gave herself entirely to him. He touched her everywhere with reverent hands and lips, murmuring
husky love words, making promises she wished he
could keep.

Her body reveled in his loving possession. When
he thrust that last time, carrying her to dizzying

heights of pleasure and soul-deep awareness of how special he was, she broke down and whispered, ''I love you. I love you.''

Not that he seemed to hear. He was shuddering, holding her tightly. Afterward, he lay in the dark, pressing her close. She lay beside him, stunned by the immensity of her emotional turmoil.

I love him.

The next morning she felt a little shy around him. Maybe he did, too. Neither of them said much as they filled the Porsche with gas and then left for Corpus. She and Campbell and the kids led the way in the Porsche. Taz and Chuck trailed behind them on their bikes. Luckily, the kids enjoyed each other without bickering and the only noise above the roar of the engine were electronic beeps and the children's voices from the back seat as they played some game Campbell had bought Joey.

The weekend had been a wonderful break, Georgina thought as she watched the land flatten as they headed south toward the coast. Nevertheless, she found herself glancing at Campbell's hard, dark profile, worrying about what the future held.

A week passed. A week in which Guy James learned to walk on a walker in the hospital hall. His doctor now predicted Guy would make a full recovery. Not that it would be fast.

Campbell drove Georgina out to the beach house with two men in a truck he'd borrowed from Bob Africa. Quickly, because the beach house made her tense, the four of them packed all her belongings that hadn't been shredded or broken into boxes and brought them back to his house. Mrs. T. came over and helped, but the woman was nerve-racking with her constant chatter about the police and their questions.

Mrs. T. couldn't quit staring at Georgina piercingly. "So, you're Lady Phillips. *That* model. I've been reading all about you in the newspapers." Matilda was racing about, yapping enthusiastically. "You're all over TV, too."

"Don't believe everything you read or see on TV, Mrs. T.," Campbell said curtly as he grabbed the last box. "I think that's it, Georgina. Mrs. T., I'm good for whatever it costs to repair this place."

"I'll pay you back," Georgina said hastily, following him down the stairs with the single white cup with blue gulls that hadn't been smashed.

Mrs. T. could have talked all day about how terrified she'd been when she'd heard gunshots. But Campbell helped Georgina into the truck, waved at the landlady breezily and drove away.

They were soon home. The men unloaded all the boxes and stacked them in Campbell's garage. As they watched the men, Georgina began to feel guilty.

"I know you hate stacks."

His eyes had crinkled at the corners. "That should give you incentive to unpack."

"I won't be staying…long."

"Right."

He'd said nothing more, and she hadn't been able to see his eyes in the dark garage. But he'd turned abruptly and climbed into the truck to get a box.

Another week went by. Nothing happened other than that Georgina felt more profoundly involved with Campbell than ever. Every glance and every touch and every conversation she shared with him made her long for a normal future. Since neither of them was working, the weeks spent sailing and swimming would have seemed like a honeymoon if they'd been married. But they weren't.

Then Bob Africa called. Georgina answered the phone and didn't hang up even after Campbell picked up.

"The firm wants you back," Africa said. When Campbell said nothing, Africa continued, "Your clients don't want other lawyers. They want you."

"How very refreshing."

So the next morning Campbell went to his office. Even when Georgina complained that evening that she was lonely without him and wanted to go back to work herself, he said she'd be too vulnerable out showing houses.

"Not until we figure out what your husband, who slashed your panties and trashed your beach house, intends."

"He wants to hurt me, to punish me. I know that." She sighed. Because of the happy weeks with Campbell, Dom suddenly seemed very far away and unreal. Her terror of him had lessened.

It was strange, but she could barely remember him now. Maybe because she didn't want to. She was enjoying Campbell and their life together too much. Rapidly, she was moving past all the bad stuff.

The next night when Georgina flew to greet him at the door, Campbell came inside grinning.

He swept her into his arms and kissed her. When he let her go, he was still smiling.

"You're usually tense when you get in," she said

as he shrugged out of his jacket under the bright chandelier in the foyer.

"The meatpacking company settled. They're paying big time for Maria Gastar losing that leg."

"They should."

"She'll have money for college...and for a down payment on the home of her dreams."

"Because of you. That's wonderful. So wonderful."

He beamed. "So lawyers aren't always bad, are they?"

"Not always." Wanting to touch him again, she reached up and loosened his tie.

"Yes. For the first time in a long time I felt like I was doing something I was proud of." He yanked his tie off and unbuttoned the top button.

Her face softened. "I'm proud of you, too. So, let's celebrate Maria's good fortune...due to your hard work...by eating by candlelight in the dining room with Rebecca and the children."

"All right. What's for supper?" he asked, eyeing the kitchen.

"What an unromantic, ordinary-sounding question," she teased. But she smiled as she flipped the light switch that turned off the chandelier. "I love it...because it sounds so normal." She could almost believe Dom was gone, and she and Campbell might have a real life together, and not some temporary fantasy interlude bordered by terror.

"Make love to me," she whispered, leaning back against the shadowy wall.

"Now? Here?"

"Upstairs. Think of it as part of our celebration."

"That won't be difficult."

At the touch of his hard mouth on hers, she melted against him. In an instant her desperate need for him infected him, too, and his tongue thrust into her mouth. Her tongue flicked against the tip of his.

"God," he whispered. "What the hell has gotten into you?"

"I told you I got lonely when you're at the office."

"So kids aren't enough?"

"Not by a long shot."

He caught her hand fiercely in his and pulled her deeper inside the house, across the den, up the swirling flight of stairs, as eager now as she was to get to their bedroom and lock themselves inside. Once inside, he shot the bolt. Without leaving the door, they stripped each other. When he drove into her, she came, standing against the wall, the pleasure exquisite. She clung to him, not letting him go even when it was over.

Laughing, he carried her to bed as she kissed his lips endlessly.

"What was that?" he whispered when she finally quieted.

"An explosion. Lightning bolts. Great sex."

"It was more than great sex, you little minx, and you know it."

She said nothing, afraid that if she admitted all she felt, her happiness would go up in smoke.

Twenty-Two

The hot, muggy Monday morning felt even muggier in the garage where Georgina was working. Even though she was wearing a tank top and short shorts and had two fans going full blast as she unpacked Georgia's dolls, she constantly had to stop and wipe perspiration off her brow with the back of her hand. Georgina had had another unbearably sweet weekend with Campbell and the children, and she couldn't stop smiling as she remembered making love to him last night. The rest of the weekend had been normal family life. Normal. That was a first.

Patches had streaked out of the patio door late Saturday afternoon and had run away and hidden when they'd call him.

Campbell had cursed and said, "Typical cat."

As a result, Patches had been out all night. When Joey had cried himself to sleep, Campbell had sat on his bed for a long time in the dark, smoothing his wayward cowlick, promising to find Patches.

"Patches is fine."

"You hate him," Joey had wailed.

"You don't know that."

"Why is he so upset?" Campbell had asked Georgina later when he'd finally come to bed. "The beast

is just a cat. The ugliest cat and with the worst dis-
position... A monster that is hell on upholstery. Hell
on wallpaper, too. Not to mention lizards.''

"Remember that rule you made...not to insult
Patches.''

"Right. Even when he hisses at me and claws my
foot.''

"Joey is upset because he loves Patches. He
doesn't want to lose something he loves so much.''

"We can get another cat.''

"Not Patches.''

"Way better than Patches. The pound is full of
them.''

"Not Patches, though. Joey's suffered tremendous
losses. The divorce. He lost his mother.'' Georgina
had hesitated. "I know you dislike Patches.''

"I don't dislike stupid Patches,'' Campbell had
grumbled as he thrust out his chin and leaned back
against the headboard.

"That's the first time you've admitted that, even if
you did call him stupid. He loves *this* cat.''

"All right. I get it. He doesn't want to lose something he loves.''

"Would you?'' As she waited for his answer, the
sudden tension in his eyes put her heart into turmoil.

He stared at her for an endless time across the darkness. "No. I wouldn't want to lose anything...or anyone I loved.''

"Hold me,'' she whispered, wondering what he
meant but hoping. "Just hold me.''

Without a word, his arms had circled her shoulders.

The next morning, Campbell had gotten up early

and searched the grounds, yelling Patches's name while she cooked breakfast. He'd called all the neighbors, which hadn't been easy, since he'd never bothered to get to know them in the past. Still, he'd left friendly neighborly messages. Joey had been thrilled when the lady next door finally called back an hour later and said a cat that looked exactly like Patches was in her flower bed playing with a lizard's tail.

"It has to be Patches," Campbell said. "There can't be two cats that ugly in the world that are hell on lizards."

Campbell had insisted on going over himself and on carrying Patches home himself. Then he'd forgotten his rule and insulted the cat for the rest of the afternoon.

"You're insulting him to hide the fact you were worried about him. You like him, too," Georgina said.

"Is that really why?" Joey had whispered.

"Hell, no," Campbell had said. But with a smile. After that Joey had laughed at every insult.

We're becoming a family, she thought as she lifted the box of dolls. At the same moment her cell phone rang.

Expecting Campbell, who usually called her on his way to work, she got Dom's thready, singsong voice.

"Have you been waiting breathlessly for my call, love?"

In an instant the garage felt suffocating. As if she could already feel ribbons or scarves or his large fingers, her hand went protectively to her throat.

"Dom—"

"You can't be with *him*, darling. You know that. Not when I…still *crave* you." His tender voice mocked all that was sacred.

A chill swept her and she wiped her brow, suddenly too aware of how hot it was in Campbell's garage. She could feel her control giving way to panic and she clenched her hands.

"Did you shoot Guy Jones? Who gave you this number?"

A burst of maniacal laughter jarred her.

"Did you call those TV people? Did you give them our names? My photograph?

"What if I did? I *crave* you. That's all that matters. If you come to me alone, I won't hurt Georgia or him. If you don't…"

Some part of Georgina refused to believe the disembodied voice on the phone was Dom's. These past few weeks with Campbell had almost made her believe she could lead a normal life with the man she loved.

"If you don't…" Dom repeated. Then rage that must have been bubbling just below the surface exploded, and he began to yell obscenities and list in horrifying detail exactly what he would do to Georgia if Georgina didn't do as he said.

Georgina gasped and felt sickened and shivery. All of a sudden Dom was as real as ever.

"Abstinence has whetted my taste for you, love. I want to tie—"

"You were never abstinent when we were married."

"Nobody counts but you. If I could do without

you, would I have followed you here to this hellhole? You are to come now—''

''Where?''

''Don't call the police. I'll know if you do. I'm a powerful man.''

''A sick, crazy man who needs help.''

He chuckled. ''Georgia will never be safe anywhere....''

She was covered with goose bumps and shivering despite the heat.

''Not until you're dead or locked away!''

Again he chuckled. ''After I punish you, I'll forgive you.''

Georgia. Georgia was all that mattered. And Campbell. She had to keep Campbell safe, even if it meant...the unspeakable.

''You're to come—now. I'm waiting. If you aren't here in thirty minutes...''

''Where?''

He gave her the name of a hotel and a room number and warned her not to call the police. Vaguely she realized he was staying at the same hotel Veronica had stayed at.

''Do you need directions?'' His deep tone was so eerily polite, she shivered.

''I know where it is.'' Her own voice sounded robotic. She was conditioned to obey him.

''Correct. You've been here before.'' He laughed. ''I was here. I watched you in the bar with your friends.''

''You were that jogger?''

''It was amusing that night, watching you.''

She hung up the phone slowly and got into her Mercedes. Rebecca was inside with the children. She didn't trust herself to go say goodbye. If she left quietly, maybe she could keep everybody she loved safe.

A tear streaked her face as she turned the key in the ignition.

When nothing happened, panic engulfed her.

She tried the key again, but the battery was dead or something. She pounded on the steering wheel. Not once had she driven the car since she'd been staying with Campbell. She looked at her watch. She had less than thirty minutes now. Quickly, she dialed a cab. Still holding her mobile phone, she ran out to the curb to wait. She crouched behind a palm tree, so Rebecca wouldn't see her if she chanced to look out.

When a battered yellow Chevy finally pulled alongside her, she jumped in and gave the driver the name of the hotel. Her teeth began to chatter as the cab sped away.

As if in slow motion she saw Campbell in his Porsche this morning in the garage. She remembered leaning down, kissing his lips, lingering near him in the garage, waving long after he'd disappeared before she'd lowered the garage door. He'd been wearing a red shirt and that loud yellow tie.

High on coke, Dom raced anxiously about the bedroom, tying red ribbons to the corners of the bed. A school uniform with a white shirt and navy plaid shorts and knee-high navy socks like the one he used to wear was laid carefully in the center of the bed. He'd had it made in Georgina's size. He'd had one

made for Georgia, too. Only hers was still in his over-
night bag. He was saving it for later. He smiled as he
thought of showing it to Georgina when he had her
tied up and gagged properly. He would tell her that
her little sacrifice today would not suffice for all the
heartbreak and betrayal.

The uniform made Dom remember a scruffy-
looking child, his white shirt always out of the waist-
band, his knees always scuffed and bruised. He'd
been summoned to the headmaster that first time to
be punished for torturing small animals. Strangely,
he'd learned not only to enjoy the punishments but to
crave them. Later he craved to inflict such punishment
on others.

Power. Sex was all about power. When the headmaster had chosen a new favorite, a younger boy,
Dom had felt betrayed, just as he had when his father
had died. The boy had met with an accident.

The champagne was cooling. Chilled strawberries
dusted with sugar were in the refrigerator. Everything
was perfect.

Dom was a planner. He liked to organize in metic-
ulous detail. He didn't like surprises. He wished now
he'd told her an hour. He felt rattled. He wanted to
review his plan for the perfect fantasy—sexual murder. He would kill her at the moment when his ecstasy
peaked.

But when a light, feminine knock sounded at the
door, he almost laughed as he flung it open. Then his
face changed and he began to whimper as he had as
a boy in the headmaster's closet.

"Please, sir...don't..."

* * *

At nine o'clock, Campbell was standing before his desk in his office when Chuck called him on his cell. Maria's file was in front of him, lying open. There were still a few loose ends that needed to be tied up, a few calls to make to the lawyers on the other side. At the sound of Chuck's panicked voice, he tossed the file aside, frowning.

"She's where?"

Campbell grabbed his jacket and car keys and was out the door.

"I was taking a leak. Hell, man, I thought she was in the garage."

Muriel called to him, but Campbell shook his head and held up his hand and kept running. "Where the hell are you going?"

"The hotel. Taking the stairs to the floor where the elevator she took stopped."

The door to Dom's hotel room stood ajar.

Georgina was nearly choking on her fear as she stepped soundlessly across the threshold. The walls pressed closer. Something felt wrong.

Everything felt wrong. What if Dom killed her? Georgia. Who would take care of her? And she would never see Campbell again.

She took another step. Her heart racing, she took yet another. Then she saw the rumpled sheets. Pillows and spread lay in a tangle all over the floor. Dom's open eyes stared at her.

He was tied with red ribbons. He was wearing a pair of navy plaid shorts and a white shirt and knee-

high socks. It was a uniform he used to make
her wear.

She felt sick. Tears stung her eyes. Like waves, the
terrible memories of all that he had done to her
washed over her.

She had never wanted to think of those things
again. Bile rose in her stomach as she fought to block
them out. But they kept sliding through her mind like
scenes from a horror film. All she knew was that she
had to get away. The door... She had to make it to
the door.

She was shaking. Her knees were buckling. The
walls of the room zoomed toward her and seemed to
close her inside. Dom used to lock her inside that
awful closet after he'd tied her up.

An invisible hand seemed to close around her
throat. The floor rocked beneath her. The walls! The
terrible walls were squeezing in tighter.

Then she was falling into darkness.

Georgina was lying down on the den couch with
her head in Campbell's lap. Taz and Chuck had taken
the children off to the movies to distract them.

"I can't stop thinking about Dom," Georgina said.
"About everything he did to me. I didn't realize how
scared I was of him until I saw him on that bed. I
kept thinking he'd cross the line and somebody would
find me in a bed like that."

"He's gone."

"Are all the police gone, too?" she whispered,
feeling strange, as if her brain were in a foggy daze.

"Dawson just left."

"I can't stand him."

"He's just doing his job."

"He asked a million questions. I had to repeat myself over and over again. I don't care who asks. There's so much I can't tell anybody...so much I can't bear to think about."

"I know. I have a lot of garbage in my own head."

"Who do you think killed him?"

"He was a psycho. Maybe he made somebody mad. Maybe he just died of a heart attack. There wasn't a mark on him. You said he used a lot of coke. Maybe he died of natural causes."

"I—I don't think he died of natural causes."

"He was using. Dawson said they found a lot of cocaine."

"But somebody was there. Somebody tied him. And...who shot Guy?" she asked.

"Maybe Dom. Maybe whoever was sending me death threats. Maybe we'll never know. Bottom line, you're safe now." He smoothed her hair out of her eyes.

"Am I? Is it really over?"

"I think so."

She'd thought Dom had receded because of her happiness with Campbell. Now she knew he'd left a mark. Because of him, deep in her bones, Georgina knew that the human heart contained both evil and good. At some point, one had to choose. Dom had made his choices long before he'd met her. She hadn't brought the evil out. She'd just been too young and naive to believe evil really existed.

"I feel too numb to feel safe," she said. *Too numb to feel anything.*

"I know."

"Just stay here with me," she said, closing her eyes, wondering if she would ever feel normal again, praying that Dom would recede again. "I can't forget the way he seemed to stare at me. Those eyes."

"He's dead."

"But the memories..."

"They'll fade."

"I hope so." She remembered her birthday. Dom had stabbed her cake over and over. He'd tied her up and done awful things.

"Dom hated mirrors. He said he couldn't see himself in mirrors. Did I ever tell you that?"

"Hush. Hush."

Hours later when she opened her eyes again, Campbell was still there.

Dom was dead. She should be happy. But she wasn't. She was sad. Dom had had such a terrible childhood. His father and the headmaster had done terrible things to him. Dom felt sorry for people who suffered atrocities like the land-mine victims. Yet he'd craved power, too.

She'd made a terrible mistake, a terrible miscalculation in marrying him, and it had changed her, maybe forever.

"Maybe if Dom hadn't married me, he would still be alive. Maybe I brought out the monster.... He wasn't all bad, you know."

Campbell put a fingertip to her lips. "Don't torture

yourself. He made his choices. You've paid for your mistakes.''

"Have I?"

"If you don't let go, you'll be paying for them for the rest of your life.''

Campbell was speaking softly into his kitchen phone. "So, is this thing ever going to be over?" Campbell demanded of the female cop who leaked stuff when he needed it. "There's an army of press people camped in front of my house.''

"Sir Dominic Phillips was famous, a paragon. The Hot Lady thing caught on.''

"Was he murdered? Or did he die of natural causes?''

"I got this from Dawson. The bartender, Mac, says he picked up several women. Phillips slept with that famous writer, one of the Hot Ladies. He scared the hell out of her. Somebody sent those files you received over the Internet from Veronica's computer.''

"Veronica Holiday?''

"A clerk at the desk said she looked like hell the next day. She checked out early. He said she was terrified.''

"Page went up to Austin and interrogated her. Not that she gave him much. Said Phillips was sick in the head. When Page asked her about the red ribbons, she became hysterical. She said he used her computer and stole the list. She gave Phillips all the women's names. She has an airtight alibi. She was with her therapist. Apparently, she had some sort of break-down after Phillips. Another thing. Phillips picked up another woman since Miss Holiday, according to Mac. Good-looking. Short, getting a little bit older, but built. He saw them together twice.''

"Does Dawson think Dom shot James?"

"We don't have a murder weapon."

"Phillips could have gotten rid of it."

"Maybe. Or maybe he isn't the perp. Maybe whoever was sending you the death threats is still out there."

"I don't want to believe that. I want this over."

"We all do."

"You people need to do your jobs."

"Make it easy for us, Counselor. Be nice to people. Don't get on any more hit lists.''

Campbell was still furious because Georgina had gone to meet Dom at the hotel. At the sound of her Mercedes in the drive, he opened the front door in time to see Georgina deliberately park twenty feet from his garage.

Now, why the hell… Then he saw her and forgot why he was so angry.

Wow! She damn sure wasn't in hiding now.

Her honey-gold hair tumbled around her fine-boned face and shoulders like a bright, soft cloud. She'd done it, and boy was she dazzling with the sunlight in her hair. Campbell blinked in sheer self-defense.

Taz and Chuck were on their motorcycles. Chuck followed Georgina everywhere these days. Apparently Taz was riding along today.

When Georgina got out of the car, she showed a lot of leg. Then she was racing up his drive, turning around once and smiling so the reporters outside could snap dozens of pictures of her as a blonde.

Why the hell was she doing that? His anger returned. Showing off? Didn't she know that tomorrow those pictures would be on every tabloid cover in London? They didn't need any more bad press. Lord knows, he'd had his fill.

Campbell was really fuming when he pushed the door wider so that Georgina could step inside the foyer. Then he waved goodbye to Chuck and Taz.

"Like my makeover?" she asked, kissing his cheek.

"I like it too damn much."

"Is that a compliment or an insult?"

"Both."

Her laughter stung him, maybe because he was able to feel again. For days after Dom's death, his emotions had been on ice. Now he was mad, really mad— furious at her.

When she'd slipped out this morning, she hadn't told him where she was going. He hadn't known she was gone until Chuck had called him on his cell. When that had happened he'd relived the other time she'd just run off to Dom.

"Why the hell did you run to Dom like that?"

"Wow. You're hot. You've hardly said a word in days. Don't be mad because I left today. I wanted to surprise you." She fluffed her hair.

"If I'm hot it's because every time I think about what might have happened to you at the hotel—"

She wore a gray, clingy knit dress that clung to her curves. "But nothing happened," she purred.

"You left me—for him."

"I went to him because I thought then maybe he would let you and Georgia and Joey go. Maybe. You know what really scares me...I don't think he would have."

Her skirt was short; her legs endless. "Damn it, you could have called me."

"I didn't see it that way." She hesitated. "You could say thank you, Georgina."

"For what?"

Her lips looked pink and soft as she grinned up at him.

"Thank you for being suicidal?"

"I couldn't risk your life, too, Campbell. I just couldn't."

"Maybe I can't stand the fact that you risked yours."

"He's dead, Campbell. I'm okay. I'm here."

"But you look haunted. You barely speak to me."

"I'm speaking to you now."

"We don't know who shot James, either. We don't know if Dom was murdered."

"You know you're not the most popular guy in town, now, are you? We know you were receiving death threats." She stopped. "Why are we bickering?" she asked. "We sound like Joey and Georgia."

"Because I want to know, damn it. Because you nearly went out and got yourself killed."

"I didn't die. I'm here. And you're here. And maybe we won't ever know more than we do now."

"I hate this waiting."

"Do you like me better as a blonde or not?"

She was so beautiful, she took his breath away. And she knew it. "You're so damn cute you can get away with anything."

"Going to Dom scared me, too. Did you ever think that, you big handsome lug?"

She reached up and brushed his cheek with her hand. It was the first time she'd been the least bit demonstrative since she'd found Dom dead, and just that warm, light caress was enough to break him.

He put his hand over hers and drew it to his lips.

"I'm sorry," she whispered. "I won't ever go off without telling you again. So…truce?"

A drift of her perfume, Chanel, wafted his way. Then she winked at him. "Truce," he finally said, surrendering.

When he pulled her into his arms, she let him kiss her, too, but only once. Not like before Dom. Nothing was like it had been before Dom, but Campbell didn't push.

Then she suggested that they have a drink out by the pool. Once they were outside, with their icy diet colas, she smiled a little wanly.

"Okay, then." She took a deep breath and gulped in a breath of air.

"What are you so nervous about all of a sudden?" he demanded.

"I—I didn't want to start this next conversation with you in a bad mood."

Oh, shit. He leaned forward and pressed his fingertips to her lips. "Don't say it."

It was her turn to kiss his fingers, and she did, just

the tips, one by one. Then she said very softly, "I bought my tickets home."

"Home?" The way she said it made him sick.

"London," she said.

"When?" His voice was low, bleak.

"Two days from now."

"Without the mystery being solved? Are you sure this is what you really want?"

Nodding, she tried to smile but couldn't quite manage it. Her fingernails tapped her glass and made quick little clinking sounds.

"Dom's dead," she said, but she kept clicking her nails on the glass. "There are a lot of legal matters about his estate I need to see about. And there's my mother."

He wanted to grab her hand and make the maddening noise stop. He wanted to take her in his arms and kiss her mouth hard, so she'd shut up. So she'd stay, damn it.

"Two days. That should give us time to pack and say goodbye," she whispered, not looking at him.

"What if…" he began.

"What if…what?" she pressed, still staring past him.

"Do you ever think about…I mean, have you ever wondered if this could work…us…if we could work on a permanent basis?" He tried to sound casual, but, of course, he wasn't.

"Of course I've wondered." Her expression softened.

She was so damned beautiful. An angel with long golden hair.

"I've brought nothing but chaos into your life. James was shot. Dom was stalking us.... Now he's dead, and I'm a widow. Everybody thinks I'm horrible to be living with you right after his death. But that isn't it. Ever since I saw him, all this stuff that I wouldn't think about before, this stuff between Dom and me, keeps bombarding me. I feel so dirty. Then there's you and me. We happened so fast. Too fast. What if I was just using you so I wouldn't have to face my relationship with Dom?"

"You weren't."

"I was sick, too, you know, to be with him. We can't possibly make a lifetime commitment this soon."

"You've brought more than chaos to me. You helped me immeasurably with Joey. And I'll wait...until you get past all the stuff with Dom."

"You always knew I lived in London and wanted to go home."

"I'm not talking about where you live. I'm talking about how you feel now, what you want—now."

"What if I don't know? What if I go home and we slow this down for a while? What if we take a little time for ourselves, to adjust to who we really are, now. I wrap up Dom's estate.... Then if you still want...and I still want..."

There was a hopeful note in her voice that he didn't dare let himself believe in.

"Maybe," she continued, "maybe then you could call me up one day. Ask me out..."

"And what would you say?" he whispered, leaning forward.

"Call me up in a month or so…and find out."

Not good enough.

She was running out on him. He wanted to push, but he thought about Dom. Dom had pushed and never listened to her.

"All right. But if you change your mind, I mean before…the month is up…you can call me… anytime."

"I know."

I love you, he thought, realizing how much he did love her now that he was losing her.

Twenty-Three

Feeling jumpy and sick to her stomach after a sandwich for a late lunch, Georgina stared at her packed suitcases lined up against the door of Campbell's bedroom. Even though all her clothes had been slashed at her beach house, she had to run to the mall and buy extra suitcases and duffel bags because Campbell had bought Georgia and her so many new clothes.

At the sound of running footsteps in the hall, Georgina looked up from the stacked suitcases.

"Me don't want to go home, Mommy," Georgia said, tilting her chin a little defiantly and squaring her thin shoulders in the doorway. "Me want to go sailing." Georgina was wearing her toe shoes. Only as usual she hadn't bothered to tie the satin ribbons.

Georgina ignored the baby talk, which Georgia had never used—not even once around Campbell—since they'd moved in with him.

"You need to comb your hair. It's all gold tangles. And tie your shoes. And...where's Joey?"

"Me don't know, but me want to stay here."

"But you hate it here, darling. You've said over and over again that Texas is too hot and too bright and too sticky."

"Me no say it anymore. I want Campbell to be my

new daddy and I want Joey to be my new brother. Me like Rebecca and Patches, too.''

''But you and Joey bicker all the time.''

''Me like to bicker. Me bored at the beach house before Rebecca and Taz and Joey and Campbell....''

''Yes, it was boring....'' If scary could be boring. But what had scared her most then had been her memories. No matter what she'd said, they were receding now. Every day her life with Campbell felt more real.

Campbell was spending today at the office. He'd grown dark and moody when she hadn't still been in bed this morning when he'd brought her a cup of coffee. He'd found her in the closet, yanking clothes off hangers. He'd skipped breakfast by the pool and left early, saying he didn't like goodbyes, but he would be coming home himself to drive them to the airport for their late afternoon flight.

The thought of leaving him and flying across a cold, dark ocean filled Georgina with dread, even though her mother was happy she was coming home. Not that Georgina had admitted how she hated leaving him.

But she had to do it. There was the estate to settle, and she needed space and time to figure out her life. She wasn't sure she'd ever get over Dom and what had happened to her. She couldn't just dash into another committed relationship as heedlessly as she had when she'd been a girl. She'd be using Campbell if she did that.

''Will we ever come back?'' Georgia asked, fingering the doorjamb.

''I don't know, darling.''

"But maybe?" Georgia persisted.

"Maybe," her mother replied gently.

"I'm going to go find Patches."

After Georgia clomped noisily down the hall, Georgina did a final tour of the house and grounds. Feeling increasingly depressed, she drifted through the large high-beamed rooms. Staring out at the pool and Campbell's yacht, trying to memorize it all, she wondered what the future would hold once she got back to her world. It came to her that she'd really enjoyed her work here. Her guilt about Dom really would recede. Maybe the confusion she felt today would come clear later. Would a month be enough? Or would a week be more than she needed?

When the phone rang, she flew down the stairs into the kitchen to catch it, hoping against hope it would be Campbell.

With difficulty she suppressed her disappointment when it was her secretary.

"Alice?"

"I'm going to miss you. I was half hoping you'd get off your stubborn high horse and change your mind."

"And stay here with that awful lawyer who might bamboozle me?"

"I've changed my mind about him, and so have you."

"You flirted with him shamelessly when I brought him by the office the other day."

"He flirted with me."

"Well, the womanizing flirt is all yours. I'm flying home today."

"I know this place isn't going to be the same without you," Alice said rather mournfully.

She hadn't confided in Alice there was even the slightest possibility she might return. "I'll miss you, too," Georgina admitted softly. "How's everything going?"

"Katherine Rosner wants to sign the contract on that house on Ocean Drive."

"So, she finally made up her mind without me."

"No. She's frantic you're leaving today. She wants to see the house again. I told her I'd schedule her with somebody for tomorrow...that I don't have a free agent. But she got very upset. In fact, she may call you."

Halfway through Alice's next sentence, Georgina got a beep which proved to be Katherine, who was even pushier than usual.

"Please, I know you could meet me there if you wanted to. Three-thirty?"

Georgina hesitated. "I have a plane to catch."

"This won't take long. Just a final look at the place before I make up my mind. And...and I'd like to see you before you go. I've got a little going-away present for you."

"You don't take no for an answer, do you?"

Katherine laughed. "My father used to say that, too. Three-thirty, then?"

Georgina hung up, wishing she'd had the gumption to say no. Then she wandered through the big rooms one last time. If thinking about leaving Campbell made her feel dark and lonely, what must Katherine feel? She'd been with her husband much longer, and he was leaving her.

Georgina knew too well what it was like to be all alone and to feel needy. She went to every window, looking out, touching a curtain here, a bronze sculpture of a sailboat there. In the foyer, she knelt to smell the yellow roses that Campbell had brought her last night. They'd been wrapped in tissue and tied with a yellow satin ribbon.

With a pang she realized, she wanted to stay here with him more than anything—which was exactly why she had to go. No more leaning on anybody until she could stand on her own two feet.

The doorbell rang. As she went to answer it, she glanced at her watch. It was nearly three. She'd have to hurry to show the house and get back in time to drive to the airport and make her flight.

When she opened the door, Veronica stood outside looking pale and lost. "We have to talk," she said.

"I—I don't understand." Georgina glanced at her watch again. Her nerves were in knots, but Veronica, who was wearing a baggy T-shirt and wrinkled jeans, looked so different, so strung out, she couldn't tell her she didn't have time to talk.

"I don't know why I'm here, really, but I saw the news. I feel to blame for that list and for that boy who was shot. I was joking when I thought up that hit list. Joking…I'm good at fantasy…at writing silly novels, but not good at reality. I never thought where that list could lead. Everything got all mixed up."

"I know." Georgina touched her shoulder and then stepped back, so Veronica could come inside.

"My books are the only thing that's ever worked out for me, but my characters aren't real. Not like me, anyway. They take charge. They can face anything. And there's always a happy ending. I like to live in their world better than I do mine."

Twisting her hands, Veronica prowled the foyer. Georgina looked at her watch again as she shut the front door.

"I saw your husband's picture on TV." Veronica stopped and stared at her. "He was with me when the doctor told me his idea about the kill-a-lawyer club. He was in the bar, too, watching us, watching us shoot darts, watching everything we did. He was that jogger on the beach. And later that same night, I saw him again. That night...he..." Veronica's voice broke as she struggled with some terrible memory. "He was so awful, and I—I let him... I'll never forgive myself for letting..."

The panic in Veronica's eyes brought Dom and all the pain she'd let Dom inflict upon her back as nothing else could. More than anything, Georgina wanted to tell her to go, so she could meet Katherine and make her plane—so she wouldn't have to remember Dom.

Instead, she put her arms around Veronica and held her until they both stopped shaking.

"He was after you. He was pretending I was you—"

"He's gone," Georgina said. "He can't hurt us anymore." Strangely, as she said those words, she almost felt a weight lift from her heart and mind. "We're free," she whispered, realizing to her amazement that it was really true. "We can do anything and be anything we want to be."

Slowly Veronica got control of herself. "Do you really think so?"

Georgina continued to hold her. "I have a house to show and a plane to catch. We can talk more in the car if you'd like."

When Veronica shook her head, hesitating and yet not wanting to go, Georgina took her hand and led her blindly to the garage.

Campbell stepped out of the elevator when his cell rang. The note of alarm in Chuck's voice had him sprinting toward the parking garage.

"You followed her where? She's with who?"

"Veronica Holiday. They left together.

"They're meeting who?"

"Rosner." As usual, the name ticked in the back of Campbell's mind, and he tensed. Where had he heard it before? Where? He knew he'd seen that name. "What does Katherine Rosner look like?"

"Short. Attractive. Tight black stretch pants. A red knit top. Gymnast's body."

"Sounds like the same description somebody gave me of the last woman Dom was seen with alive." Another memory niggled like a loose wire, shooting sparks in the back of his brain.

"Oh, God— No—"

Against Campbell's will the image of Kay Crocker's ferocious eyes giving him a lurid once-over when he'd turned from the jury to stare at her husband rose in Campbell's mind's eye. During the trial he'd

kept wondering how Crocker had ever fallen victim
to a shark like her. Finally, he'd decided she'd come
on to the old doctor hard, pounced him sexually or
something.

*No, it couldn't be. But it was. Katherine Rosner
Crocker. Kay from Katherine.*

Rosner? Crocker? Why the two names?

He didn't like the way the crazy puzzle suddenly
made a weird kind of sense when he added Kay as a
key piece. Dom's death was too convenient. Kay had
been the last woman he'd picked up. She was the type
to hold a grudge. She was a nurse. She would know
how to kill somebody without leaving a trace.

How the hell did Veronica Holiday fit in with Kay?

The afternoon was gorgeous—low humidity, bright
blue sky, puffy clouds. Campbell gunned the Porsche,
opening her up. Tires squealing, he swung onto
Shoreline into the sunlight and screamed through a
yellow light.

A twelve-knot breeze was stirring up ripples on the
green bay. It was a perfect afternoon for sailing. Not
that Campbell was thinking about *Victory* as the nee-
dle of his speedometer climbed and other cars flicked
by in his rearview mirror way too fast.

Where the hell were the cops when he wanted one
to follow him? When he reached the address Chuck
had given him, he swerved across oncoming traffic,
burning rubber, bouncing over a curb into the drive.

The bay-front mansion had that forlorn look un-
lived-in houses quickly get. Leaves littered the sidewalk and crunched under his loafers when he got out.

Paper cups and other bits of trash fluttered in the flower beds. The grass was a little too long, also. When he saw the front door hanging open, Campbell banged into the house, his footsteps echoing like hollow drumbeats on the lower floor. The house was empty, so he rushed outside again.

Shit. Where was Georgina? Where the hell was Chuck?

When Campbell rounded the southern corner of the house, he saw three women at the end of the pier. He shouted and waved, but the wind was blowing and they couldn't hear him.

Georgina's bright head was bent over a document. The pages were fluttering. When he raced down the bluff toward them, Kay saw him, and all hell broke loose.

Kay opened her purse and pulled out a handgun. Next, somebody moaned on the ground to his left. Campbell was running so fast, he nearly tripped on a motorcycle boot sticking out of the flower bed onto the brick path.

The boot was attached to a man's heavy, denim-clad leg.

Oh, God!

"She fucking nailed me," Chuck whispered when Campbell pulled back a few straggling branches of an immense hibiscus bush dripping with murder-red blossoms. Chuck lay facedown in the dirt.

Swamped with fear and guilt, torn between Chuck and Georgina, Campbell knelt. Blood streamed into Chuck's eyes.

"The women were in the house. I was watching

them through the window. One minute Crocker was there. The next she was behind me. She has a silencer. She knows what she's doing.''

Campbell ripped off his bright red tie and mopped at Chuck's head. "You're a lucky son of a bitch. Scalp wound. Looks like hell, but all she did was graze you.''

"Lucky? She knocked me flat on my ass.''

"Call 9-1-1. Tell them there's been a shooting. Leave the phone on.''

Georgina hesitated when she came to the buyer's name on the contract, which read Katherine Rosner Crocker. "Crocker? Isn't that—''

Veronica screamed. There was a splash.

Georgina looked up from the contract. Veronica was gone, and Katherine was holding something in her hand.

"Where's Veronica?'' Instinctively she began backing away from Katherine even before she realized the thing in Katherine's hand was the long black barrel of the gun.

"The bitch panicked when she saw the gun. Dove into the water. But I'll get her.''

"Crocker?'' Georgina whispered. "Your name is Crocker, too. Campbell sued you. He said you...''

"When Al left me, I took my maiden name back. Why add insult to injury by keeping the jerk's name?''

The hand that held the gun was shaking, and Katherine's eyes burned her just as Dom's used to.

This wasn't the Katherine she knew. This Katherine had snapped. A wild, terrible emotion was driving this woman. Again she was reminded of Dom. Somehow Georgina knew she had to keep this Katherine talking.

"Why?" Georgina managed to say in a hoarse croak.

"You shouldn't have made friends with Joe. Because now you're in the way, too. Just like your husband, Dominic, was."

"Dom?" Georgina couldn't believe what she was hearing. "I don't understand."

"My husband was stalking Joe. Dom was stalking you. Sir Dominic got in the way."

"I still don't get it."

"Since Dom was tracking you, and you were with Joe, whom Al was stalking, my husband started tracking Dom, too. Al even made a point of chatting him up at a bar in the hotel where he was staying. They even got drunk together. Al told Dom about his stupid lawyer-murder-club idea. That same crazy night, Dom picked up Veronica Holiday. Maybe none of this would have happened if your writer friend hadn't stolen Al's idea. Al was furious. He couldn't stop ranting about her stealing his wonderful idea. I'm glad she's here. She deserves to die, too."

"I still don't get it."

"We were sued by Joe just like you were. The avaricious bastard... When is enough ever enough? My husband was very angry.... So was I. Joe Campbell ruined everything, but Al, for all his bravado, is too big a wimp to make him pay."

"And you're not?"

Katherine's smile sent a chill through Georgina.

"Look, I have a little girl. I'm supposed to fly home today.... I'm getting out of your way...."

"You'd tell him." Katherine smiled. "Dom shouldn't have stolen that list from the writer and given it to the press just to see where they'd go with it. He wanted to scare you out into the open. He told me all about it...and all the crazy things he did to that writer in bed because she was your friend.... How he tied her up. All the things he planned to do to you." Katherine leaned over the pier railing. "Did you hear that, Veronica? I know all about you."

Georgina squeezed her eyes shut, not wanting to hear more. "How do you know him...Dom?"

"When the list made television, it got me thinking. You Hot Ladies had a point. It'd be fun. It'd be the right thing, really, to blow Joe Campbell away. I'd sent him a few death threats just to scare him. Why not be a gutsy Hot Lady and do it for real?"

"We were joking. It was fantasy."

"You do a lot of thinking when you're all alone. Every time I saw Joe's face plastered to those billboards, I got so mad. He wanted you, not me. I felt better when I began to think maybe there was a way I could bring Joe down."

"But your husband won."

"Campbell flirted with me all through the trial. I figured a hot, rich lawyer might be even better than some old doctor. Then Joe told me to go to hell, too."

"Before the trial, I had a husband, a maid, a gardener, a glamorous place to live on the water. I had a life."

"I know."

"I don't want to be a nurse again…struggling to pay bills…just getting by. I spent my whole life struggling. Why should some rich, greedy, fast-talking, womanizing creep like Joe Campbell come along and destroy everything? I knew my husband didn't have the guts to do what it takes…to get even."

"But you do?"

"Al could never have shot that kid.…"

"You shot Guy James?"

"I went there with my husband's Sako to blow Joe away, figuring they'd get you somehow for doing it since you put him on that hit list. The kid turned around, and I'd pulled the trigger before I realized it wasn't Joe."

"And Dom?"

"My husband talked about him a lot. I kept wondering where he fit in, wondering why he was stalking Joe, too. So, I went to his hotel and watched him a night or two. I even picked him up in the bar. He tied me up the first time, did awful things…things he said he wanted to do to you."

"I don't want to hear." Black panic nearly overwhelmed Georgina as she remembered Dom.

Katherine laughed. "You're probably as sick as he was."

"How did you kill him?"

"I'm a nurse. He snorted coke. Coke does bad things to your vascular system. He told me that you'd come running when he called…to save your precious little girl. So, I thought, what if he was dead when you got there? What if you and Campbell thought you were safe and could be happy together? Wouldn't it be worse to think you could finally be happy and then lose everything...?''

''But what do you get out of it?''

''Closure, maybe.'' She took a breath. ''I thought probably I should figure out a way to get Dom to overdose on his drug of choice.... But as a backup plan I simply went to a hospital and stole some epinephrine off a crash cart.''

Georgina saw Campbell running down the bluff behind Katherine. But where was Veronica?

''A crash cart?''

''One of those carts with medicines nurses need if a patient has a bad reaction to a drug. Crash carts are everywhere. Nobody counts epinephrine vials. Epinephrine is a natural substance in the body. I figured an examiner would assume a fatal heart problem would be due to cocaine and not look for abnormally high epinephrine levels. I had just been with Dom right before he said he was going to call you, so I listened at his door when he made the call. I knew you were coming. He thought I was gone. But I came back. He was wild to see you...and furious to see me, but he was high, too, and quite rattled because I'd blown his perfect plan. So, I asked him if I could tie him up...the way he'd tied me up...and make love to him. He didn't want to, but I said I'd leave first thing. I dressed up in a school uniform.... He could never resist that.... Then he had to wear the uniform, of course.''

Her voice no longer sounded like Katherine Rosner's, but someone else's. ''When he was helpless, I gave him an injection, ten milligrams of epinephrine. Both cocaine and epinephrine raise blood pressure and cause extremely fast heart rates. When he saw the syringe he turned purple and began to fight the ribbons.'' Katherine smiled. ''It was all over in a matter of seconds.''

''Why me? I'm your friend.''

Campbell was on the dock, moving silently toward them.

''You and Joe Campbell ruined everything,'' Katherine said, unaware of the man behind them.

''But how? He sued you. You won.''

''Joe stopped taking my calls after I told him how I felt about him.''

''You're in love with him.''

''He should have called me, the bastard. Not *you*.'' Her voice changed. ''My husband told me how different he was with *you* in the parking garage the day your husband let the air out of your tires. Told me how sweetly Joe put air in your tire.''

''Let me go. Don't you see that none of this makes any sense?''

''To me it does.''

''Because you're crazy.''

''Shut up. Shut up.''

''Why would Campbell want you? He's had enough craziness in his life.''

''Damn you.'' Katherine lifted the gun and aimed at the center of Georgina's chest.

''Leave her alone,'' Campbell yelled. ''It's me you want.'' He was running hard now, his thundering footsteps shaking the dock.

Katherine turned, and Georgina realized the woman would kill Campbell without a qualm.

"You're sick, sick, sick," Georgina began, her mind racing with terror.

A hand grabbed the railing. Wet and dripping, Veronica crawled up a ladder and swung herself onto the pier.

Kay ignored Georgina and pointed the gun at Campbell. "I knew you'd come after her. Why her and not me?"

She fired just as he lunged, rolling to the left, almost sliding under the rail into the water, but deliberately catching himself and sprawling toward her across the dock. Blood was all over the slippery boards as he began to crawl toward Katherine.

She'd shot him.

Before Katherine could fire again, Georgina and Veronica threw themselves at her. The three of them went down together locked in a desperate embrace, rolling over twice, arm-wrestling each other for control of the gun.

Katherine's eyes were feral. Her nails ripped Georgina's blouse and clawed at Veronica's eyes. Katherine was powerful and wiry, and she was panting like a tigress. Froth foamed at her lips.

She raised the gun toward Georgina's face just as Campbell grabbed Katherine's leg. When the crazed woman curled into a ball and took aim at him, he yanked her leg fiercely, swinging her around. "Run, Georgina. Run—"

Katherine flailed like a hooked fish slung up on the

dock. Then, amazingly, she propped her wrist on the deck and aimed at Campbell again.

Boom!

Veronica threw herself at Katherine, who collapsed face forward onto the dock. Her arm went limp, and her gun slid into the water. Blood dripped underneath her. But she was very much alive. Veronica's hands closed around Katherine's larynx and she began to squeeze.

Dawson, his gun still raised, was sprinting toward them as Georgina scrambled across the rough planks and pulled Campbell's dark, bleeding head into her lap.

"Get her off me," Katherine pleaded.

"I'm not going to kill you," Veronica said. "I could. But I'm going to hand you over to the law. You love lawyers so much, I'll let them crucify you."

Campbell wasn't feeling all that much. He knew one thing. Dawson had shot Kay. She was in custody. It was over. Georgina was safe.

She was holding his face in her hands. She was crying and her hands were bloody. He wanted to hold her and kiss her, but a tight band squeezed his chest and cut off his breath. Suddenly the warm sea breeze felt so icy he began to shiver.

A man yelled, "Get a medic. We've got three people hurt. Campbell's been shot! He's going into shock! Get blankets!"

"I love you," a woman said in a hoarse, low voice. "I won't leave you. Because I love you too much.

You made all the bad things go away. Don't leave me! Don't you dare leave me!''

He got one last look at her. Her terrified eyes were livid blue; her cheeks pale as death. Then, even though the sun was shining, darkness closed over him.

The transition from consciousness to unconsciousness was so fast he didn't have time to say he heard her or even to say goodbye.

"Why don't they hurry? He's so white," Georgina whispered as the medics strapped Campbell onto the gurney. "Why is he so white?"

"He's not bleeding anymore and they have him hooked up to an IV." Veronica wrapped Georgina in her arms. "It's over. We did it."

"If he lives—"

"He will. He has to." Veronica looked up at the brilliant sun and then at the bay. "I feel… I feel like one of my heroines. I feel like I can do anything. He has to live. I only write happy endings."

"This isn't a book."

"Who says real life can't be happy? Who says I can't be happy?"

"Nobody."

Then the medics began to run. Holding hands, Veronica and Georgina raced to keep up with them.

Surrounded by huge bouquets and lavish baskets of fruit and nuts and candy, Campbell was feeling no pain as Georgina turned on the television so they could watch the news.

Everybody, Georgina, their children, Georgina's grandmother from San Antonio, Patches, Rebecca,

Taz, Chuck and Veronica, had been camped at his bedside for two days. They'd eaten every meal in his bedroom, refusing to allow him to go anywhere other than his bathroom. Georgina, who was thrilled he was alive, had canceled her plane tickets and personally attended to his every need. The bullet had grazed him, but he'd broken two ribs when he'd thrown himself onto the dock. That was the worst, and he was sore as hell.

Dawson had been by a couple of times. Kay's handwriting matched that of the death threats. "She confessed everything. She was the shooter."

Al Crocker had come by to see Campbell and had apologized. "I was a bigmouthed blowhard. The kid got shot and now you.... I didn't realize what I was married to until the trial. Funny how a crisis can make you see more clearly. I should never have told anybody about a crazy murder club. Least of all Kay."

"It's even more dangerous to confide in a novelist," Veronica advised.

The newscaster on TV was interviewing an attractive, middle-aged brunette, who claimed to be Kay Crocker's oldest and dearest friend.

"Okay, everybody quiet," Georgina said.

"Yes, I knew Kay Crocker all her life," the woman smiled. "Only she was Kathy Rosner back then. She had the worst kind of life when she was in elementary school. She was smart and beautiful, but her parents didn't have much. Even in junior high, she always had airs, ambitions. In high school, all the boys liked her, but if one didn't like her, especially if he came from a good family, he was always the one she had to have. She would do anything to get him, too. Her parents died in a fire. She was the only one to get out of the house alive. She went to nursing school on the insurance money. She was supposed to save lives, not—"

"Were you surprised to learn that your old friend was the one who shot Guy James, the law clerk?" the newscaster asked.

"Definitely. She was a nurse. She married a doctor. Why couldn't she just be happy with what she had? I've started thinking about the fire. The cops said it was arson. They never caught the arsonist. I wonder—"

The show broke for a commercial and Georgina leapt up and shut the television set off.

"Everybody out," she said, her eyes huge as if she were chilled at the thought that Katherine might have killed her parents, too. "It's time for Campbell's nap."

"Past time," he affirmed, his eyes on Georgina as he flashed her a wicked grin. "And I don't want to nap alone."

Taz and Chuck, his head bandaged, herded the children out the door. When Georgina went to the bed to kiss his cheek, he grabbed her hand.

"You stay," he whispered, holding on to her slim fingers tightly and pulling her closer.

"Forever," she whispered, sitting on the mattress beside him.

"You're sure?" he murmured. "Corpus instead of London?"

"I'm sure."

"You said you needed space."

"That was before Katherine shot you. When you were lying on that dock bleeding all over me, and I thought you might die, I knew what I wanted. And it was you—alive. With me. And our children—in this house. I want a normal, ordinary life here together."

"Are you asking me to marry you?"

She bent her golden head to his, and he buried his face in her hair. "You reinvented my life for me, too," he said. "How will I ever thank you?"

"You showed there's such a thing as a new beginning. I'm going to start over, and this time I'm going to believe in me a little bit more."

"Will you marry me?" he whispered.

"As soon as possible."

"I love you," he murmured, grinning again before he kissed her.

"I love you more."

They hugged each other and laughed. Then he kissed her again.

"I love you much more," he countered.

"Just like a lawyer. You don't know when to stop."

"Yeah, I do. I've won this one—big time. We'll go to London together. I can help you with your legal problems over there. We'll bring your mother here."

"I love you so much," she said. "More every day. No more ghosts. No more Dom. Just you."

"Good."

"You know, I think it was worth even the agony with Dom if running from him and coming here brought you into my life."

He pulled her closer. "Careful, you're going to make me even more conceited than I already am."

"You're wonderful."

"Even if I'm a dirty rotten lawyer who sues people."

She clung to him. "I'm sorry I was so terrible to you. You once said, there are two sides to every argument. Oh, dear, I'm already sounding like a lawyer's wife."

He laughed. Paradise was holding her in his arms, was feeling her lips on his, was listening to her proclaim her love and his virtues as a human being.

So what if their new beginning had sprung from a terrible time in both their lives. With Georgina he would have a long and happy marriage. They would be like the normal couples he'd watched and marveled at and envied.

Good things were possible if you never gave up.

Yes, they would love each other until they were very, very old. He was sure of it.

Then she climbed into bed and kissed him hard and in such a way that he was totally convinced of it.

New York Times bestselling author

DIANA PALMER

Even the most passionate enemies sometimes
become lovers…after midnight.

After Midnight

"Ms. Palmer masterfully weaves a tale that entices on many levels,
blending adventure and strong human emotion into a great read."
—*Romantic Times* on *Desperado*

Available the first week of November 2003, wherever paperbacks are sold!

A sweeping novel of passion,
love and defiance...

from *New York Times*
bestselling author

ELAINE COFFMAN

When the naked body of beautiful, French royal-in-hiding
Sophie d'Alembert washes ashore beneath the castle of James,
Earl of Monleigh, he quickly discovers that Sophie is almost more
woman than he can handle. Terrified and stranded in the wild land
of the Scots, Sophie is unwilling to trust James...but reluctantly
finds herself falling in love with the rugged Highlander.

Can James resist Sophie, or will he choose to defy the might of
England and France for a lover as wild and passionate as himself?

THE HIGHLANDER

"Coffman's writing enriches the historical romance genre..."
—*Publishers Weekly*

MIRA®

*Available the first week of November,
wherever paperbacks are sold!*

MEC738